William James Rolfe, William Wordsworth, Bruce Rogers

Select Poems of William Wordsworth

William James Rolfe, William Wordsworth, Bruce Rogers

Select Poems of William Wordsworth

ISBN/EAN: 9783337408206

Printed in Europe, USA, Canada, Australia, Japan

Cover: Foto ©Andreas Hilbeck / pixelio.de

More available books at **www.hansebooks.com**

SELECT POEMS

OF

WILLIAM WORDSWORTH.

EDITED, WITH NOTES,

BY

WILLIAM J. ROLFE, LITT. D.,

FORMERLY HEAD MASTER OF THE HIGH SCHOOL, CAMBRIDGE, MASS.

WITH ENGRAVINGS.

NEW YORK:

HARPER & BROTHERS, PUBLISHERS,

FRANKLIN SQUARE.

1889.

ENGLISH CLASSICS.

Edited by WM. J. ROLFE, Litt. D.

Illustrated. 16mo, Cloth, 56 cents per volume; Paper, 40 cents per volume.

Shakespeare's Works.

The Merchant of Venice.
Othello.
Julius Cæsar.
A Midsummer-Night's Dream.
Macbeth.
Hamlet.
Much Ado about Nothing.
Romeo and Juliet.
As You Like It.
The Tempest.
Twelfth Night.
The Winter's Tale.
King John.
Richard II.
Henry IV. Part I.
Henry IV. Part II.
Henry V.
Henry VI. Part I.
Henry VI. Part II.
Henry VI. Part III.

Richard III.
Henry VIII.
King Lear.
The Taming of the Shrew.
All 's Well that Ends Well.
Coriolanus.
The Comedy of Errors.
Cymbeline.
Antony and Cleopatra.
Measure for Measure.
Merry Wives of Windsor.
Love's Labour 's Lost.
Two Gentlemen of Verona.
Timon of Athens.
Troilus and Cressida.
Pericles, Prince of Tyre.
The Two Noble Kinsmen.
Venus and Adonis, Lucrece, etc.
Sonnets.
Titus Andronicus.

GOLDSMITH'S SELECT POEMS.   BROWNING'S SELECT POEMS.
GRAY'S SELECT POEMS.   BROWNING'S SELECT DRAMAS.
MINOR POEMS OF JOHN MILTON.   MACAULAY'S LAYS OF ANCIENT ROME.
              WORDSWORTH'S SELECT POEMS.

Published by HARPER & BROTHERS, New York.

☞ *Any of the above works will be sent by mail, postage prepaid, to any part of the United States, on receipt of the price.*

PREFACE.

THE poems for this volume were selected several years ago, but the list has been revised again and again. Some pieces have been changed for one reason and another, and some have been necessarily omitted to avoid making the book too large. Among those which I thought could best be spared from a selection for students in high schools and academies as well as for maturer readers, were poems like *The Pet Lamb*, *The Kitten and the Falling Leaves*, etc., which are to be found in most collections of verse for young children. "*We are Seven*" was retained as perhaps the best example of this class of compositions.

The exquisite address *To the Cuckoo* (see "Addenda" to *Notes*, p. 254) was accidentally left out in sending the "copy" to the printer, and I did not discover the omission until the *notes* upon it were being put in type for page 211.

The order of the poems is chronological, as in Knight's monumental edition, Macmillan's excellent one-volume edition, and the *Selections* (see page 166) edited by Knight and others. The text is generally that of the author's last revision; but in a few instances, which are duly explained in the *Notes*, I have ventured to follow the example of Matthew Arnold and Knight (in his *Selections*) in adopting an earlier reading that was manifestly better than the later one. The punctuation of fifty years ago, retained in all the standard editions, has been made to conform to present usage.

In the *Notes* I have been mainly indebted to Knight for the collation of the texts. I have verified his work as far as I could, but there are very few of the *early* editions of Wordsworth in our American libraries. In occasional instances I have suspected inaccuracies or omissions in Knight's transcript of the readings (see foot-notes on pages 177, 178, and 194, etc.), but have not had the means of settling the question. For other matter taken from Knight due credit has been given, as to the other authorities I have cited.

The beautiful illustrations by Abbey, Parsons, and others, with the descriptive comments in the "Addenda" to the *Notes*, will give the reader who has not seen "Wordsworthshire" some slight idea of its attractions, and may possibly lead him to take the book along with him if he ever visits the district.

CAMBRIDGE, *July* 10, 1889.

HONISTER CRAG AND VALE.

CONTENTS.

RYDAL MOUNT.

WORDSWORTH'S WALK, RYDAL MOUNT.

INTRODUCTION

TO

SELECT POEMS OF WORDSWORTH.

I. THE LIFE OF WORDSWORTH.

WORDSWORTH'S life was quiet and uneventful. The main facts are given in the following memoranda dictated by the poet himself, in November, 1847, at the request of his nephew and biographer, Rev. Christopher Wordsworth, D.D. :*

"I was born at Cockermouth, in Cumberland, on April 7th, 1770, the second son of John Wordsworth, attorney-at-law—as lawyers of this class were then called—and law-agent to Sir James Lowther, afterwards Earl of Lonsdale. My mother was Anne, only daughter of William Cookson, mercer, of Penrith, and of Dorothy, born Crackanthorp, of the ancient family of that name, who from the times of Edward the Third had lived in Newbiggen Hall, Westmoreland. My grandfather was the first of the name of Wordsworth who came into Westmoreland, where he purchased the small estate of Sockbridge. He was descended from a family who had been settled at Peniston, in Yorkshire, near the sources of the Don, probably before the Norman Conquest. Their names appear on different occasions in all the transactions, personal and public, connected with that parish ; and I possess, through the kindness of Colonel Beaumont, an almery, made in 1525, at the expense of a William Wordsworth, as is expressed in a Latin inscription carved upon it, which carries the pedigree of the family back four generations from himself. The time of my infancy and early boyhood was passed partly at Cockermouth, and partly with my mother's parents at Penrith, where my mother, in the year 1778, died of a decline, brought on by a cold, in consequence of being put, at a friend's house in London, in what used to be called 'a best bedroom.' My father never recovered his usual cheerfulness of mind after this loss, and died

---

* For a fuller treatment of the subject see *Memoirs of William Wordsworth*, by Christopher Wordsworth, D.D. (London, 1851 ; reprinted in Boston same year), or better, the *Wordsworth* by F. W. H. Myers in the "English Men of Letters" series (London, 1884 ; reprinted by the Harpers same year, and in cheaper form in their "Handy Series," 1887) ; also *The Prelude*, of which there is an excellent American edition with notes by Mr. A. J. George (Boston, 1887).

when I was in my fourteenth year, a school-boy, just returned from Hawkshead, whither I had been sent with my elder brother Richard in my ninth year.

" I remember my mother only in some few situations, one of which was her pinning a nosegay to my breast, when I was going to say the catechism in the church, as was customary before Easter. An intimate friend of hers told me that she once said to her that the only one of her five children about whose future life she was anxious was William; and he, she said, would be remarkable either for good or for evil. The cause of this was that I was of a stiff, moody, and violent temper; so much so that I remember going once into the attics of my grandfather's house at Penrith, upon some indignity having been put upon me, with an intention of destroying myself with one of the foils which I knew was kept there. I took the foil in hand, but my heart failed. Upon another occasion, while I was at my grandfather's house at Penrith, along with my eldest brother, Richard, we were whipping tops together in the large drawing-room, on which the carpet was only laid down upon particular occasions. The walls were hung round with family pictures, and I said to my brother, ' Dare you strike your whip through that old lady's petticoat?' He replied, ' No, I won't.' ' Then,' said I, ' here goes !' and I struck my lash through her hooped petticoat; for which, no doubt, though I have forgotten it, I was properly punished. But, possibly from some want of judgment in punishments inflicted, I had become perverse and obstinate in defying chastisement, and rather proud of it than otherwise.

"Of my earliest days at school I have little to say, but that they were very happy ones, chiefly because I was left at liberty then, and in the vacations, to read whatever books I liked. For example, I read all Fielding's works, *Don Quixote*, *Gil Blas*, and any part of Swift that I liked—*Gulliver's Travels* and the *Tale of a Tub* being both much to my taste.

It may be, perhaps, as well to mention that the first verses which I wrote were a task imposed by my master—the subject, *The Summer Vacation;* and of my own accord I added others upon *Return to School.* There was nothing remarkable in either poem ; but I was called upon, among other scholars, to write verses upon the completion of the second centenary from the foundation of the school in 1585 by Archbishop Sandys. These verses were much admired—far more than they deserved, for they were but a tame imitation of Pope's versification, and a little in his style. This exercise, however, put it into my head to compose verses from the impulse of my own mind, and I wrote, while yet a school-boy, a long poem running upon my own adventures and the scenery of the country in which I was brought up. The only part of that poem which has been preserved is the conclusion of it, which stands at the beginning of my collected poems.*

"In the month of October, 1787, I was sent to St. John's College, Cambridge, of which my uncle, Dr. Cookson, had been a fellow. The master, Dr. Chevallier, died very soon after ; and, according to the custom of the time, his body, after being placed in the coffin, was removed to the hall of the college, and the pall spread over the coffin was stuck over by copies of verses, English or Latin, the composition of the students of St. John's. My uncle seemed mortified when upon inquiry he learned that none of these verses were from my pen, 'because,' said he, 'it would have been a fair opportunity for distinguishing yourself.' I did not, however, regret that I had been silent on the occasion, as I felt no interest in the deceased person, with whom I had had no intercourse, and whom I had never seen but during his walks in the college grounds.

"When at school I, with the other boys of the same standing, was put upon reading the first six books of Euclid, with

* Also the first poem in the present selection.

the exception of the fifth ; and also in algebra I learnt simple and quadratic equations ; and this was for me unlucky, because I had a full twelvemonth's start of the freshmen of my year, and accordingly got into rather an idle way ; reading nothing but classical authors according to my fancy, and Italian poetry. My Italian master was named Isola,* and had been well acquainted with Gray the poet. As I took to these studies with much interest, he was proud of the progress I made. Under his correction I translated the *Vision of Mirza*, and two or three other papers of the *Spectator*, into Italian. In the month of August, 1790, I set off for the Continent in companionship with Robert Jones, a Welshman, a fellow-collegian. We went staff in hand, without knapsacks, and carrying each his needments tied up in a pocket handkerchief, with about twenty pounds apiece in our pockets. We crossed from Dover and landed at Calais on the eve of the day when the king was to swear fidelity to the new constitution, an event which was solemnized with due pomp at Calais. On the afternoon of that day we started, and slept at Ardres. For what seemed best to me worth recording in this tour, see the Poem of my own Life.†

"After taking my degree in January, 1791, I went to London, stayed there some time, and then visited my friend Jones, who resided in the Vale of Clwydd, North Wales. Along with him I made a pedestrian tour through North Wales, for which also see the Poem.‡

"In the autumn of 1791 I went to Paris, where I stayed some little time, and then went to Orleans, with a view of

---

* "Agostino Isola had been compelled to fly from Milan, because a friend took up an English book in his apartment, which he had carelessly left in view. This good old man numbered among his pupils Gray the poet, Mr. Pitt, and, in his old age, Wordsworth " (Talfourd's *Letters of Charles Lamb*). His granddaughter Emma was adopted by the Lambs, and became the wife of Moxon the publisher.

† *Prelude*, book vi.   ‡ *Id.*, book xiv.

I —2

being out of the way of my own countrymen, that I might learn to speak the language fluently.   At Orleans and Blois, and Paris, on my return, I passed fifteen or sixteen months.* It was a stirring time.   The king was dethroned when I was at Blois, and the massacres of September took place when I was at Orleans.   But for these matters see also the Poem. I came home before the execution of the king, and passed the subsequent time among my friends in London and else-where, till I settled with my only sister at Racedown in Dor-setshire, in the year 1796.

" Here we were visited by Mr. Coleridge, then residing at Bristol ; and for the sake of being near him when he had removed to Nether-Stowey, in Somersetshire, we removed to Alfoxden, three miles from that place.   This was a very pleasant and productive time of my life.   Coleridge, my sis-ter, and I set off on a tour to Linton and other places in Devonshire ; and in order to defray his part of the expense, Coleridge on the same afternoon commenced his poem of *The Ancient Mariner ;* in which I was to have borne my part, and a few verses were written by me, and some assistance given in planning the poem ; but our styles agreed so little that I withdrew from the concern, and he finished it him-self.†

---

* The actual time was about thirteen months.

† Wordsworth has elsewhere given the following particulars as to his share in the composition : "Much the greatest part of the story was Mr. Coleridge's invention ; but certain parts I suggested : for example, some crime was to be committed which was to bring upon the Old Navigator, as Coleridge afterwards delighted to call him, the spectral persecution, as a consequence of that crime and his own wanderings.   I had been reading in Shelvocke's *Voyages,* a day or two before, that while doubling Cape Horn they frequently saw albatrosses in that latitude, the largest sort of sea-fowl, some extending their wings twelve or thirteen feet. ' Suppose,' said I, ' you represent him as having killed one of these birds on entering the South Sea, and that the tutelary spirits of these regions take upon them to avenge the crime.'   The incident was thought fit for the purpose, and adopted accordingly.   I also suggested the navigation

"In the course of that spring I composed many poems, most of which were printed at Bristol, in one volume, by my friend Joseph Cottle, along with Coleridge's *Ancient Mariner* and two or three other of his pieces.

"In the autumn of 1798, Mr. Coleridge, a friend of his, Mr. Chester, my sister, and I crossed from Yarmouth to Hamburg, where we remained a few days, and saw several times Klopstock the poet. Mr. Coleridge and his friend went to Ratzburg, in the north of Germany, and my sister and I preferred going southward; and for the sake of cheapness, and the neighbourhood of the Hartz Mountains, we spent the winter at the old imperial city of Goslar. The winter was perishingly cold—the coldest of the century; and the good people with whom we lodged told me one morning that they expected to find me frozen to death, my little sleeping-room being immediately over an archway. However neither my sister nor I took any harm.

"We returned to England in the following spring, and went to visit our friends the Hutchinsons at Sockburn-on-Tees, in the county of Durham, with whom we remained till the 19th of December. We then came on St. Thomas's Day, the 21st, to a small cottage at Town-end, Grasmere, which, in the course of a tour some months previously with Mr. Coleridge, I had been pleased with and had hired. This we furnished for about a hundred pounds, which sum had come to my sister by a legacy from her uncle Crackanthorp. I fell to composition immediately, and published in 1800 the second volume of the *Lyrical Ballads*.

"In the year 1802 I married Mary Hutchinson, at Bromp-

of the ship by the dead men, but do not recollect that I had anything more to do with the scheme of the poem. We began the composition together, on that to me memorable evening. I furnished two or three lines at the beginning of the poem, in particular—

> 'And listened like a three years' child;
> The Mariner had his will.' "

ton, near Scarborough, to which part of the country the family had removed from Sockburn. We had known each other from childhood, and had practised reading and spelling with the same old dame at Penrith, a remarkable personage, who had taught three generations, of the upper classes generally, of the town of Penrith and its neighbourhood.

"After our marriage we dwelt, together with our sister, at Town-end, where three of our children were born. In the spring of 1808 the increase of our family caused us to move to a larger house, then just built, Allan Bank, in the same vale; where our two younger children were born, and who died at the rectory, the house we afterwards occupied for two years. They died in 1812, and in 1813 we came to Rydal Mount, where we have since lived with no further sorrow until 1836, when my sister became a confirmed invalid, and our sister Sarah Hutchinson died. She lived alternately with her brother and with us."

Two years and a half after these autobiographical notes were dictated, the poet died of a pleurisy resulting from a cold. "On Tuesday, April 23, 1850, as his favourite cuckoo-clock struck the hour of noon, his spirit passed away. His body was buried, as he had wished, in Grasmere churchyard. Around him the dalesmen of Grasmere lie beneath the shade of sycamore and yew; and Rotha's murmur mourns the passing of that 'music sweeter than her own'" (Myers).

II. HAWKSHEAD.*

This village presents more of the signs of antiquity than any other in the Lakes; there are probably few in England that can show such quaint old houses, with so much well-carved wood-work about them. Here is an ancient Baptist chapel, and I can well believe in the justice of its reputation as among the oldest of the Dissenting places of wor-

* *The English Lakes and their Genii,* by Moncure D. Conway (*Harper's Magazine,* vol. lxii. p. 170 fol.).

HAWKSHEAD SCHOOL-HOUSE.

ship in this kingdom. There is also an old meeting-house of the Quakers, standing apart, snow-white, in its peaceful grove. Yet these buildings are mere things of yesterday compared with a farm-house near the road, whose mullioned window arrested our attention. In this house several of the monks of Furness Abbey resided, and the abbots held their manor courts in the room lighted by that mullioned window. It was in this ancient town that Wordsworth was sent to school, and by far the best of his poetry is connected with it, and the development of his mind in boyhood under the influence of nature.

We carried some introduction to the master of the famous school, Mr. H. T. Baines, whom we found thoroughly informed about all we desired to know in that neighborhood. The ancient school-room is kept so clean and ventilated that one could not imagine its great age were it not for the desks and benches. These have been so notched, dated, auto-graphed, by many generations of boys, that an urchin now could hardly find space for the smallest initial. Perhaps the care with which the masters have for a long time guard-ed with pride the signatures of the brothers Wordsworth may have given rise to a notion among the lads that to cut one's name there is the first step toward becoming a poet or a bishop. There can have been few Hawkshead boys, judg-ing by the wood-cuts they have left, who have not shown some-thing of the Wordsworthian aspiration to make a name in the world, and date it.

Mr. Baines takes great care of the archives of his school. In one of the upper rooms there is a library of old and well-bound books. The school was founded by Edwyne Sandys, Archbishop of York, in 1585. The large and elaborate char-ter issued by Queen Elizabeth is still perfect. The parch-ment is decorated with a contemporary full-length portrait of Elizabeth on her throne, and with the symbols of her kingdom, as described in her title — "Elizabeth Regina, Anglie, Francie, et Hiberne." The lion and unicorn, harp and shamrock, are there, but instead of the Scotch thistle there is the French lily. All these illuminations, including the portrait, were made by the hand. The ancient "Rules" of the school are in Archbishop Sandys's handwriting ; they prescribe, among other queer things, that the master must not enter public-houses on the days of fairs, nor participate in cock-fights, nor wear a dagger. Hawkshead was a market-town, with four fairs a year, and such regulations were very important. The archbishop's Bible, metal-bound (1572), con-taining his family register, is also kept here. Among the sponsors for his grandchildren I observed the name of Wash-ington recurring : Sir John Washington, 1621 ; Lady Wash-ington, 1629 ; Mrs. Margaret Washington, 1632 and 1636. It was pleasant to see this name associated with that of

WORDSWORTH'S DESK.

the brave chancellor who preferred going to the Tower rather than proclaim Mary queen, and helped to translate the "Bishop's Bible." Edwyne Sandys was born at Hawkshead, and his devotion to the culture of the young was rewarded in his son George, called by Dryden "the ingenious and learned Sandys, the best versifier of the former age." George was also an accomplished traveller, and wrote a good book about the East. The ancient seal of the "Grammar School" represented a master with a boy before him; the master's left hand points upward, his right grasps a bundle of birch rods. The motto is, *Docendo discimus*. Mr. Baines has learned enough by teaching to allow the birch to remain an antiquarian feature of the school on its seal. Altogether this school-house, with its surrounding larches, and the swallows flitting around it, and the clustering memories, was a very pleasant object.

As we looked, a tall and aged gentleman passed its door, supporting himself by a cane, whom one could almost imagine to be Wordsworth himself revisiting the scenes of his boyhood. He was presently followed by a quaintly dressed old lady. They were on their way to the church, which is on the hill in a field near by. I was eager to see the Hawkshead church, remembering the little picture of it in the " Prelude :"

> " The snow-white church upon the hill
> Sits like a throned lady, sending out
> A gracious look all over her domain."

A "restoration " has changed this snow-white to stone-gray, but it has also added a very sweet chime of bells, which ring out solemnly on the clear air. Around this church sheep and lambs are grazing, even up to its doors. Its Norman character is preserved. The decorations inside are rather too new and bright, consisting chiefly of colored frescoes framing texts. While I was there alone a man entered and pulled at the ropes which rang the bells ; then this bell-ringer disappeared into a room beside him, and presently reappeared in his gown, and moved up the aisle. Bell-ringer and clergyman were one and the same. Seven persons came to hear him read the daily morning service.

Ann Tyson was the name of the woman in whose cottage Wordsworth boarded. The house remains unchanged, and the room where the young poet

> " so oft
> Had lain awake on summer nights to watch
> The moon in splendour couched among the leaves
> Of a tall ash, that near our cottage stood."

Of Ann he wrote,

> " The thoughts of gratitude shall fall like dew
> Upon thy grave, good creature."

"Fair seed-time had my soul," wrote Wordsworth of his life at Hawkshead. Rambling in this neighborhood he felt the

> " first virgin passion of his soul
> Communing with this glorious universe."

It was on neighbouring Esthwaite Water that occurred the famous skating scene described in the first book of the " Prelude." Even then, amid the merry scene and the glad voices of the boys, for this boy

> " far distant hills
> Into the tumult sent an alien sound
> Of melancholy;"

and it would not have been Wordsworth had he not sometimes retired from the uproar into some silent bay " to cut across the reflex of a star." In his tenth year it was, and in this vale of Esthwaite, that he felt

> " Gleams like the flashings of a shield, the earth
> And common face of Nature spake to him
> Rememberable things."

Among the boys was a beloved minstrel (Robert Greenwood, afterward Senior Fellow of Trinity, Cambridge), who used to take his flute when they went to row. They used to leave him on an island rock and go off a little way to listen ; and

> " while he blew his flute,
> Alone upon the rock—O, then the calm
> And dead still water lay upon my mind
> Even with a weight of pleasure, and the sky,
> Never before so beautiful, sank down
> Into my heart, and held me like a dream !"

But it is also pleasant to know from the poet that there was a house in this vale where, during summer vacation,

> "mid a throng
> Of maids and youths, old men and matrons staid,
> A medley of all tempers, he had passed
> A night in dancing, gayety, and mirth."

III. FROM MATTHEW ARNOLD'S ESSAY ON WORDSWORTH.[*]

I cannot think that Wordsworth has, up to this time, at all obtained his deserts. "Glory," said M. Renan the other day—"glory, after all, is the thing which has the best chance of not being altogether vanity." Wordsworth was a homely man, and himself would certainly never have thought of talking of glory as that which, after all, has the best chance of not being altogether vanity. Yet we may well allow that few things are less vain than *real* glory. Let us conceive of the whole group of civilized nations as being, for intellectual and spiritual purposes, one great confederation, bound to a joint action and working towards a common result—a confederation whose members have a due knowledge both of the past, out of which they all proceed, and of one another. This was the ideal of Goethe, and it is an ideal which will impose itself upon the thoughts of our modern societies more and more. Then to be recognized by the verdict of such a confederation as a master, or even as a seriously and eminently worthy workman, in one's own line of intellectual or spiritual activity, is indeed glory—a glory which it would be difficult to rate too highly. For what could be more beneficent, more salutary? The world is forwarded by having its attention fixed on the best things; and here is a tribunal, free from all suspicion of national and provincial partiality, putting a stamp on the best things, and recommending them for general honour and acceptance. A nation, again, is furthered by recognition of its real gifts and successes; it is

[*] Extracts from the Preface to *Poems of Wordsworth* edited by Matthew Arnold (London, 1879; reprinted in "Franklin Square Library," 1881).

encouraged to develop them further. And here is an honest verdict, telling us which of our supposed successes are really, in the judgment of the great impartial world, and not in our own private judgment only, successes, and which are not. . . .

I come back to M. Renan's praise of glory, from which I started. Yes, real glory is a most serious thing, glory authenticated by the Amphictyonic court of final appeal—definitive glory. And even for poets and poetry, long and difficult as may be the process of arriving at the right award, the right award comes at last; the definitive glory rests where it is deserved. Every establishment of such a real glory is good and wholesome for mankind at large, good and wholesome for the nation which produced the poet crowned with it. To the poet himself it can seldom do harm ; for he, poor man, is in his grave, probably, long before his glory crowns him.

Wordsworth has been in his grave for some thirty years, and certainly his lovers and admirers cannot flatter themselves that this great and steady light of glory as yet shines over him. He is not fully recognized at home ; he is not recognized at all abroad. Yet I firmly believe that the poetical performance of Wordsworth is, after that of Shakespeare and Milton, of which all the world now recognizes the worth, undoubtedly the most considerable in our language from the Elizabethan age to the present time. Chaucer is anterior ; and on other grounds, too, he cannot well be brought into the comparison. But taking the roll of our chief poetical names, besides Shakespeare and Milton, from the age of Elizabeth downwards, and going through it—Spenser, Dryden, Pope, Gray, Goldsmith, Cowper, Burns, Coleridge, Campbell, Moore, Byron, Shelley, Keats (I mention those only who are dead), I think it certain that Wordsworth's name deserves to stand, and will finally stand, above them all. Several of the poets named have gifts and excellences which Wordsworth has not. But taking the performance of each as a

whole, I say that Wordsworth seems to me to have left a
body of poetical work superior in power, in interest, in the
qualities which give enduring freshness, to that which any
one of the others has left.

But this is not enough to say.   I think it certain, further,
that if we take the chief poetical names of the Continent
since the death of Molière, and, omitting Goethe, confront
the remaining names with that of Wordsworth, the result is
the same.   Let us take Klopstock, Lessing, Schiller, Uhland,
Rückert, and Heine for Germany; Filicaja, Alfieri, Manzoni,
and Leopardi for Italy; Racine, Boileau, Voltaire, André
Chenier, Béranger, Lamartine, Musset, and Victor Hugo for
France.   Several of these, again, have evidently gifts and excellences to which Wordsworth can make no pretension.
But in real poetical achievement it seems to me indubitable
that to Wordsworth here again belongs the palm.   It seems
to me that Wordsworth has left behind him a body of poetical work which wears, and will wear, better, on the whole,
than the performance of any one of these personages, so far
more brilliant and celebrated, most of them, than the homely poet of Rydal.   Wordsworth's performance in poetry is,
on the whole, in power, in interest, in the qualities which
give enduring freshness, superior to theirs.

This is a high claim to make for Wordsworth.   But if
it is a just claim—if Wordsworth's place among the poets
who have appeared in the last two or three centuries is after
Shakespeare, Molière, Milton, Goethe, indeed, but before all
the rest, then in time Wordsworth will have his due.   We
shall recognize him in his place, as we recognize Shakespeare and Milton; and not only we ourselves shall recognize him, but he will be recognized by Europe also. . . .

The *Excursion* and the *Prelude*, his poems of greatest bulk,
are by no means Wordsworth's best work.   His best work
is in his shorter pieces, and many, indeed, are there of these
which are of first-rate excellence.   But in his seven volumes

the pieces of high merit are mingled with a mass of pieces very inferior to them ; so inferior to them that it seems won- derful how the same poet should have produced both. Shakespeare frequently has lines and passages in a strain quite false, and which are entirely unworthy of him. But one can imagine his smiling if one could meet him in the Elysian Fields and tell him so ; smiling, and replying that he knew it perfectly well himself, and what did it matter? But with Wordsworth the case is different. Work altogether inferior, work quite uninspired, flat, and dull, is produced by him with evident unconsciousness of its defects, and he pre- sents it to us with the same faith and seriousness as his best work. Now, a drama or an epic fills the mind, and one does not look beyond them ; but in a collection of short pieces the impression made by one piece requires to be continued and sustained by the piece following. In reading Words- worth the impression made by one of his fine pieces is too often dulled and spoiled by a very inferior piece coming after it.

Wordsworth composed verses during a space of some sixty years ; and it is not much of an exaggeration to say that within one single decade of those years, between 1798 and 1808, almost all his really first-rate work was produced. A mass of inferior work remains, work done before and after this golden prime, imbedding the first-rate work and clog- ging it, obstructing our approach to it, chilling not unfre- quently the high-wrought mood with which we leave it. To be recognized far and wide as a great poet, to be possible and receivable as a classic, Wordsworth needs to be relieved of a great deal of the poetical baggage which now encumbers him. To administer this relief is indispensable, unless he is to continue to be a poet for the few only, a poet valued far below his real worth by the world. . . .

Naturally grouped, and disengaged, moreover, from the quantity of inferior work which now obscures them, the best poems of Wordsworth, I hear many people say, would indeed stand out in great beauty, but they would prove to be very few in number, scarcely more than half a dozen.   I maintain, on the other hand, that what strikes me with admiration, what establishes in my opinion Wordsworth's superiority, is the great and ample body of powerful work which remains to him, even after all his inferior work has been cleared away.   He gives us so much to rest upon, so much which communicates his spirit and engages ours ! . . .

To exhibit this body of Wordsworth's best work, to clear away obstructions from around it, and to let it speak for itself, is what every lover of Wordsworth should desire.   Until this has been done, Wordsworth, whom we, to whom he is dear, all of us know and feel to be so great a poet, has not had a fair chance before the world.   When once it has been done, he will make his way best not by our advocacy of him, but by his own worth and power.   We may safely leave him to make his way thus, we who believe that a superior worth and power in poetry finds in mankind a sense responsive to it and disposed at last to recognize it.   Yet at the outset, before he has been duly known and recognized, we may do Wordsworth a service, perhaps, by indicating in what his superior power and worth will be found to consist, and in what it will not.

Long ago, in speaking of Homer, I said that the noble and profound application of ideas to life is the most essential part of poetic greatness.   I said that a great poet receives his distinctive character of superiority from his application, under the conditions immutably fixed by the laws of poetic beauty and poetic truth, from his application, I say, to his subject, whatever it may be, of the ideas

> "On man, on nature, and on human life,"

which he has acquired for himself.   The line quoted is Wordsworth's own ; and his superiority arises from his powerful use, in his best pieces, his powerful application to his subject, of ideas "on man, on nature, and on human life."

Voltaire, with his signal acuteness, most truly remarked that "no nation has treated in poetry moral ideas with more energy and depth than the English nation." And he adds: "There, it seems to me, is the great merit of the English poets." Voltaire does not mean, by "treating in poetry moral ideas," the composing moral and didactic poems— that brings us but a very little way in poetry. He means just the same thing as was meant when I spoke above "of the noble and profound application of ideas to life;" and he means the application of these ideas under the conditions fixed for us by the laws of poetic beauty and poetic truth. If it is said that to call these ideas *moral* ideas is to introduce a strong and injurious limitation, I answer that it is to do nothing of the kind, because moral ideas are really so main a part of human life. The question *how to live* is itself a moral idea; and it is the question which most interests every man, and with which, in some way or other, he is perpetually occupied. A large sense is, of course, to be given to the term *moral*. Whatever bears upon the question "how to live" comes under it.

> "Nor love thy life, nor hate; but, what thou liv'st,
>   Live well; how long or short, permit to Heaven."

In those fine lines Milton utters, as every one at once perceives, a moral idea. Yes, but so, too, when Keats consoles the forward-bending lover on the Grecian Urn, the lover arrested and presented in immortal relief by the sculptor's hand before he can kiss, with the line,

> "Forever wilt thou love, and she be fair"—

he utters a moral idea. When Shakespeare says that "we are such stuff as dreams are made of, and our little life is rounded with a sleep," he utters a moral idea.

Voltaire was right in thinking that the energetic and profound treatment of moral ideas, in this large sense, is what
distinguishes the English poetry. He sincerely meant praise,
not dispraise or hint of limitation ; and they err who suppose
that poetic limitation is a necessary consequence of the fact,
the fact being granted as Voltaire states it. If what distinguishes the greatest poets is their powerful and profound
application of ideas to life, which surely no good critic will
deny, then to prefix to the term *ideas* here the term *moral*
makes hardly any difference, because human life itself is in
so preponderating a degree moral.

It is important, therefore, to hold fast to this : that poetry
is at bottom a criticism of life ; that the greatness of a poet
lies in his powerful and beautiful application of ideas to life
—to the question how to live. Morals are often treated in
a narrow and false fashion ; they are bound up with systems
of thought and belief which have had their day; they are
fallen into the hands of pedants and professional dealers;
they grow tiresome to some of us. We find attraction, at
times, even in a poetry of revolt against them ; in a poetry
which might take for its motto Omar Khayyám's words: " Let
us make up in the tavern for the time which we have wasted
in the mosque." Or we find attractions in a poetry indifferent to them, in a poetry where the contents may be what they
will, but where the form is studied and exquisite. We delude
ourselves in either case ; and the best cure for our delusion
is to let our minds rest upon that great and inexhaustible
word *life*, until we learn to enter into its meaning. A poetry
of revolt against moral ideas is a poetry of revolt against
life ; a poetry of indifference towards moral ideas is a poetry
of indifference towards *life.*

Epictetus had a happy figure for things like the play of
the senses, or literary form and finish, or argumentative in-
genuity, in comparison with " the best and master thing" for
us, as he called it. the concern how to live. Some people

were afraid of them, he said, or they disliked and undervalued them. Such people were wrong; they were unthankful or cowardly. But the things might also be over-prized, and treated as final when they are not. They bear to life the relation which inns bear to home. "As if a man, journeying home, and finding a nice inn on the road, and liking it, were to stay forever at the inn! Man, thou hast forgotten thine object; thy journey was not *to* this, but *through* this. 'But this inn is taking.' And how many other inns, too, are taking, and how many fields and meadows! but as places of passage merely. ·You have an object, which is this: to get home, to do your duty to your family, friends, and fellow-countrymen; to attain inward freedom, serenity, happiness, contentment. Style takes your fancy, arguing takes your fancy, and you forget your home and want to make your abode with them and to stay with them, on the plea that they are taking. Who denies that they are taking? but as places of passage, as inns. And when I say this, you suppose me to be attacking the care for style, the care for argument. I am not; I attack the resting in them, the not looking to the end which is beyond them."

Now, . . . when we come across a poet like Wordsworth, who sings,

> "Of truth, of grandeur, beauty, love, and hope,
> And melancholy fear subdued by faith,
> Of blessed consolations in distress,
> Of moral strength and intellectual power,
> Of joy in widest commonalty spread "—

then we have a poet intent on "the best and master thing," and who prosecutes his journey home. We say, for brevity's sake, that he deals with *life*, because he deals with that in which life really consists. This is what Voltaire means to praise in the English poets—this dealing with what is really life. But always it is the mark of the greatest poets that they deal with it; and to say that the English poets are remarkable for dealing with it, is only another way of saying, what is true, that in poetry the English genius has especially shown its power.

Wordsworth deals with it, and his greatness lies in his dealing with it so powerfully. I have named a number of celebrated poets, above all of whom he, in my opinion, deserves to be placed. He is to be placed above poets like Voltaire, Dryden, Pope, Lessing, Schiller, because these famous personages, with a thousand gifts and merits, never, or scarcely ever, attain the distinctive accent and utterance of the high and genuine poets—

       " Quique pii vates et Phœbo digna locuti "—

at all. Burns, Keats, Heine, not to speak of others in our list, have this accent; who can doubt it? And at the same time they have treasures of humour, felicity, passion, for which in Wordsworth we shall look in vain. Where, then, is Wordsworth's superiority? It is here: he deals with more of *life* than they do; he deals with *life*, as a whole, more powerfully. . . .

Wordsworth's poetry is great because of the extraordinary power with which Wordsworth feels the joy offered to us in nature, the joy offered to us in the simple elementary affections and duties; and because of the extraordinary power with which, in case after case, he shows us this joy, and renders it so as to make us share it.

The source of joy from which he thus draws is the truest and most unfailing source of joy accessible to man. It is also accessible universally. Wordsworth brings us word, therefore, according to his own strong and characteristic line—he brings us word

      " Of joy in widest commonalty spread."

Here is an immense advantage for a poet. Wordsworth tells of what all seek, and tells of it at its truest and best source, and yet a source where all may go and draw for it.

Nevertheless, we are not to suppose that everything is precious which Wordsworth, standing even at this perennial and beautiful source, may give us. . . . To give aright what he wishes to give, to interpret and render successfully, is not always within Wordsworth's own command. It is within no poet's command; here is the part of the Muse, the inspiration, the God, the "not ourselves." In Wordsworth's case, the accident—for so it may almost be called—of inspiration is of peculiar importance. No poet, perhaps, is so evidently filled with a new and sacred energy when the inspiration is upon him; no poet, when it fails him, is so left "weak as is a breaking wave." I remember hearing him say that "Goethe's poetry was not inevitable enough." The remark is striking and true; no line in Goethe, as Goethe said himself, but its maker knew well how it came there. Wordsworth is right, Goethe's poetry is not inevitable; not inevitable enough. But Wordsworth's poetry, when he is at his best, is inevitable, as inevitable as Nature herself. It might seem that Nature not only gave him the matter for his poem, but wrote his poem for him. He has no style. He was too conversant with Milton not to catch at times his master's manner, and he has fine Miltonic lines; but he has no assured poetic style of his own, like Milton. . . .

Wordsworth owed much to Burns, and a style of perfect plainness, relying for effect solely on the weight and force of that which with entire fidelity it utters, Burns could show him.

> " The poor inhabitant below
> Was quick to learn and wise to know,
> And keenly felt the friendly glow
>   And softer flame ;
> But thoughtless follies laid him low
>   And stain'd his name."

Every one will be conscious of a likeness here to Words-

worth; and if Wordsworth did great things with this nobly
plain manner, we must remember, what indeed he himself
would always have been forward to acknowledge, that Burns
used it before him.

Still Wordsworth's use of it has something unique and un-
matchable.   Nature herself seems, I say, to take the pen
out of his hand, and to write for him with her own bare,
sheer, penetrating power.   This arises from two causes—
from the profound sincereness with which Wordsworth feels
his subject, and also from the profoundly sincere and natural character of his subject itself.   He can and will treat
such a subject with nothing but the most plain, first-hand,
almost austere naturalness.   His expression may often be
called bald, as, for instance, in the poem of *Resolution and
Independence;* but it is bald as the bare mountain-tops are
bald, with a baldness which is full of grandeur. . . .

On the whole, then, as I said at the beginning, not only
is Wordsworth eminent by reason of the goodness of his
best work, but he is eminent also by reason of the great
body of good work which he has left to us.   With the ancients I will not compare him.   In many respects the ancients are far above us, and yet there is something that we
demand which they can never give.   Leaving the ancients,
let us come to the poets and poetry of Christendom.   Dante,
Shakespeare, Molière, Milton, even Goethe, are altogether
larger and more splendid luminaries in the poetical heaven
than Wordsworth.   But I know not where else, among the
moderns, we are to find his superiors. . . .

Wordsworth is something more than the pure and sage
master of a small band of devoted followers, and we ought
not to rest satisfied until he is seen to be what he is.   He is
one of the very chief glories of English poetry; and by nothing is England so glorious as by her poetry.   Let us lay
aside every weight which hinders our getting him recognized as this, and let our one study be to bring to pass,

as widely as possible and as truly as possible, his own word concerning his poems : " They will co-operate with the benign tendencies in human nature and society, and will, in their degree, be efficacious in making men wiser, better, and happier."

IV. FROM JAMES RUSSELL LOWELL'S ADDRESS AS PRESIDENT OF THE WORDSWORTH SOCIETY, 1884.*

As in Catholic countries men go for a time into retreat from the importunate dissonances of life to collect their better selves again by communion with things that are heavenly and therefore eternal, so this Chartreuse of Wordsworth, dedicated to the Genius of Solitude, will allure to its imperturbable calm the finer natures and the more highly tempered intellects of every generation, so long as man has any intuition of what is most sacred in his own emotions and sympathies, or of whatever in outward nature is the most capable of awakening them and making them operative, whether to console or strengthen. And over the entrance-gate to that purifying seclusion shall be inscribed,

> " Minds innocent and quiet take
> This for a hermitage."

* *Wordsworthiana* (London, 1889), p. 177.

TO THE MEMORY OF
WILLIAM WORDSWORTH,
A TRUE PHILOSOPHER AND POET,
WHO, BY THE SPECIAL GIFT AND CALLING OF
ALMIGHTY GOD,
WHETHER HE DISCOURSED ON MAN OR NATURE,
FAILED NOT TO LIFT UP THE HEART
TO HOLY THINGS,
TIRED NOT OF MAINTAINING THE CAUSE
OF THE POOR AND SIMPLE;
AND SO, IN PERILOUS TIMES WAS RAISED UP
TO BE A CHIEF MINISTER,
NOT ONLY OF NOBLEST POESY,
BUT OF HIGH AND SACRED TRUTH.

THIS MEMORIAL
IS PLACED HERE BY HIS FRIENDS AND NEIGHBOURS,
IN TESTIMONY OF
RESPECT, AFFECTION, AND GRATITUDE,
ANNO MDCCCLI

MEMORIAL TABLET, ST. OSWALD'S.

SELECT POEMS OF WORDSWORTH.

LOWER RYDAL FALLS.

WINDERMERE, SOUTHWARD VIEW.

EXTRACT

FROM THE CONCLUSION OF A POEM, COMPOSED IN ANTICIPA-
TION OF LEAVING SCHOOL.

DEAR native regions, I foretell,
From what I feel at this farewell,
That, wheresoe'er my steps may tend,
And whensoe'er my course shall end,
If in that hour a single tie
Survive of local sympathy,
My soul will cast the backward view,
The longing look alone on you.

Thus, while the sun sinks down to rest
Far in the regions of the west,
Though to the vale no parting beam
Be given, not one memorial gleam,

A lingering light he fondly throws
On the dear hills where first he rose.

WRITTEN IN VERY EARLY YOUTH.

CALM is all nature as a resting wheel.
The kine are couched upon the dewy grass ;
The horse alone, seen dimly as I pass,
Is cropping audibly his later meal :
Dark is the ground ; a slumber seems to steal
O'er vale, and mountain, and the starless sky.
Now, in this blank of things, a harmony,
Home-felt and home-created, comes to heal
That grief for which the senses still supply
Fresh food ; for only then, when memory
Is hushed, am I at rest.   My friends ! restrain
Those busy cares that would allay my pain ;
O, leave me to myself, nor let me feel
The officious touch that makes me droop again !

THE REVERIE OF POOR SUSAN.

AT the corner of Wood Street, when daylight appears,
Hangs a thrush that sings loud, it has sung for three years :
Poor Susan has passed by the spot, and has heard
In the silence of morning the song of the bird.

'T is a note of enchantment ; what ails her?   She sees
A mountain ascending, a vision of trees ;
Bright volumes of vapour through Lothbury glide,
And a river flows on through the vale of Cheapside.

Green pastures she views in the midst of the dale,
Down which she so often has tripped with her pail ;
And a single small cottage, a nest like a dove's,
The one only dwelling on earth that she loves.

She looks, and her heart is in heaven : but they fade,
The mist and the river, the hill and the shade ;
The stream will not flow, and the hill will not rise,
And the colours have all passed away from her eyes !

———

'WE ARE SEVEN.'

————A simple child,
   That lightly draws its breath,
And feels its life in every limb,
   What should it know of death ?

I met a little cottage girl :
   She was eight years old, she said ;
Her hair was thick with many a curl
   That clustered round her head.

She had a rustic, woodland air,
   And she was wildly clad :
Her eyes were fair, and very fair ;—
   Her beauty made me glad.

' Sisters and brothers, little maid,
   How many may you be ?'
' How many?   Seven in all,' she said,
   And wondering looked at me.

'And where are they?   I pray you tell.'
  She answered, 'Seven are we;
And two of us at Conway dwell,
  And two are gone to sea.   20

'Two of us in the churchyard lie,
  My sister and my brother;
And in the churchyard cottage I
  Dwell near them with my mother.'

'You say that two at Conway dwell,
  And two are gone to sea,
Yet ye are seven!—I pray you tell,
  Sweet maid, how this may be.'

Then did the little maid reply,
  'Seven boys and girls are we;   30
Two of us in the churchyard lie,
  Beneath the churchyard tree.'

'You run about, my little maid,
  Your limbs they are alive;
If two are in the churchyard laid,
  Then ye are only five.'

'Their graves are green, they may be seen,'
  The little maid replied,
'Twelve steps or more from my mother's door,
  And they are side by side.   40

'My stockings there I often knit,
  My kerchief there I hem;
And there upon the ground I sit,
  And sing a song to them.

'And often after sunset, sir,
  When it is light and fair,
I take my little porringer,
  And eat my supper there.

'The first that died was sister Jane ;
  In bed she moaning lay   50
Till God released her of her pain,
  And then she went away.

'So in the churchyard she was laid ;
  And, when the grass was dry,
Together round her grave we played,
  My brother John and I.

'And when the ground was white with snow,
  And I could run and slide,
My brother John was forced to go,
  And he lies by her side.'   60

'How many are you then,' said I,
  'If they two are in heaven?'
Quick was the little maid's reply,
  'O Master, we are seven !'

'But they are dead ; those two are dead !
  Their spirits are in heaven !'
'T was throwing words away ; for still
The little maid would have her will,
  And said, 'Nay, we are seven !'

LINES WRITTEN IN EARLY SPRING.

I HEARD a thousand blended notes
    While in a grove I sat reclined,
In that sweet mood when pleasant thoughts
    Bring sad thoughts to the mind.

To her fair works did Nature link
    The human soul that through me ran;
And much it grieved my heart to think
    What man has made of man.

Through primrose tufts in that green bower
    The periwinkle trailed its wreaths;   10
And 't is my faith that every flower
    Enjoys the air it breathes.

The birds around me hopped and played;
    Their thoughts I cannot measure:
But the least motion which they made,
    It seemed a thrill of pleasure.

The budding twigs spread out their fan
    To catch the breezy air;
And I must think, do all I can,
    That there was pleasure there.   20

If this belief from heaven be sent,
    If such be Nature's holy plan,
Have I not reason to lament
    What man has made of man?

TO · MY SISTER.

WRITTEN AT A SMALL DISTANCE FROM MY HOUSE, AND SENT
BY MY LITTLE BOY.

It is the first mild day of March,
　Each minute sweeter than before ;
The redbreast sings from the tall larch
　That stands beside our door.

There is a blessing in the air,
　Which seems a sense of joy to yield
To the bare trees and mountains bare,
　And grass in the green field.

My sister !—'t is a wish of mine—
　Now that our morning meal is done,　　10
Make haste, your morning task resign ;
　Come forth and feel the sun.

Edward will come with you ; and, pray,
　Put on with speed your woodland dress ;
And bring no book : for this one day
　We 'll give to idleness.

No joyless forms shall regulate
　Our living calendar ;
We from to-day, my friend, will date
　The opening of the year.　　20

Love, now a universal birth,
　From heart to heart is stealing,
From earth to man, from man to earth ;
　It is the hour of feeling.

One moment now may give us more
 Than years of toiling reason;
Our minds shall drink at every pore
 The spirit of the season.

Some silent laws our hearts will make,
 Which they shall long obey;   30
We for the year to come may take
 Our temper from to-day.

And from the blessed power that rolls
 About, below, above,
We 'll frame the measure of our souls;
 They shall be tuned to love.

Then come, my sister! come, I pray,
 With speed put on your woodland dress;
And bring no book: for this one day
 We 'll give to idleness.   40

EXPOSTULATION AND REPLY.

'WHY, William, on that old gray stone,
 Thus for the length of half a day,
Why, William, sit you thus alone,
 And dream your time away?

'Where are your books?—that light bequeathed
 To beings else forlorn and blind!
Up! up! and drink the spirit breathed
 From dead men to their kind.

' You look round on your Mother Earth,
   As if she for no purpose bore you ;   10
As if you were her first-born birth,
   And none had lived before you !'

One morning thus, by Esthwaite lake,
   When life was sweet, I knew not why,
To me my good friend Matthew spake,
   And thus I made reply :

' The eye—it cannot choose but see ;
   We cannot bid the ear be still ;
Our bodies feel, where'er they be,
   Against or with our will.   20

' Nor less I deem that there are powers
   Which of themselves our minds impress ;
That we can feed this mind of ours
   In a wise passiveness.

' Think you, 'mid all this mighty sum
   Of things forever speaking,
That nothing of itself will come,
   But we must still be seeking?

' Then ask not wherefore, here, alone,
   Conversing as I may,   30
I sit upon this old gray stone,
   And dream my life away.'

RYDAL WATER.

THE TABLES TURNED.

AN EVENING SCENE ON THE SAME SUBJECT.

Up! up! my friend, and quit your books,
　Or surely you 'll grow double:
Up! up! my friend, and clear your looks;
　Why all this toil and trouble?

The sun, above the mountain's head,
　A freshening lustre mellow
Through all the long green fields has spread,
　His first sweet evening yellow.

Books! 't is a dull and endless strife:
　Come, hear the woodland linnet,　　　　10
How sweet his music! on my life
　There 's more of wisdom in it.

And hark! how blithe the throstle sings!
　He, too, is no mean preacher:
Come forth into the light of things,
　Let Nature be your teacher.

She has a world of ready wealth,
　Our minds and hearts to bless—
Spontaneous wisdom breathed by health,
　Truth breathed by cheerfulness.　　　　20

One impulse from a vernal wood
　May teach you more of man,
Of moral evil and of good,
　Than all the sages can.

Sweet is the lore which Nature brings ;
　　Our meddling intellect
Misshapes the beauteous forms of things :—
　　We murder to dissect.

Enough of science and of art !
　　Close up those barren leaves ;　　　　　30
Come forth, and bring with you a heart
　　That watches and receives.

———

THE COMPLAINT

OF A FORSAKEN INDIAN WOMAN.

BEFORE I see another day,
O, let my body die away !
In sleep I heard the northern gleams ;
The stars, they were among my dreams ;
In rustling conflict through the skies,
　　I heard, I saw, the flashes drive,
And yet they are upon my eyes,
　　And yet I am alive ;
Before I see another day,
O, let my body die away !　　　　　　　10

My fire is dead : it knew no pain ;
Yet is it dead, and I remain.
All stiff with ice the ashes lie ;
And they are dead, and I will die.
When I was well I wished to live,
　　For clothes, for warmth, for food, and fire ;
But they to me no joy can give,
　　No pleasure now, and no desire.
Then here contented will I lie !
Alone I cannot fear to die.　　　　　　20

Alas! ye might have dragged me on
Another day, a single one!
Too soon I yielded to despair;
Why did ye listen to my prayer?
When ye were gone my limbs were stronger;
  And O, how grievously I rue
That, afterwards, a little longer,
  .My friends, I did not follow you!
For strong and without pain I lay,
Dear friends, when ye were gone away.   30

My child! they gave thee to another,
A woman who was not thy mother.
When from my arms my babe they took,
On me how strangely did he look!
Through his whole body something ran,
  A most strange working did I see,
As if he strove to be a man,
  That he might pull the sledge for me;
And then he stretched his arms, how wild!
O mercy! like a helpless child.   40

My little joy! my little pride!
In two days more I must have died.
Then do not weep and grieve for me;
I feel I must have died with thee.
O wind, that o'er my head art flying
  The way my friends their course did bend,
I should not feel the pain of dying,
  Could I with thee a message send!
Too soon, my friends, ye went away;
For I had many things to say.   50

I'll follow you across the snow;
Ye travel heavily and slow;

4

In spite of all my weary pain,
I 'll look upon your tents again.—
My fire is dead, and snowy-white
    The water which beside it stood ;
The wolf has come to me to-night,
    And he has stolen away my food.
Forever left alone am I,
Then wherefore should I fear to die ?   60

Young as I am, my course is run,
I shall not see another sun ;
I cannot lift my hands to know
If they have any life or no.
My poor forsaken child, if I
    For once could have thee close to me,
With happy heart I then would die,
    And my last thought would happy be ;
But thou, dear babe, art far away,
Nor shall I see another day.   70

————

LINES

COMPOSED A FEW MILES ABOVE TINTERN ABBEY, ON REVIS-
ITING THE BANKS OF THE WYE DURING A TOUR.

JULY 13, 1798.

FIVE years have past ; five summers, with the length
Of five long winters ! and again I hear
These waters, rolling from their mountain-springs
With a sweet inland murmur.   Once again
Do I behold these steep and lofty cliffs,
That on a wild secluded scene impress
Thoughts of more deep seclusion, and connect
The landscape with the quiet of the sky.

TINTERN ABBEY.

The day is come when I again repose
Here under this dark sycamore, and view   10
These plots of cottage-ground, these orchard-tufts,
Which at this season, with their unripe fruits,
Are clad in one green hue, and lose themselves
Among the woods and copses, nor disturb
The wild green landscape.   Once again I see
These hedgerows—hardly hedgerows—little lines
Of sportive wood run wild; these pastoral farms,
Green to the very door; and wreaths of smoke
Sent up in silence from among the trees,
With some uncertain notice, as might seem   20
Of vagrant dwellers in the houseless woods,
Or of some hermit's cave, where by his fire

The hermit sits alone.
                    These beauteous forms,
Through a long absence, have not been to me
As in a landscape to a blind man's eye ;
But oft, in lonely rooms and 'mid the din
Of towns and cities, I have owed to them,
In hours of weariness, sensations sweet,
Felt in the blood and felt along the heart,
And passing even into my purer mind   30
With tranquil restoration ; feelings too
Of unremembered pleasure, such, perhaps,
As have no slight or trivial influence
On that best portion of a good man's life—
His little, nameless, unremembered acts
Of kindness and of love.   Nor less, I trust,
To them I may have owed another gift,
Of aspect more sublime—that blessed mood,
In which the burden of the mystery,
In which the heavy and the weary weight   40
Of all this unintelligible world
Is lightened ; that serene and blessed mood
In which the affections gently lead us on
Until, the breath of this corporeal frame
And even the motion of our human blood
Almost suspended, we are laid asleep
In body and become a living soul,
While with an eye made quiet by the power
Of harmony and the deep power of joy
We see into the life of things.
                              If this   50
Be but a vain belief, yet, O, how oft
In darkness and amid the many shapes
Of joyless daylight, when the fretful stir
Unprofitable and the fever of the world
Have hung upon the beatings of my heart—

How oft in spirit have I turned to thee,
O sylvan Wye! Thou wanderer through the woods,
How often has my spirit turned to thee!

And now, with gleams of half-extinguished thought,
With many recognitions dim and faint,   60
And somewhat of a sad perplexity,
The picture of the mind revives again
While here I stand, not only with the sense
Of present pleasure, but with pleasing thoughts
That in this moment there is life and food
For future years.   And so I dare to hope,
Though changed, no doubt, from what I was when first
I came among these hills, when like a roe
I bounded o'er the mountains, by the sides
Of the deep rivers and the lonely streams,   70
Wherever Nature led, more like a man
Flying from something that he dreads than one
Who sought the thing he loved.   For Nature then—
The coarser pleasures of my boyish days
And their glad animal movements all gone by—
To me was all in all.   I cannot paint
What then I was.   The sounding cataract
Haunted me like a passion; the tall rock,
The mountain, and the deep and gloomy wood,
Their colours and their forms, were then to me   80
An appetite—a feeling and a love,
That had no need of a remoter charm
By thought supplied nor any interest
Unborrowed from the eye.   That time is past,
And all its aching joys are now no more,
And all its dizzy raptures.   Not for this
Faint I, nor mourn nor murmur; other gifts
Have followed, for such loss, I would believe,
Abundant recompense.   For I have learned

To look on Nature, not as in the hour   90
Of thoughtless youth, but hearing oftentimes
The still, sad music of humanity,
Nor harsh nor grating, though of ample power
To chasten and subdue.   And I have felt
A presence that disturbs me with the joy
Of elevated thoughts , a sense sublime
Of something far more deeply interfused,
Whose dwelling is the light of setting suns,
And the round ocean and the living air
And the blue sky, and in the mind of man—   100
A motion and a spirit, that impels
All thinking things, all objects of all thought,
And rolls through all things.   Therefore am I still
A lover of the meadows and the woods
And mountains, and of all that we behold
From this green earth, of all the mighty world
Of eye and ear, both what they half create
And what perceive ; well pleased to recognize
In Nature and the language of the sense
The anchor of my purest thoughts, the nurse,   110
The guide, the guardian of my heart, and soul
Of all my moral being.
                         Nor perchance,
If I were not thus taught, should I the more
Suffer my genial spirits to decay ;
For thou art with me here upon the banks
Of this fair river, thou, my dearest friend,
My dear, dear friend and in thy voice I catch
The language of my former heart and read
My former pleasures in the shooting lights
Of thy wild eyes.   O, yet a little while   120
May I behold in thee what I was once,
My dear, dear sister ! and this prayer I make,
Knowing that Nature never did betray

The heart that loved her : 't is her privilege,
Through all the years of this our life, to lead
From joy to joy ; for she can so inform
The mind that is within us, so impress
With quietness and beauty, and so feed
With lofty thoughts, that neither evil tongues,
Rash judgments, nor the sneers of selfish men,   130
Nor greetings where no kindness is, nor all
The dreary intercourse of daily life,
Shall e'er prevail against us, or disturb
Our cheerful faith that all which we behold
Is full of blessings.   Therefore let the moon
Shine on thee in thy solitary walk,
And let the misty mountain winds be free
To blow against thee ; and in after years,
When these wild ecstasies shall be matured
Into a sober pleasure, when thy mind   140
Shall be a mansion for all lovely forms,
Thy memory be as a dwelling-place
For all sweet sounds and harmonies, O, then,
If solitude or fear or pain or grief
Should be thy portion, with what healing thoughts
Of tender joy wilt thou remember me
And these my exhortations!   Nor perchance,
If I should be where I no more can hear
Thy voice, nor catch from thy wild eyes these gleams
Of past existence, wilt thou then forget   150
That on the banks of this delightful stream
We stood together ; and that I, so long
A worshipper of Nature, hither came
Unwearied in that service · rather say
With warmer love—O, with far deeper zeal
Of holier love !   Nor wilt thou then forget,
That after many wanderings, many years
Of absence, these steep woods and lofty cliffs,

And this green pastoral landscape, were to me
More dear, both for themselves and for thy sake.   160

'SHE DWELT AMONG THE UNTRODDEN WAYS.'

SHE dwelt among the untrodden ways
   Beside the springs of Dove,
A maid whom there were none to praise
   And very few to love:

A violet by a mossy stone
   Half hidden from the eye !—
Fair as a star, when only one
   Is shining in the sky.

She lived unknown, and few could know
   When Lucy ceased to be ;
But she is in her grave, and, O,
   The difference to me !

'I TRAVELLED AMONG UNKNOWN MEN.'

I TRAVELLED among unknown men,
   In lands beyond the sea ;
Nor, England, did I know till then
   What love I bore to thee !

LODORE ~   BORRUNDALE~

Derwentwate ~

'T is past, that melancholy dream !
  Nor will I quit thy shore
A second time ; for still I seem
  To love thee more and more.

Among thy mountains did I feel
  The joy of my desire ;
And she I cherished turned her wheel
  Beside an English fire.

Thy mornings showed, thy nights concealed
  The bowers where Lucy played ;
And thine too is the last green field
  That Lucy's eyes surveyed.

'THREE YEARS SHE GREW.'

THREE years she grew in sun and shower,
Then Nature said, ' A lovelier flower
  On earth was never sown !
This child I to myself will take ;
She shall be mine, and I will make
  A lady of my own.

' Myself will to my darling be
Both law and impulse ; and with me
  The girl, in rock and plain,
In earth and heaven, in glade and bower,
Shall feel an overseeing power   10
  To kindle or restrain.

'She shall be sportive as the fawn
That wild with glee across the lawn
   Or up the mountain springs ;
And hers shall be the breathing balm,
And hers the silence and the calm
   Of mute insensate things.

'The floating clouds their state shall lend
To her, for her the willow bend ;   20
   Nor shall she fail to see
Even in the motions of the storm
Grace that shall mould the maiden's form
   By silent sympathy.

'The stars of midnight shall be dear
To her ; and she shall lean her ear
   In many a secret place
Where rivulets dance their wayward round,
And beauty born of murmuring sound
   Shall pass into her face.   30

'And vital feelings of delight
Shall rear her form to stately height,
   Her virgin bosom swell ;
Such thoughts to Lucy I will give
While she and I together live
   Here in this happy dell.'

Thus Nature spake.—The work was done—
How soon my Lucy's race was run !
   She died, and left to me
This heath, this calm and quiet scene ;   40
The memory of what has been,
   And never more will be.

'A SLUMBER DID MY SPIRIT SEAL.'

A SLUMBER did my spirit seal;
　　I had no human fears:
She seemed a thing that could not feel
　　The touch of earthly years.

No motion has she now, no force;
　　She neither hears nor sees,
Rolled round in earth's diurnal course
　　With rocks and stones and trees.

———

MATTHEW.

IF Nature, for a favourite child,
　　In thee hath tempered so her clay
That every hour thy heart runs wild,
　　Yet never once doth go astray,

Read o'er these lines; and then review
　　This tablet, that thus humbly rears
In such diversity of hue
　　The history of two hundred years.

When through this little wreck of fame,
　　Cipher and syllable, thine eye
Has travelled down to Matthew's name,
　　Pause with no common sympathy.

And, if a sleeping tear should wake,
  Then be it neither checked nor stayed:
For Matthew a request I make
  Which for himself he had not made.

Poor Matthew, all his frolics o'er,
  Is silent as a standing pool;
Far from the chimney's merry roar,
  And murmur of the village school.   20

The sighs which Matthew heaved were sighs
  Of one tired out with fun and madness;
The tears which came to Matthew's eyes
  Were tears of light, the dew of gladness.

Yet, sometimes, when the secret cup
  Of still and serious thought went round,
It seemed as if he drank it up,
  He felt with spirit so profound.

Thou soul of God's best earthly mould!
  Thou happy soul! and can it be   30
That these two words of glittering gold
  Are all that must remain of thee?

THE FOUNTAIN.

A CONVERSATION.

WE talked with open heart, and tongue
   Affectionate and true—
A pair of friends, though I was young
   And Matthew seventy-two.

We lay beneath a spreading oak,
   Beside a mossy seat ;
And from the turf a fountain broke,
   And gurgled at our feet.

'Now, Matthew,' said I, 'let us match
   This water's pleasant tune   10
With some old Border-song, or catch
   That suits a summer's noon ;

'Or of the church-clock and the chimes
   Sing here beneath the shade,
That half-mad thing of witty rhymes
   Which you last April made.'

In silence Matthew lay, and eyed
   The spring beneath the tree ;
And thus the dear old man replied,
   The gray-haired man of glee :   20

'Down to the vale this water steers,
   How merrily it goes !
'T will murmur on a thousand years,
   And flow as now it flows.

'And here, on this delightful day,
    I cannot choose but think
How oft, a vigorous man, I lay
    Beside this fountain's brink.

' My eyes are dim with childish tears,
    My heart is idly stirred;   30
For the same sound is in my ears
    Which in those days I heard.

'Thus fares it still in our decay;
    And yet the wiser mind
Mourns less for what age takes away
    Than what it leaves behind.

'The blackbird in the summer trees,
    The lark upon the hill,
Let loose their carols when they please,
    Are quiet when they will.   40

'With Nature never do *they* wage
    A foolish strife: they see
A happy youth, and their old age
    Is beautiful and free;

' But we are pressed by heavy laws,
    And often, glad no more,
We wear a face of joy because
    We have been glad of yore.

' If there be one who need bemoan
    His kindred laid in earth,   50
The household hearts that were his own,
    It is the man of mirth.

'My days, my friend, are almost gone ;
   My life has been approved,
And many love me, but by none
   Am I enough beloved.'

'Now both himself and me he wrongs,
   The man who thus complains !
I live and sing my idle songs
   Upon these happy plains ;   60

'And, Matthew, for thy children dead
   I 'll be a son to thee !'
At this he grasped my hand and said,
   'Alas ! that cannot be.'

We rose up from the fountain-side,
   And down the smooth descent
Of the green sheep-track did we glide,
   And through the wood we went ;

And ere we came to Leonard's rock,
   He sang those witty rhymes   70
About the crazy old church-clock,
   And the bewildered chimes.

———

THE TWO APRIL MORNINGS.

WE walked along, while bright and red
   Uprose the morning sun ;
And Matthew stopped, he looked and said,
   'The will of God be done !'

A village schoolmaster was he,
  With hair of glittering gray,
As blithe a man as you could see
  On a spring holiday.

And on that morning through the grass
  And by the steaming rills,
We travelled merrily to pass
  A day among the hills.

' Our work,' said I, ' was well begun ;
  Then, from thy breast what thought,
Beneath so beautiful a sun,
  So sad a sigh has brought ?'

A second time did Matthew stop,
  And fixing still his eye
Upon the eastern mountain-top,
  To me he made reply :

' Yon cloud with that long purple cleft
  Brings fresh into my mind
A day like this which I have left
  Full thirty years behind.

' And just above yon slope of corn
  Such colours, and no other,
Were in the sky that April morn,
  Of this the very brother.

' With rod and line I sued the sport
  Which that sweet season gave,
And, coming to the church, stopped short
  Beside my daughter's grave.

5

' Nine summers had she scarcely seen,
    The pride of all the vale ;
And then she sang—she would have been
    A very nightingale.

' Six feet in earth my Emma lay ;
    And yet I loved her more—
For so it seemed—than till that day
    I e'er had loved before.   40

' And, turning from her grave, I met
    Beside the churchyard yew
A blooming girl, whose hair was wet
    With points of morning dew.

' A basket on her head she bare,
    Her brow was smooth and white :
To see a child so very fair,
    It was a pure delight.

' No fountain from its rocky cave
    E'er tripped with foot so free ;   50
She seemed as happy as a wave
    That dances on the sea.

' There came from me a sigh of pain
    Which I could ill confine ;
I looked at her, and looked again—
    And did not wish her mine.'

Matthew is in his grave, yet now
    Methinks I see him stand,
As at that moment, with a bough
    Of wilding in his hand.   60

HART-LEAP WELL.

PART FIRST.

THE knight had ridden down from Wensley Moor
    With the slow motion of a summer's cloud;
He turned aside towards a vassal's door,
    And 'Bring another horse!' he cried aloud.

'Another horse!' That shout the vassal heard,
    And saddled his best steed, a comely gray.
Sir Walter mounted him; he was the third
    Which he had mounted on that glorious day.

Joy sparkled in the prancing courser's eyes;
    The horse and horseman are a happy pair;   10
But, though Sir Walter like a falcon flies,
    There is a doleful silence in the air.

A rout this morning left Sir Walter's hall
    That as they galloped made the echoes roar;
But horse and man are vanished, one and all;
    Such race, I think, was never seen before.

Sir Walter, restless as a veering wind,
    Calls to the few tired dogs that yet remain;
Blanch, Swift, and Music, noblest of their kind,
    Follow, and up the weary mountain strain.   20

The knight hallooed, he cheered and chid them on
    With suppliant gestures and upbraidings stern;
But breath and eyesight fail, and, one by one,
    The dogs are stretched among the mountain fern.

Where is the throng, the tumult of the race?
  The bugles that so joyfully were blown?
This chase it looks not like an earthly chase ;
  Sir Walter and the hart are left alone.

The poor hart toils along the mountain-side ;
  I will not stop to tell how far he fled.   30
Nor will I mention by what death he died ;
  But now the knight beholds him lying dead.

Dismounting then, he leaned against a thorn ;
  He had no follower, dog, nor man, nor boy :
He neither cracked his whip nor blew his horn,
  But gazed upon the spoil with silent joy.

Close to the thorn on which Sir Walter leaned,
  Stood his dumb partner in this glorious feat,
Weak as a lamb the hour that it is yeaned,
  And white with foam as if with cleaving sleet.   40

Upon his side the hart was lying stretched ;
  His nostril touched a spring beneath a hill,
And with the last deep groan his breath had fetched
  The waters of the spring were trembling still.

And now, too happy for repose or rest—
  Never had living man such joyful lot—
Sir Walter walked all round, north, south, and west,
  And gazed and gazed upon that darling spot.

And climbing up the hill—it was at least
  Four roods of sheer ascent—Sir Walter found   50
Three several hoof-marks which the hunted beast
  Had left imprinted on the grassy ground.

Sir Walter wiped his face and cried, ' Till now
   Such sight was never seen by human eyes ;
Three leaps have borne him from this lofty brow
   Down to the very fountain where he lies.

' I 'll build a pleasure-house upon this spot,
   And a small arbour, made for rural joy ;
'T' will be the traveller's shed, the pilgrim's cot,
   A place of love for damsels that are coy.   60

' A cunning artist will I have to frame
   A basin for that fountain in the dell ;
And they who do make mention of the same
   From this day forth shall call it HART-LEAP WELL.

' And, gallant stag, to make thy praises known,
   Another monument shall here be raised —
Three several pillars, each a rough-hewn stone,
   And planted where thy hoofs the turf have grazed.

' And in the summer-time when days are long
   I will come hither with my paramour ;   70
And with the dancers and the minstrel's song
   We will make merry in that pleasant bower.

' Till the foundations of the mountains fail
   My mansion with its arbour shall endure —
The joy of them who till the fields of Swale,
   And them who dwell among the woods of Ure !'

Then home he went, and left the hart, stone-dead,
   With breathless nostrils stretched above the spring.
Soon did the knight perform what he had said,
   And far and wide the fame thereof did ring.   80

Ere thrice the moon into her port had steered,
    A cup of stone received the living well;
Three pillars of rude stone Sir Walter reared,
    And built a house of pleasure in the dell.

And near the fountain flowers of stature tall
    With trailing plants and trees were intertwined,
Which soon composed a little sylvan hall—
    A leafy shelter from the sun and wind.

And thither, when the summer days were long,
    Sir Walter led his wondering paramour,   90
And with the dancers and the minstrel's song
    Made merriment within that pleasant bower.

The knight, Sir Walter, died in course of time,
    And his bones lie in his paternal vale.—
But there is matter for a second rhyme,
    And I to this would add another tale.

PART SECOND.

The moving accident is not my trade;
    To freeze the blood I have no ready arts:
'T is my delight, alone in summer shade,
    To pipe a simple song for thinking hearts.   100

As I from Hawes to Richmond did repair,
    It chanced that I saw standing in a dell
Three aspens at three corners of a square,
    And one, not four yards distant, near a well.

What this imported I could ill divine;
    And, pulling now the rein my horse to stop,
I saw three pillars standing in a line,
    The last stone pillar on a dark hill-top.

The trees were gray, with neither arms nor head,
    Half-wasted the square mound of tawny green ;   110
So that you just might say, as then I said,
    ' Here in old time the hand of man hath been.'

I looked upon the hill both far and near,
    More doleful place did never eye survey ;
It seemed as if the spring-time came not here,
    And Nature here were willing to decay.

I stood in various thoughts and fancies lost,
    When one who was in shepherd's garb attired
Came up the hollow ; him did I accost,
    And what this place might be I then inquired.   120

The shepherd stopped, and that same story told
    Which in my former rhyme I have rehearsed.
' A jolly place,' said he, ' in times of old !
    But something ails it now ; the spot is curst.

' You see these lifeless stumps of aspen wood—
    Some say that they are beeches, others elms—
These were the bower ; and here a mansion stood,
    The finest palace of a hundred realms !

' The arbour does its own condition tell ;
    You see the stones, the fountain, and the stream ;   130
But as to the great lodge, you might as well
    Hunt half a day for a forgotten dream.

' There 's neither dog nor heifer, horse nor sheep,
    Will wet his lips within that cup of stone ;
And oftentimes, when all are fast asleep,
    This water doth send forth a dolorous groan.

'Some say that here a murder has been done,
  And blood cries out for blood ; but, for my part,
I 've guessed, when I 've been sitting in the sun,
  That it was all for that unhappy hart.   140

'What thoughts must through the creature's brain have passed !
  Even from the topmost stone upon the steep
Are but three bounds ; and look, sir, at this last—
  O master, it has been a cruel leap !

'For thirteen hours he ran a desperate race ;
  And in my simple mind we cannot tell
What cause the hart might have to love this place,
  And come and make his death-bed near the well.

'Here on the grass perhaps asleep he sank,
  Lulled by the fountain in the summer-tide ;   150
This water was perhaps the first he drank
  When he had wandered from his mother's side.

'In April here beneath the scented thorn
  He heard the birds their morning carols sing ;
And he, perhaps, for aught we know, was born
  Not half a furlong from that selfsame spring.

'Now, here is neither grass nor pleasant shade,
  The sun on drearier hollow never shone ;
So will it be, as I have often said,
  Till trees and stones and fountain all are gone.'   160

'Gray-headed shepherd, thou hast spoken well ;
  Small difference lies between thy creed and mine :
This beast not unobserved by Nature fell ;
  His death was mourned by sympathy divine.

'The Being that is in the clouds and air,
   That is in the green leaves among the groves,
Maintains a deep and reverential care
   For the unoffending creatures whom he loves.

'The pleasure-house is dust—behind, before,
   This is no common waste, no common gloom ;   170
But Nature, in due course of time, once more
   Shall here put on her beauty and her bloom.

'She leaves these objects to a slow decay,
   That what we are and have been may be known ;
But, at the coming of the milder day,
   These monuments shall all be overgrown.

'One lesson, shepherd, let us two divide,
   Taught both by what she shows and what conceals—
Never to blend our pleasure or our pride
   With sorrow of the meanest thing that feels.'   180

———

THE SPARROW'S NEST.

BEHOLD, within the leafy shade,
Those bright blue eggs together laid !
On me the chance-discovered sight
Gleamed like a vision of delight.
I started—seeming to espy
   The home and sheltered bed,
The sparrow's dwelling, which, hard by
My father's house, in wet or dry
My sister Emmeline and I
    Together visited.   10

She looked at it and seemed to fear it,
Dreading, though wishing, to be near it ;
Such heart was in her, being then
A little prattler among men.
The blessing of my later years
  Was with me when a boy:
She gave me eyes, she gave me ears ;
And humble cares, and delicate fears :
A heart, the fountain of sweet tears ;
  And love, and thought, and joy.   20

TO A BUTTERFLY.

STAY near me—do not take thy flight !
A little longer stay in sight !
Much converse do I find in thee,
Historian of my infancy !
Float near me ; do not yet depart !
  Dead times revive in thee :
Thou bring'st, gay creature as thou art,
A solemn image to my heart,
  My father's family !

O, pleasant, pleasant were the days,   10
The time when in our childish plays
My sister Emmeline and I
Together chased the butterfly !
A very hunter did I rush
  Upon the prey :—with leaps and springs
I followed on from brake to bush ;
But she, God love her, feared to brush
  The dust from off its wings !

BUTTERMERE.

"MY HEART LEAPS UP WHEN I BEHOLD."

My heart leaps up when I behold
    A rainbow in the sky:
So was it when my life began;
So is it now I am a man;
So be it when I shall grow old,
    Or let me die!
The child is father of the man;
And I could wish my days to be
Bound each to each by natural piety.

TO A BUTTERFLY.

I 'VE watched you now a full half-hour,
Self-poised upon that yellow flower,
And, little butterfly, indeed
I know not if you sleep or feed.
How motionless!—not frozen seas
    More motionless! and then
What joy awaits you, when the breeze
Hath found you out among the trees,
    And calls you forth again!

This plot of orchard-ground is ours;   10
My trees they are, my sister's flowers;
Here rest your wings when they are weary;
Here lodge as in a sanctuary!

Come often to us, fear no wrong;
　Sit near us on the bough!
We 'll talk of sunshine and of song,
And summer days when we were young;
Sweet childish days, that were as long
　As twenty days are now.

———

TO THE SMALL CELANDINE.

PANSIES, lilies, kingcups, daisies,
Let them live upon their praises;
Long as there 's a sun that sets,
　Primroses will have their glory;
Long as there are violets,
　They will have a place in story:
There 's a flower that shall be mine,
'T is the little celandine.

Eyes of some men travel far
For the finding of a star;　　　　　　10
Up and down the heavens they go,
　Men that keep a mighty rout!
I 'm as great as they, I trow,
　Since the day I found thee out,
Little flower!—I 'll make a stir,
Like a sage astronomer.

Modest, yet withal an elf
Bold and lavish of thyself,
Since we needs must first have met
　I have seen thee, high and low,　　　20

Thirty years or more, and yet
　"T' was a face I did not know ;
Thou hast now, go where I may,
Fifty greetings in a day.

Ere a leaf is on a bush,
In the time before the thrush
Has a thought about her nest,
　Thou wilt come with half a call,
Spreading out thy glossy breast
　Like a careless prodigal,   30
Telling tales about the sun
When we 've little warmth or none.

Poets—vain men in their mood—
Travel with the multitude :
Never heed them ; I aver
　That they all are wanton wooers ;
But the thrifty cottager,
　Who stirs little out of doors,
Joys to see thee near her home ;
Spring is coming, thou art come !   40

Comfort have thou of thy merit,
Kindly, unassuming spirit !
Careless of thy neighbourhood,
　Thou dost show thy pleasant face
On the moor, and in the wood,
　In the lane—there 's not a place,
Howsoever mean it be,
But 't is good enough for thee.

Ill befall the yellow flowers,
Children of the flaring hours !   50

Buttercups, that will be seen,
  Whether we will see or no ;
Others, too, of lofty mien ;
  They have done as worldlings do,
Taken praise that should be thine,
Little, humble celandine !

Prophet of delight and mirth,
Ill-requited upon earth ;
Herald of a mighty band,
  Of a joyous train ensuing,   60
Serving at my heart's command,
  Tasks that are no tasks renewing,
I will sing, as doth behoove,
Hymns in praise of what I love !

TO THE SAME FLOWER.

PLEASURES newly found are sweet
When they lie about our feet :
February last, my heart
  First at sight of thee was glad ;
All unheard of as thou art,
  Thou must needs, I think, have had,
Celandine, and long ago,
Praise of which I nothing know.

I have not a doubt but he,
Whosoe'er the man might be,   10
Who the first with pointed rays—
  Workman worthy to be sainted- ·

Set the sign-board in a blaze
    When the rising sun he painted,
Took the fancy from a glance
At thy glittering countenance.

Soon as gentle breezes bring
News of winter's vanishing,
And the children build their bowers,
    Sticking kerchief-plots of mould   20
All about with full-blown flowers,
    Thick as sheep in shepherd's fold,
With the proudest thou art there,
Mantling in the tiny square.

Often have I sighed to measure
By myself a lonely pleasure,
Sighed to think I read a book
    Only read, perhaps, by me ;
Yet I long could overlook
    Thy bright coronet and thee,   30
And thy arch and wily ways,
And thy store of other praise.

Blithe of heart, from week to week
Thou dost play at hide-and-seek ;
While the patient primrose sits
    Like a beggar in the cold,
Thou, a flower of wiser wits,
    Slipp'st into thy sheltering hold,
Liveliest of the vernal train
When ye all are out again.   40

Drawn by what peculiar spell,
By what charm of sight or smell,

Does the dim-eyed curious bee,
    Labouring for her waxen cells,
Fondly settle upon thee,
    Prized above all buds and bells
Opening daily at thy side,
By the season multiplied?

Thou art not beyond the moon,
But a thing ' beneath our shoon :'   50
Let the bold discoverer thrid
    In his bark the polar sea ;
Rear who will a pyramid ;
    Praise it is enough for me,
If there be but three or four
Who will love my little flower?

THE LEECH-GATHERER ;

Or, Resolution and Independence.

There was a roaring in the wind all night,
    The rain came heavily and fell in floods ;
But now the sun is shining calm and bright ;
    The birds are singing in the distant woods ;
    Over his own sweet voice the stock-dove broods ;
The jay makes answer as the magpie chatters ;
And all the air is filled with pleasant noise of waters.

All things that love the sun are out of doors ;
    The sky rejoices in the morning's birth ;
The grass is bright with rain-drops ; on the moors   10
    The hare is running races in her mirth ;
    And with her feet she from the plashy earth

6

Raises a mist that, glittering in the sun,
Runs with her all the way, wherever she doth run.

I was a traveller then upon the moor,
   I saw the hare that raced about with joy ;
I heard the woods and distant waters roar,
   Or heard them not, as happy as a boy.
   The pleasant season did my heart employ ;
My old remembrances went from me wholly,   20
And all the ways of men, so vain and melancholy.

But, as it sometimes chanceth, from the might
   Of joy in minds that can no further go,
As high as we have mounted in delight
   In our dejection do we sink as low :
   To me that morning did it happen so,
And fears and fancies thick upon me came,
Dim sadness—and blind thoughts I knew not nor could
    name.

I heard the skylark warbling in the sky,
   And I bethought me of the playful hare :   30
Even such a happy child of earth am I,
   Even as these blissful creatures do I fare ;
   Far from the world I walk, and from all care ;
But there may come another day to me—
Solitude, pain of heart, distress, and poverty.

My whole life I have lived in pleasant thought,
   As if life's business were a summer mood ;
As if all needful things would come unsought
   To genial faith, still rich in genial good ;
   But how can he expect that others should   40
Build for him, sow for him, and at his call
Love him, who for himself will take no heed at all?

I thought of Chatterton, the marvellous boy,
　The sleepless soul that perished in his pride ;
Of him who walked in glory and in joy
　Following his plough along the mountain-side.
　By our own spirits are we deified ;
We poets in our youth begin in gladness,
But thereof comes in the end despondency and madness.

Now, whether it were by peculiar grace,　　　　　　　50
　A leading from above, a something given,
Yet it befell that in this lonely place,
　When I with these untoward thoughts had striven,
　Beside a pool bare to the eye of heaven
I saw a man before me unawares ;
The oldest man he seemed that ever wore gray hairs.

As a huge stone is sometimes seen to lie
　Couched on the bald top of an eminence,
Wonder to all who do the same espy,
　By what means it could thither come and whence,　60
　So that it seems a thing endued with sense,
Like a sea-beast crawled forth, that on a shelf
Of rock or sand reposeth, there to sun itself ;

Such seemed this man, not all alive nor dead,
　Nor all asleep—in his extreme old age.
His body was bent double, feet and head
　Coming together in life's pilgrimage ;
　As if some dire constraint of pain, or rage
Of sickness felt by him in times long past,
A more than human weight upon his frame had cast.　70

Himself he propped, limbs, body, and pale face,
　Upon a long gray staff of shaven wood ;
And, still as I drew near with gentle pace,

Upon the margin of that moorish flood
Motionless as a cloud the old man stood,
That heareth not the loud winds when they call
And moveth all together, if it move at all.

At length, himself unsettling, he the pond
Stirred with his staff, and fixedly did look
Upon the muddy water, which he conned   80
As if he had been reading in a book ;
And now a stranger's privilege I took,
And, drawing to his side, to him did say,
'This morning gives us promise of a glorious day.'

A gentle answer did the old man make,
In courteous speech which forth he slowly drew ;
And him with further words I thus bespake,
'What occupation do you there pursue ?
This is a lonesome place for one like you.'
Ere he replied a flash of mild surprise   90
Broke from the sable orbs of his yet vivid eyes.

His words came feebly from a feeble chest,
But each in solemn order followed each,
With something of a lofty utterance drest —
Choice word and measured phrase, above the reach
Of ordinary men ; a stately speech,
Such as grave livers do in Scotland use,
Religious men, who give to God and man their dues.

He told, that to these waters he had come
To gather leeches, being old and poor—   100
Employment hazardous and wearisome !
And he had many hardships to endure :
From pond to pond he roamed, from moor to moor,

Housing, with God's good help, by choice or chance,
And in this way he gained an honest maintenance.

The old man still stood talking by my side,
  But now his voice to me was like a stream
Scarce heard, nor word from word could I divide ;
  And the whole body of the man did seem
  Like one whom I had met with in a dream,   110
Or like a man from some far region sent,
To give me human strength by apt admonishment.

My former thoughts returned—the fear that kills,
  And hope that is unwilling to be fed ;
Cold, pain, and labour, and all fleshly ills,
  And mighty poets in their misery dead.
  Perplexed and longing to be comforted,
My question eagerly did I renew,
'How is it that you live, and what is it you do?"

He with a smile did then his words repeat,   120
  And said that, gathering leeches, far and wide
He travelled, stirring thus about his feet
  The waters of the pools where they abide.
  'Once I could meet with them on every side,
But they have dwindled long by slow decay ;
Yet still I persevere and find them where I may.'

While he was talking thus, the lonely place,
  The old man's shape and speech—all troubled me :
In my mind's eye I seemed to see him pace
  About the weary moors continually,   130
  Wandering about alone and silently.
While I these thoughts within myself pursued,
He, having made a pause, the same discourse renewed.

And soon with this he other matter blended,
  Cheerfully uttered, with demeanour kind,
But stately in the main ; and when he ended,
  I could have laughed myself to scorn to find
  In that decrepit man so firm a mind.
'God,' said I, 'be my help and stay secure ;
I 'll think of the leech-gatherer on the lonely moor !'   140

COMPOSED UPON WESTMINSTER BRIDGE,

SEPT. 3, 1802.

EARTH has not anything to show more fair ;
Dull would he be of soul who could pass by
A sight so touching in its majesty.
This city now doth like a garment wear
The beauty of the morning ; silent, bare,
Ships, towers, domes, theatres, and temples lie
Open unto the fields and to the sky,
All bright and glittering in the smokeless air.
Never did sun more beautifully steep
In his first splendour valley, rock, or hill ;   10
Ne'er saw I, never felt, a calm so deep !
The river glideth at his own sweet will.
Dear God ! the very houses seem asleep,
And all that mighty heart is lying still !

'IT IS A BEAUTEOUS EVENING, CALM AND FREE.'

IT is a beauteous evening, calm and free ;
The holy time is quiet as a nun
Breathless with adoration ; the broad sun
Is sinking down in its tranquillity ;

LANGDALE PIKES.

The gentleness of heaven is on the sea.
Listen! the mighty being is awake,
And doth with his eternal motion make
A sound like thunder everlastingly.
Dear child! dear girl! that walkest with me here,
If thou appear untouched by solemn thought,
Thy nature is not therefore less divine.
Thou liest in Abraham's bosom all the year,
And worshipp'st at the temple's inner shrine,
God being with thee when we know it not.

ON THE EXTINCTION OF THE VENETIAN REPUBLIC.

ONCE did she hold the gorgeous East in fee
And was the safeguard of the West; the worth
Of Venice did not fall below her birth,
Venice, the eldest child of Liberty.
She was a maiden city, bright and free,
No guile seduced, no force could violate;
And, when she took unto herself a mate,
She must espouse the everlasting sea.
And what if she had seen those glories fade,
Those titles vanish, and that strength decay?
Yet shall some tribute of regret be paid
When her long life hath reached its final day.
Men are we, and must grieve when even the shade
Of that which once was great is passed away.

TO TOUSSAINT L'OUVERTURE.

TOUSSAINT, the most unhappy man of men!
Whether the whistling rustic tend his plough
Within thy hearing, or thy head be now
Pillowed in some deep dungeon's earless den—
O miserable chieftain, where and when
Wilt thou find patience? Yet die not; do thou
Wear rather in thy bonds a cheerful brow:
Though fallen thyself, never to rise again,
Live, and take comfort. Thou hast left behind
Powers that will work for thee—air, earth, and skies;
There's not a breathing of the common wind
That will forget thee. Thou hast great allies;
Thy friends are exultations, agonies,
And love, and man's unconquerable mind.

————

WRITTEN IN LONDON, SEPTEMBER, 1802.

O FRIEND, I know not which way I must look
For comfort, being, as I am, opprest,
To think that now our life is only drest
For show—mean handiwork of craftsman, cook,
Or groom! We must run glittering like a brook
In the open sunshine, or we are unblest;
The wealthiest man among us is the best;
No grandeur now in nature or in book
Delights us. Rapine, avarice, expense,
This is idolatry, and these we adore;
Plain living and high thinking are no more;
The homely beauty of the good old cause
Is gone—our peace, our fearful innocence,
And pure religion breathing household laws.

LONDON, 1802.

MILTON, thou shouldst be living at this hour!
England hath need of thee : she is a fen
Of stagnant waters ; altar, sword, and pen,
Fireside, the heroic wealth of hall and bower,
Have forfeited their ancient English dower
Of inward happiness.   We are selfish men ;
O, raise us up, return to us again,
And give us manners, virtue, freedom, power !
Thy soul was like a star, and dwelt apart ;
Thou hadst a voice whose sound was like the sea.
Pure as the naked heavens, majestic, free,
So didst thou travel on life's common way
In cheerful godliness ; and yet thy heart
The lowliest duties on itself did lay.

'IT IS NOT TO BE THOUGHT OF.'

IT is not to be thought of that the flood
Of British freedom, which to the open sea
Of the world's praise from dark antiquity
Hath flowed, 'with pomp of waters, unwithstood,'
Roused though it be full often to a mood
Which spurns the check of salutary bands—
That this most famous stream in bogs and sands
Should perish, and to evil and to good
Be lost forever.   In our halls is hung
Armoury of the invincible knights of old :

We must be free or die who speak the tongue
That Shakespeare spake, the faith and morals hold
Which Milton held. In everything we are sprung
Of Earth's first blood, have titles manifold.

'WHEN I HAVE BORNE IN 'MEMORY.'

WHEN I have borne in memory what has tamed
Great nations, how ennobling thoughts depart
When men change swords for ledgers, and desert
The student's bower for gold, some fears unnamed
I had, my country!—am I to be blamed?
Now, when I think of thee and what thou art,
Verily, in the bottom of my heart
Of those unfilial fears I am ashamed!
For dearly must we prize thee, we who find
In thee a bulwark for the cause of men;
And I by my affection was beguiled.
What wonder if a poet now and then,
Among the many movements of his mind,
Felt for thee as a lover or a child?

TO THE DAISY.

'Her divine skill taught me this,
  That from everything I saw
  I could some instruction draw,
  And raise pleasure to the height
  Through the meanest object's sight.
  By the murmur of a spring,
  Or the least bough's rustling,

By a daisy whose leaves spread
Shut when Titan goes to bed,
Or a shady bush or tree,
She could more infuse in me
Than all Nature's beauties can
In some other wiser man.'

G. WITHER.

In youth from rock to rock I went,
From hill to hill in discontent
Of pleasure high and turbulent,
    Most pleased when most uneasy ;
But now my own delights I make,—
My thirst at every rill can slake,
And gladly Nature's love partake
    Of thee, sweet daisy !

Thee Winter in the garland wears
That thinly decks his few gray hairs ;   10
Spring parts the clouds with softest airs,
    That she may sun thee ;
Whole summer fields are thine by right ;
And Autumn, melancholy wight,
Doth in thy crimson head delight
    When rains are on thee.

In shoals and bands, a morrice train,
Thou greet'st the traveller in the lane,
Pleased at his greeting thee again,
    Yet nothing daunted   20
Nor grieved if thou be set at nought ;
And oft alone in nooks remote
We meet thee, like a pleasant thought,
    When such are wanted.

Be violets in their secret mews
The flowers the wanton Zephyrs choose ;

EAGLE CRAG.

Proud be the rose, with rains and dews
　　Her head impearling!
Thou liv'st with less ambitious aim,
Yet hast not gone without thy fame ;　　　　30
Thou art indeed by many a claim
　　The poet's darling.

If to a rock from rains he fly,
Or, some bright day of April sky,
Imprisoned by hot sunshine lie
　　Near the green holly,
And wearily at length should fare,
He needs but look about and there
Thou art—a friend at hand, to scare
　　His melancholy.　　　　40

A hundred times, by rock or bower,
Ere thus I have lain couched an hour,
Have I derived from thy sweet power
　　Some apprehension,
Some steady love, some brief delight,
Some memory that had taken flight,
Some chime of fancy wrong or right,
　　Or stray invention.

If stately passions in me burn,
And one chance look to thee should turn,　　50
I drink out of an humbler urn
　　A lowlier pleasure—
The homely sympathy that heeds
The common life our nature breeds,
A wisdom fitted to the needs
　　Of hearts at leisure.

Fresh-smitten by the morning ray,
When thou art up, alert and gay,

Then, cheerful flower, my spirits play
    With kindred gladness ;   60
And when at dusk by dews opprest
Thou sink'st, the image of thy rest
Hath often eased my pensive breast
    Of careful sadness.

And all day long I number yet,
All seasons through, another debt,
Which I, wherever thou art met,
    To thee am owing—
An instinct call it, a blind sense,
A happy, genial influence,   70
Coming one knows not how nor whence,
    Nor whither going.

Child of the year, that round dost run
Thy pleasant course, when day 's begun
As ready to salute the sun
    As lark or leveret,
Thy long-lost praise thou shalt regain,
Nor be less dear to future men
Than in old time ; thou not in vain
    Art Nature's favourite.   80

TO THE SAME FLOWER.

WITH little here to do or see
Of things that in the great world be,
Daisy, again I talk to thee,
    For thou art worthy,

Thou unassuming common-place
Of nature, with that homely face,
And yet with something of a grace
    Which Love makes for thee!

Oft on the dappled turf at ease
I sit and play with similes,
Loose types of things through all degrees,   10
    Thoughts of thy raising;
And many a fond and idle name
I give to thee for praise or blame,
As in the humour of the game,
    While I am gazing.

A nun demure of lowly port;
Or sprightly maiden of Love's court,
In thy simplicity the sport
    Of all temptations;   20
A queen in crown of rubies drest;
A starveling in a scanty vest;
Are all, as seems to suit thee best,
    Thy appellations.

A little Cyclops, with one eye
Staring to threaten and defy,
That thought comes next—and instantly
    The freak is over,
The shape will vanish—and behold
A silver shield with boss of gold,   30
That spreads itself, some faery bold
    In fight to cover!

I see thee glittering from afar,
And then thou art a pretty star;
Not quite so fair as many are
    In heaven above thee,

Yet like a star, with glittering crest,
Self-poised in air thou seem'st to rest ;—
May peace come never to his nest
 Who shall reprove thee !   40

Bright *flower!* for by that name at last,
When all my reveries are past,
I call thee, and to that cleave fast !
 Sweet silent creature,
That breath'st with me in sun and air,
Do thou, as thou art wont, repair
My heart with gladness and a share
 Of thy meek nature !

TO THE DAISY.

Bright Flower, whose home is everywhere,
Bold in maternal Nature's care,
And all the long year through the heir
 Of joy or sorrow !
Methinks that there abides in thee
Some concord with humanity,
Given to no other flower I see
 The forest thorough.

Is it that man is soon deprest—
A thoughtless thing, who, once unblest,   10
Does little on his memory rest
 Or on his reason?
And thou wouldst teach him how to find
A shelter under every wind,
A hope for times that are unkind
 And every season?

7

Thou wander'st the wide world about,
Unchecked by pride or scrupulous doubt,
With friends to greet thee or without,
    Yet pleased and willing;   20
Meek, yielding to the occasion's call,
And all things suffering from all,
Thy function apostolical
    In peace fulfilling.

THE GREEN LINNET.

BENEATH these fruit-tree boughs that shed
Their snow-white blossoms on my head,
With brightest sunshine round me spread
    Of spring's unclouded weather,
In this sequestered nook how sweet
To sit upon my orchard-seat,
And birds and flowers once more to greet,
    My last year's friends together!

One have I marked, the happiest guest
In all this covert of the blest: 10
Hail to thee, far above the rest
    In joy of voice and pinion!
Thou, linnet, in thy green array,
Presiding spirit here to-day,
Dost lead the revels of the May,
    And this is thy dominion.

While birds and butterflies and flowers
Make all one band of paramours,
Thou, ranging up and down the bowers,
    Art sole in thy employment;   20

A life, a presence like the air,
Scattering thy gladness without care,
Too blest with any one to pair,
    Thyself thy own enjoyment.

Amid yon tuft of hazel-trees,
That twinkle to the gusty breeze,
Behold him perched in ecstasies,
    Yet seeming still to hover—
There! where the flutter of his wings
Upon his back and body flings   30
Shadows and sunny glimmerings, .
    That cover him all over.

My dazzled sight he oft deceives,
A brother of the dancing leaves,
Then flits and from the cottage-eaves
    Pours forth his song in gushes;
As if by that exulting strain
He mocked and treated with disdain
The voiceless form he chose to feign
    While fluttering in the bushes.   40

TO A HIGHLAND GIRL

(AT INVERSNAID, UPON LOCH LOMOND).

SWEET Highland girl, a very shower
Of beauty is thy earthly dower!
Twice seven consenting years have shed
Their utmost bounty on thy head;
And these gray rocks, that household lawn,
Those trees, a veil just half withdrawn,

This fall of water that doth make
A murmur near the silent lake,
This little bay, a quiet road
That holds in shelter thy abode—   10
In truth, together do ye seem
Like something fashioned in a dream,
Such forms as from their covert peep
When earthly cares are laid asleep.
Yet, dream or vision as thou art,
I bless thee with a human heart :
God shield thee to thy latest years !
Thee neither know I nor thy peers,
And yet my eyes are filled with tears.

With earnest feeling I shall pray   20
For thee when I am far away ;
For never saw I mien or face
In which more plainly I could trace
Benignity and home-bred sense
Ripening in perfect innocence.
Here scattered like a random seed,
Remote from men, thou dost not need
The embarrassed look of shy distress
And maidenly shamefacedness ;
Thou wear'st upon thy forehead clear   30
The freedom of a mountaineer—
A face with gladness overspread,
Soft smiles by human kindness bred ;
And seemliness complete that sways
Thy courtesies about thee plays,
With no restraint but such as springs
From quick and eager visitings
Of thoughts that lie beyond the reach
Of thy few words of English speech—

A bondage sweetly brooked, a strife   40
That gives thy gestures grace and life !
So have I, not unmoved in mind,
Seen birds of tempest-loving kind
Thus beating up against the wind.

What hand but would a garland cull
For thee who art so beautiful ?
O, happy pleasure here to dwell
Beside thee in some heathy dell,
Adopt your homely ways and dress,
A shepherd, thou a shepherdess !   50
But I could frame a wish for thee
More like a grave reality :
Thou art to me but as a wave
Of the wild sea, and I would have
Some claim upon thee, if I could,
Though but of common neighbourhood.
What joy to hear thee, and to see !
Thy elder brother I would be,
Thy father—anything to thee !

Now thanks to Heaven that of its grace   60
Hath led me to this lonely place !
Joy have I had, and going hence
I bear away my recompense.
In spots like these it is we prize
Our memory, feel that she hath eyes ;
Then why should I be loath to stir ?
I feel this place was made for her ;
To give new pleasure like the past,
Continued long as life shall last.
Nor am I loath, though pleased at heart,   70
Sweet Highland girl, from thee to part ;

For I, methinks, till I grow old,
As fair before me shall behold
As I do now the cabin small,
The lake, the bay, the waterfall,
And thee, the spirit of them all !

THE SOLITARY REAPER.

Behold her, single in the field,
    Yon solitary Highland lass,
Reaping and singing by herself;
    Stop here, or gently pass !
Alone she cuts and binds the grain
And sings a melancholy strain ;
O, listen, for the vale profound
Is overflowing with the sound !

No nightingale did ever chant
    So sweetly to reposing bands   10
Of travellers in some shady haunt
    Among Arabian sands :
A voice so thrilling ne'er was heard
In springtime from the cuckoo-bird,
Breaking the silence of the seas
Among the farthest Hebrides.

Will no one tell me what she sings ?
    Perhaps the plaintive numbers flow
For old, unhappy, far-off things,
    And battles long ago ;   20
Or is it some more humble lay,
Familiar matter of to-day ?

Some natural sorrow, loss, or pain,
That has been, and may be again?

Whate'er the theme, the maiden sang
  As if her song could have no ending;
I saw her singing at her work,
  And o'er the sickle bending.
I listened till I had my fill;
And when I mounted up the hill,   30
The music in my heart I bore
Long after it was heard no more.

———

YARROW UNVISITED.

From Stirling Castle we had seen
  The mazy Forth unravelled,
Had trod the banks of Clyde and Tay,
  And with the Tweed had travelled;
And when we came to Clovenford,
  Then said my 'winsome Marrow,'
'Whate'er betide, we'll turn aside
  And see the Braes of Yarrow.'

'Let Yarrow folk, frae Selkirk town,
  Who have been buying, selling,   10
Go back to Yarrow—'t is their own—
  Each maiden to her dwelling!
On Yarrow's banks let herons feed,
  Hares couch, and rabbits burrow!
But we will downward with the Tweed,
  Nor turn aside to Yarrow.

'There 's Galla Water, Leader Haughs,
    Both lying right before us;
And Dryborough, where with chiming Tweed
    The lintwhites sing in chorus;   20
There 's pleasant Tiviotdale, a land
    Made blithe with plough and harrow:
Why throw away a needful day
    To go in search of Yarrow?

'What 's Yarrow but a river bare,
    That glides the dark hills under?
There are a thousand such elsewhere
    As worthy of your wonder.'
Strange words they seemed of slight and scorn;
    My true-love sighed for sorrow,   30
And looked me in the face, to think
    I thus could speak of Yarrow!

'O, green,' said I, 'are Yarrow's holms,
    And sweet is Yarrow flowing!
Fair hangs the apple frae the rock,
    But we will leave it growing.
O'er hilly path and open strath
    We 'll wander Scotland thorough;
But, though so near, we will not turn
    Into the dale of Yarrow.   40

'Let beeves and home-bred kine partake
    The sweets of Burn-mill meadow,
The swan on still Saint Mary's Lake
    Float double, swan and shadow!
We will not see them, will not go
    To-day, nor yet to-morrow;
Enough if in our hearts we know
    There 's such a place as Yarrow.

WINDERMEER.

' Be Yarrow stream unseen, unknown !
   It must, or we shall rue it :   50
We have a vision of our own ;
   Ah ! why should we undo it ?
The treasured dreams of times long past,
   We 'll keep them, winsome Marrow !
For when we 're there, although 't is fair,
   'T will be another Yarrow !

' If care with freezing years should come
   And wandering seem but folly,
Should we be loath to stir from home
   And yet be melancholy,   60
Should life be dull and spirits low,
   'T will soothe us in our sorrow
That earth has something yet to show,
   The bonny holms of Yarrow !'

———

'SHE WAS A PHANTOM OF DELIGHT.'

SHE was a phantom of delight
When first she gleamed upon my sight,
A lovely apparition, sent
To be a moment's ornament :
Her eyes as stars of twilight fair,
Like twilight's, too, her dusky hair ;
But all things else about her drawn
From May-time and the cheerful dawn—
A dancing shape, an image gay,
To haunt, to startle, and waylay.   10

I saw her upon nearer view,
A spirit, yet a woman too !

Her household motions light and free,
And steps of virgin liberty;
A countenance in which did meet
Sweet records, promises as sweet;
A creature not too bright or good
For human nature's daily food;
For transient sorrows, simple wiles,
Praise, blame, love, kisses, tears, and smiles.　20

And now I see with eye serene
The very pulse of the machine;
A being breathing thoughtful breath,
A traveller between life and death;
The reason firm, the temperate will,
Endurance, foresight, strength, and skill;
A perfect woman, nobly planned,
To warn, to comfort, and command;
And yet a spirit still, and bright
With something of an angel light.　30

'I WANDERED LONELY AS A CLOUD.'

I WANDERED lonely as a cloud
　That floats on high o'er vales and hills,
When all at once I saw a crowd,
　A host of golden daffodils,
Beside the lake, beneath the trees,
　Fluttering and dancing in the breeze.

Continuous as the stars that shine
　And twinkle on the Milky Way,
They stretched in never-ending line
　Along the margin of a bay:　10

Ten thousand saw I at a glance,
Tossing their heads in sprightly dance.

The waves beside them danced, but they
  Outdid the sparkling waves in glee.
A poet could not but be gay
  In such a jocund company;
I gazed and gazed, but little thought
What wealth the show to me had brought.

For oft, when on my couch I lie
  In vacant or in pensive mood,   20
They flash upon that inward eye
  Which is the bliss of solitude,
And then my heart with pleasure fills,
And dances with the daffodils.

THE AFFLICTION OF MARGARET.

WHERE art thou, my beloved son,
  Where art thou, worse to me than dead?
O, find me, prosperous or undone!
  Or, if the grave be now thy bed,
Why am I ignorant of the same,
That I may rest, and neither blame
Nor sorrow may attend thy name?

Seven years, alas! to have received
  No tidings of an only child;
To have despaired, and have believed,   10
  And be forevermore beguiled,
Sometimes with thoughts of very bliss!
I catch at them, and then I miss;
Was ever darkness like to this?

He was among the prime in worth,
    An object beauteous to behold :
Well born, well bred, I sent him forth
    Ingenuous, innocent, and bold :
If things ensued that wanted grace,
As hath been said, they were not base,   20
And never blush was on my face.

Ah ! little doth the young one dream,
    When full of play and childish cares,
What power is in his wildest scream,
    Heard by his mother unawares !
He knows it not, he cannot guess :
Years to a mother bring distress,
But do not make her love the less.

Neglect me ! no, I suffered long
    From that ill thought, and, being blind,   30
Said, 'Pride shall help me in my wrong:
    Kind mother have I been, as kind
As ever breathed.' And that is true ;
I 've wet my path with tears like dew,
Weeping for him when no one knew.

My son, if thou be humbled, poor,
    Hopeless of honour and of gain,
O, do not dread thy mother's door,
    Think not of me with grief and pain !
I now can see with better eyes ;   40
And worldly grandeur I despise,
And Fortune with her gifts and lies.

Alas ! the fowls of heaven have wings,
    And blasts of heaven will aid their flight;
They mount—how short a voyage brings
    The wanderers back to their delight!

Chains tie *us* down by land and sea ;
And wishes, vain as mine, may be
All that is left to comfort thee.

Perhaps some dungeon hears thee groan,   50
   Maimed, mangled by inhuman men ;
Or thou upon a desert thrown
   Inheritest the lion's den,
Or hast been summoned to the deep,
Thou, thou and all thy mates, to keep
An incommunicable sleep.

I look for ghosts, but none will force
   Their way to me : 't is falsely said
That there was ever intercourse
   Between the living and the dead ;   60
For, surely, then I should have sight
Of him I wait for day and night,
With love and longings infinite.

My apprehensions come in crowds ;
   I dread the rustling of the grass ;
The very shadows of the clouds
   Have power to shake me as they pass.
I question things, and do not find
One that will answer to my mind,
And all the world appears unkind.   70

Beyond participation lie
   My troubles, and beyond relief:
If any chance to heave a sigh,
   They pity me, and not my grief.
Then come to me, my son, or send
Some tidings that my woes may end ;
I have no other earthly friend !

ODE TO DUTY.

'Jam non consilio bonus, sed more eo perductus, ut non tantum recte
facere possim, sed nisi recte facere non possim.'

STERN daughter of the voice of God!
   O Duty! if that name thou love
Who art a light to guide, a rod
   To check the erring and reprove;
Thou, who art victory and law
When empty terrors overawe,
From vain temptations dost set free,
And calm'st the weary strife of frail humanity!

. There are who ask not if thine eye
   Be on them; who, in love and truth,   10
Where no misgiving is, rely
   Upon the genial sense of youth;
Glad hearts, without reproach or blot,
Who do thy work and know it not:
Long may the kindly impulse last!
But thou, if they should totter, teach them to stand fast!

Serene will be our days and bright,
   And happy will our nature be,
When love is an unerring light,
   And joy its own security;   20
And they a blissful course may hold
Even now who, not unwisely bold,
Live in the spirit of this creed,
Yet seek thy firm support according to their need.

I, loving freedom and untried—
  No sport of every random gust,
Yet being to myself a guide—
  Too blindly have reposed my trust;
And oft, when in my heart was heard
Thy timely mandate, I deferred   30
The task, in smoother walks to stray;
But thee I now would serve more strictly, if I may.

Through no disturbance of my soul
  Or strong compunction in me wrought,
I supplicate for thy control,
  But in the quietness of thought.
Me this unchartered freedom tires;
I feel the weight of chance desires;
My hopes no more must change their name,
I long for a repose that ever is the same.   40

Stern lawgiver! yet thou dost wear
  The Godhead's most benignant grace,
Nor know we anything so fair
  As is the smile upon thy face.
Flowers laugh before thee on their beds,
And fragrance in thy footing treads;
Thou dost preserve the stars from wrong;
And the most ancient heavens, through thee, are fresh and
     strong.

To humbler functions, awful power,
  I call thee: I myself commend   50
Unto thy guidance from this hour;
  O, let my weakness have an end!
Give unto me, made lowly wise,
The spirit of self-sacrifice;

The confidence of reason give,
And in the light of truth thy bondman let me live!

TO A YOUNG LADY

WHO HAD BEEN REPROACHED FOR TAKING LONG WALKS IN
THE COUNTRY.

DEAR child of Nature, let them rail!
There is a nest in a green dale,
   A harbour and a hold,
Where thou, a wife and friend, shalt see
Thy own delightful days, and be
   A light to young and old.

There, healthy as a shepherd-boy,
And treading among flowers of joy
   Which at no season fade,
Thou, while thy babes around thee cling,   10
Shalt show us how divine a thing
   A woman may be made.

Thy thoughts and feelings shall not die,
Nor leave thee, when gray hairs are nigh,
   A melancholy slave;
But an old age serene and bright,
And lovely as a Lapland night,
   Shall lead thee to thy grave.
   8

CHARACTER OF THE HAPPY WARRIOR.

Who is the happy warrior? Who is he
That every man in arms should wish to be?
It is the generous spirit who, when brought
Among the tasks of real life, hath wrought
Upon the plan that pleased his boyish thought;
Whose high endeavors are an inward light
That makes the path before him always bright;
Who, with a natural instinct to discern
What knowledge can perform, is diligent to learn,
Abides by this resolve, and stops not there,   10
But makes his moral being his prime care;
Who, doomed to go in company with pain
And fear and bloodshed—miserable train!—
Turns his necessity to glorious gain;
In face of these doth exercise a power
Which is our human nature's highest dower;
Controls them and subdues, transmutes, bereaves
Of their bad influence, and their good receives;
By objects which might force the soul to abate
Her feeling rendered more compassionate;   20
Is placable, because occasions rise
So often that demand such sacrifice;
More skilful in self-knowledge, even more pure,
As tempted more; more able to endure
As more exposed to suffering and distress;
Thence, also, more alive to tenderness.
'T is he whose law is reason; who depends
Upon that law as on the best of friends;
Whence, in a state where men are tempted still
To evil for a guard against worse ill,   30

HELVELLYN AND THIRLMERE.

And what in quality or act is best
Doth seldom on a right foundation rest,
He fixes good on good alone, and owes
To virtue every triumph that he knows:
Who, if he rise to station of command,
Rises by open means, and there will stand
On honourable terms, or else retire
And in himself possess his own desire;
Who comprehends his trust, and to the same
Keeps faithful with a singleness of aim,   40
And therefore does not stoop, nor lie in wait
For wealth or honours or for worldly state;
Whom they must follow, on whose head must fall
Like showers of manna, if they come at all;
Whose powers shed round him, in the common strife
Or mild concerns of ordinary life,
A constant influence, a peculiar grace;
But who, if he be called upon to face
Some awful moment to which Heaven has joined
Great issues, good or bad for human kind,   50
Is happy as a lover, and attired
With sudden brightness, like a man inspired;
And through the heat of conflict keeps the law
In calmness made, and sees what he foresaw;
Or if an unexpected call succeed,
Come when it will, is equal to the need:
He who, though thus endued as with a sense
And faculty for storm and turbulence,
Is yet a soul whose master-bias leans
To homefelt pleasures and to gentle scenes—   60
Sweet images! which, wheresoe'er he be,
Are at his heart, and such fidelity
It is his darling passion to approve;
More brave for this, that he hath much to love,
'Tis, finally, the man who, lifted high,

Conspicuous object in a nation's eye,
Or left unthought of in obscurity,—
Who, with a toward or untoward lot,
Prosperous or adverse, to his wish or not,
Plays, in the many games of life, that one   70
Where what he most doth value must be won;
Whom neither shape of danger can dismay
Nor thought of tender happiness betray;
Who, not content that former worth stand fast,
Looks forward, persevering to the last,
From well to better, daily self-surpassed;
Who, whether praise of him must walk the earth
Forever and to noble deeds give birth,
Or he must go to dust without his fame
And leave a dead unprofitable name,   80
Finds comfort in himself and in his cause,
And, while the mortal mist is gathering, draws
His breath in confidence of Heaven's applause.
This is the happy warrior; this is he
That every man in arms should wish to be.

POWER OF MUSIC.

An Orpheus! an Orpheus! yes, Faith may grow bold,
And take to herself all the wonders of old;
Near the stately Pantheon you'll meet with the same
In the street that from Oxford hath borrowed its name.

His station is there; and he works on the crowd,
He sways them with harmony merry and loud;
He fills with his power all their hearts to the brim —
Was aught ever heard like his fiddle and him?

What an eager assembly! what an empire is this!
The weary have life, and the hungry have bliss ;   10
The mourner is cheered and the anxious have rest,
And the guilt-burdened soul is no longer opprest.

As the moon brightens round her the clouds of the night,
So he, where he stands, is a centre of light ;
It gleams on the face there of dusky-browed Jack,
And the pale-visaged baker's, with basket on back.

That errand-bound 'prentice was passing in haste—
What matter? he 's caught, and his time runs to waste.
The newsman is stopped, though he stops on the fret ;
And the half-breathless lamplighter—he 's in the net !   20

The porter sits down on the weight which he bore ;
The lass with her barrow wheels hither her store ;
If a thief could be here, he might pilfer at ease ;
She sees the musician, 't is all that she sees !

He stands, backed by the wall ; he abates not his din ;
His hat gives him vigour, with boons dropping in
From the old and the young, from the poorest ; and there !
The one-pennied boy has his penny to spare.

O, blest are the hearers, and proud be the hand
Of the pleasure it spreads through so thankful a band !   30
I am glad for him, blind as he is !—all the while
If they speak 't is to praise, and they praise with a smile.

That tall man, a giant in bulk and in height,
Not an inch of his body is free from delight ;
Can he keep himself still if he would?   O, not he !
The music stirs in him like wind through a tree.

Mark that cripple who leans on his crutch; like a tower
That long has leaned forward, leans hour after hour!
That mother, whose spirit in fetters is bound,
While she dandles the babe in her arms to the sound.   40

Now, coaches and chariots, roar on like a stream!
Here are twenty souls happy as souls in a dream:
They are deaf to your murmurs—they care not for you,
Nor what ye are flying, nor what ye pursue!

SONNETS.

Nuns fret not at their convent's narrow room,
And hermits are contented with their cells,
And students with their pensive citadels;
Maids at the wheel, the weaver at his loom,
Sit blithe and happy; bees that soar for bloom
High as the highest peak of Furness Fells
Will murmur by the hour in foxglove bells.
In truth, the prison unto which we doom
Ourselves no prison is; and hence for me,
In sundry moods, 't was pastime to be bound
Within the sonnet's scanty plot of ground;
Pleased if some souls—for such there needs must be—
Who have felt the weight of too much liberty
Should find brief solace there, as I have found.

Wings have we, and as far as we can go
We may find pleasure; wilderness and wood,
Blank ocean and mere sky, support that mood

Which with the lofty sanctifies the low.
Dreams, books, are each a world; and books, we know,
Are a substantial world, both pure and good:
Round these, with tendrils strong as flesh and blood,
Our pastime and our happiness will grow.
There find I personal themes, a plenteous store,
Matter wherein right voluble I am,
To which I listen with a ready ear:
Two shall be named, pre-eminently dear—
The gentle lady married to the Moor,
And heavenly Una with her milk-white lamb.

Nor can I not believe but that hereby
Great gains are mine, for thus I live remote
From evil-speaking; rancour, never sought,
Comes to me not, malignant truth or lie.
Hence have I genial seasons, hence have I
Smooth passions, smooth discourse, and joyous thought;
And thus from day to day my little boat
Rocks in its harbour, lodging peaceably.
Blessings be with them and eternal praise,
Who gave us nobler loves and nobler cares—
The poets, who on earth have made us heirs
Of truth and pure delight by heavenly lays!
O, might my name be numbered among theirs,
Then gladly would I end my mortal days!

The world is too much with us; late and soon,
Getting and spending, we lay waste our powers.
Little we see in Nature that is ours;

We have given our hearts away, a sordid boon !
The sea that bares her bosom to the moon,
The winds that will be howling at all hours,
And are upgathered now like sleeping flowers—
For this, for everything, we are out of tune ;
It moves us not.   Great God ! I 'd rather be
A Pagan suckled in a creed outworn,
So might I, standing on this pleasant lea,
Have glimpses that would make me less forlorn,
Have sight of Proteus rising from the sea,
Or hear old Triton blow his wreathed horn.

To Sleep.

A FLOCK of sheep that leisurely pass by,
One after one ; the sound of rain and bees
Murmuring ; the fall of rivers, winds and seas,
Smooth fields, white sheets of water, and pure sky,
By turns have all been thought of, yet I lie
Sleepless, and soon the small birds' melodies
Must hear, first uttered from my orchard trees,
And the first cuckoo's melancholy cry.
Even thus last night, and two nights more, I lay,
And could not win thee, sleep, by any stealth :
So do not let me wear to-night away.
Without thee what is all the morning's wealth ?
Come, blessed barrier between day and day,
Dear mother of fresh thoughts and joyous health !

ODE.

INTIMATIONS OF IMMORTALITY FROM RECOLLECTIONS OF EARLY CHILDHOOD.

THERE was a time when meadow, grove, and stream,
    The earth, and every common sight,
        To me did seem
      Apparelled in celestial light,
The glory and the freshness of a dream.
It is not now as it hath been of yore ;
      Turn wheresoe'er I may,
        By night or day,
The things which I have seen I now can see no more.

      The rainbow comes and goes,   10
      And lovely is the rose ;
      The moon doth with delight
Look round her when the heavens are bare ;
      Waters on a starry night
      Are beautiful and fair ;
    The sunshine is a glorious birth ;
    But yet I know, where'er I go,
That there hath passed away a glory from the earth.

Now, while the birds thus sing a joyous song,
      And while the young lambs bound   20
      As to the tabor's sound,
To me alone there came a thought of grief:
A timely utterance gave that thought relief,
      And I again am strong.

BRIDGE IN ST. JOHN'S VALE.

The cataracts blow their trumpets from the steep ;
No more shall grief of mine the season wrong ;
I hear the echoes through the mountains throng ;
The winds come to me from the fields of sleep,
     And all the earth is gay ;
        Land and sea   30
    Give themselves up to jollity,
      And with the heart of May
   Doth every beast keep holiday.
      Thou child of joy,
Shout round me, let me hear thy shouts, thou happy shepherd-
    boy !

Ye blessed creatures, I have heard the call
    Ye to each other make ; I see
The heavens laugh with you in your jubilee ;
    My heart is at your festival.
    My head hath its coronal,   40
The fulness of your bliss, I feel—I feel it all.
    O evil day if I were sullen
   When Earth herself is adorning
     This sweet May morning,
   And the children are culling
      On every side,
In a thousand valleys far and wide,
    Fresh flowers, while the sun shines warm,
And the babe leaps up on his mother's arm !
    I hear, I hear, with joy I hear !   50
    But there 's a tree, of many one,
A single field which I have looked upon,
Both of them speak of something that is gone ;
     The pansy at my feet
     Doth the same tale repeat.
Whither is fled the visionary gleam ?
Where is it now, the glory and the dream ?

' Our birth is but a sleep and a forgetting:
The soul that rises with us, our life's star,
  Hath had elsewhere its setting,   60
   And cometh from afar ;
 Not in entire forgetfulness,
 And not in utter nakedness,
But trailing clouds of glory do we come
  From God, who is our home.
Heaven lies about us in our infancy !
Shades of the prison-house begin to close
  Upon the growing boy,
But he beholds the light and whence it flows,
  He sees it in his joy;   70
The youth, who daily farther from the East
 Must travel, still is nature's priest,
  And by the vision splendid
  Is on his way attended ;
At length the man perceives it die away,
And fade into the light of common day.

Earth fills her lap with pleasures of her own ;
Yearnings she hath in her own natural kind,
And even with something of a mother's mind,
  And no unworthy aim,   80
 The homely nurse doth all she can
To make her foster-child, her inmate man,
 Forget the glories he hath known
And that imperial palace whence he came.

Behold the child among his new-born blisses,
A six years' darling of a pigmy size !
See, where 'mid work of his own hand he lies,
Fretted by sallies of his mother's kisses,

With light upon him from his father's eyes!
See at his feet some little plan or chart,   90
Some fragment from his dream of human life,
Shaped by himself with newly learned art—
  A wedding or a festival.
  A mourning or a funeral;
   And this hath now his heart,
  And unto this he frames his song.
   Then will he fit his tongue
To dialogues of business, love, or strife;
   But it will not be long
   Ere this be thrown aside,   100
   And with new joy and pride
The little actor cons another part,
Filling from time to time his ' humorous stage '
With all the persons, down to palsied age.
That Life brings with her in her equipage,
   As if his whole vocation
   Were endless imitation.

Thou, whose exterior semblance doth belie
   Thy soul's immensity;
. Thou best philosopher, who yet dost keep   110
Thy heritage; thou eye among the blind,
That, deaf and silent, read'st the eternal deep,
Haunted forever by the eternal mind—
   Mighty prophet! seer blest!
   On whom those truths do rest
Which we are toiling all our lives to find,
In darkness lost, the darkness of the grave;
Thou, over whom thy immortality
Broods like the day, a master o'er a slave,
A presence which is not to be put by;   120
Thou little child, yet glorious in the might
Of heaven-born freedom on thy being's height,

Why with such earnest pains dost thou provoke
The years to bring the inevitable yoke,
Thus blindly with thy blessedness at strife?
Full soon thy soul shall have her earthly freight,
And custom lie upon thee with a weight
Heavy as frost and deep almost as life!

      O joy, that in our embers
        Is something that doth live,   130
      That nature yet remembers
        What was so fugitive!
The thought of our past years in me doth breed
Perpetual benediction; not indeed
For that which is most worthy to be blest—
Delight and liberty, the simple creed
Of childhood, whether busy or at rest,
With new-fledged hope still fluttering in his breast:
      Not for these I raise
        The song of thanks and praise;   140
    But for those obstinate questionings
    Of sense and outward things,
    Fallings from us, vanishings,
    Blank misgivings of a creature
Moving about in worlds not realized,
High instincts before which our mortal nature
Did tremble like a guilty thing surprised;
      But for those first affections,
      Those shadowy recollections, ·
      Which, be they what they may,   150
Are yet the fountain light of all our day,
Are yet a master light of all our seeing,
Uphold us, cherish, and have power to make
Our noisy years seem moments in the being
Of the eternal silence: truths that wake,
       To perish never,

Which neither listlessness, nor mad endeavour,
          Nor man nor boy,
Nor all that is at enmity with joy,
Can utterly abolish or destroy!   160
Hence, in a season of calm weather,
          Though inland far we be,
Our souls have sight of that immortal sea
          Which brought us hither,
          Can in a moment travel thither,
And see the children sport upon the shore,
And hear the mighty waters rolling evermore.

Then sing, ye birds! sing, sing a joyous song!
          And let the young lambs bound
          As to the tabor's sound!   170
We in thought will join your throng,
          Ye that pipe and ye that play,
          Ye that through your hearts to-day
          Feel the gladness of the May!
What though the radiance which was once so bright
Be now forever taken from my sight,
Though nothing can bring back the hour
Of splendour in the grass, of glory in the flower?
          We will grieve not, rather find
          Strength in what remains behind;   180
          In the primal sympathy
          Which, having been, must ever be,
          In the soothing thoughts that spring
          Out of human suffering,
          In the faith that looks through death,
In years that bring the philosophic mind.

And O ye fountains, meadows, hills, and groves,
Think not of any severing of our loves!

Yet in my heart of hearts I feel your might;
I only have relinquished one delight   190
To live beneath your more habitual sway.
I love the brooks which down their channels fret,
Even more than when I tripped lightly as they;
The innocent brightness of a new-born day
   Is lovely yet;
The clouds that gather round the setting sun
Do take a sober colouring from an eye
That hath kept watch o'er man's mortality;
Another race hath been, and other palms are won.
Thanks to the human heart by which we live,   200
Thanks to its tenderness, its joys, and fears,
To me the meanest flower that blows can give
Thoughts that do often lie too deep for tears.

WYTHBURN CHURCH.

BROUGHAM CASTLE.

SONG AT THE FEAST OF BROUGHAM CASTLE,

UPON THE RESTORATION OF LORD CLIFFORD, THE SHEPHERD,
TO THE ESTATES AND HONOURS OF HIS ANCESTORS.

HIGH in the breathless hall the minstrel sate,
   And Eamont's murmur mingled with the song.
The words of ancient time I thus translate,
   A festal strain that hath been silent long:

'From town to town, from tower to tower,
The Red Rose is a gladsome flower.
Her thirty years of winter past,
The Red Rose is revived at last;
She lifts her head for endless spring,
For everlasting blossoming.   10
Both Roses flourish, Red and White:
In love and sisterly delight

The two that were at strife are blended,
And all old troubles now are ended.
Joy, joy to both! but most to her
Who is the flower of Lancaster!
Behold her how she smiles to-day
On this great throng, this bright array!
Fair greeting doth she send to all
From every corner of the hall;   20
But chiefly from above the board,
Where sits in state our rightful lord,
A Clifford to his own restored!

'They came with banner, spear, and shield;
And it was proved in Bosworth field.
Not long the Avenger was withstood—
Earth helped him with the cry of blood.
Saint George was for us, and the might
Of blessed angels crowned the right.
Loud voice the land has uttered forth,   30
We loudest in the faithful North:
Our fields rejoice, our mountains ring,
Our streams proclaim a welcoming;
Our strong abodes and castles see
The glory of their loyalty.

'How glad is Skipton at this hour,
Though she is but a lonely tower,
To vacancy and silence left,
Of all her guardian sons bereft—
Knight, squire or yeoman, page or groom!   40
We have them at the feast of Brougham.
How glad Pendragon, though the sleep
Of years be on her! She shall reap
A taste of this great pleasure, viewing
As in a dream her own renewing.

Rejoiced is Brough, right glad I deem
Beside her little humble stream,
And she that keepeth watch and ward
Her statelier Eden's course to guard ;
They both are happy at this hour,   50
Though each is but a lonely tower :
But here is perfect joy and pride
For one fair house by Eamont's side,
This day distinguished without peer
To see her master and to cheer—
Him and his lady mother dear !

'O, it was a time forlorn
When the fatherless was born !
Give her wings that she may fly,
Or she sees her infant die !   60
Swords that are with slaughter wild
Hunt the mother and the child.
Who will take them from the light?
Yonder is a man in sight;
Yonder is a house—but where?
No, they must not enter there.
To the caves and to the brooks,
To the clouds of heaven she looks ;
She is speechless, but her eyes
Pray in ghostly agonies.   70
Blissful Mary, Mother mild,
Maid and Mother undefiled,
Save a mother and her child !

'Now who is he that bounds with joy
On Carrock's side, a shepherd-boy?
No thoughts hath he but thoughts that pass
Light as the wind along the grass.

Can this be he who hither came
In secret, like a smothered flame,
O'er whom such thankful tears were shed   80
For shelter and a poor man's bread?
God loves the child ; and God hath willed
That those dear words should be fulfilled,
The lady's words, when forced away
The last she to her babe did say,
" My own, my own, thy fellow-guest
I may not be ; but rest thee, rest,
For lowly shepherd's life is best !"

' Alas ! when evil men are strong
No life is good, no pleasure long.   90
The boy must part from Mosedale's groves,
And leave Blencathara's rugged coves,
And quit the flowers that summer brings
To Glenderamakin's lofty springs—
Must vanish, and his careless cheer
Be turned to heaviness and fear.
Give Sir Lancelot Threlkeld praise !
Hear it, good man, old in days !
Thou tree of covert and of rest
For this young bird that is distrest,   100
Among thy branches safe he lay,
And he was free to sport and play
When falcons were abroad for prey.

' A recreant harp that sings of fear
And heaviness in Clifford's ear !
I said, when evil men are strong
No life is good, no pleasure long—
A weak and cowardly untruth !
Our Clifford was a happy youth,

And thankful through a weary time   110
That brought him up to manhood's prime.
Again he wanders forth at will,
And tends a flock from hill to hill.
His garb is humble ; ne'er was seen
Such garb with such a noble mien.
Among the shepherd-grooms no mate
Hath he, a child of strength and state,
Yet lacks not friends for simple glee,
Nor yet for higher sympathy.
To his side the fallow-deer   120
Came, and rested without fear ;
The eagle, lord of land and sea,
Stooped down to pay him fealty ;
And both the undying fish that swim
Through Bowscale Tarn did wait on him.
The pair were servants of his eye
In their immortality ;
They moved about in open sight,
To and fro, for his delight.
He knew the rocks which angels haunt   130
On the mountains visitant,
He hath kenned them taking wing ;
And the caves where fairies sing
He hath entered, and been told
By voices how men lived of old.
Among the heavens his eye can see
Face of thing that is to be ;
And, if men report him right,
He could whisper words of might.
Now another day is come,   140
Fitter hope and nobler doom ;
He hath thrown aside his crook,
And hath buried deep his book.
Armour rusting in his halls

.DUNMAIL RAISE.

On the blood of Clifford calls:
"Quell the Scot," exclaims the lance;
Bear me to the heart of France,
Is the longing of the shield.
Tell thy name, thou trembling field—
Field of death, where'er thou be,   150
Groan thou with our victory!
Happy day and mighty hour,
When our Shepherd, in his power,
Mailed and horsed, with lance and sword,
To his ancestors restored
Like a reappearing star,
Like a glory from afar,
First shall head the flock of war!'

Alas! the fervent harper did not know
  That for a tranquil soul the lay was framed,   160
Who, long compelled in humble walks to go,
  Was softened into feeling, soothed, and tamed.

Love had he found in huts where poor men lie;
  His daily teachers had been woods and rills,
The silence that is in the starry sky,
  The sleep that is among the lonely hills.

In him the savage virtue of the race,
  Revenge, and all ferocious thoughts, were dead:
Nor did he change, but kept in lofty place
  The wisdom which adversity had bred.   170

Glad were the vales, and every cottage hearth;
  The shepherd lord was honoured more and more;
And, ages after he was laid in earth,
  'The good Lord Clifford' was the name he bore.

LAODAMIA.

'WITH sacrifice, before the rising morn
   Performed, my slaughtered lord have I required ;
And in thick darkness, amid shades forlorn,
   Him of the infernal gods have I desired.
Celestial pity I again implore :
Restore him to my sight, great Jove, restore !'

So speaking, and by fervent love endowed
   With faith, the suppliant heavenward lifts her hands,
While, like the sun emerging from a cloud,
   Her countenance brightens and her eye expands ;   10
Her bosom heaves and spreads, her stature grows,
And she expects the issue in repose.

O terror ! what hath she perceived ?   O joy !
   What doth she look on ? whom doth she behold ?
Her hero slain upon the beach of Troy ?
   His vital presence ? his corporeal mould ?
It is—if sense deceive her not—'t is he !
And a god leads him, winged Mercury !

Mild Hermes spake, and touched her with his wand
   That calms all fear: 'Such grace hath crowned thy prayer,
Laodamia, that at Jove's command   21
   Thy husband walks the paths of upper air.
He comes to tarry with thee three hours' space ;
Accept the gift, behold him face to face !'

Forth sprang the impassioned queen her lord to clasp ;
 Again that consummation she essayed ;
But unsubstantial form eludes her grasp
 As often as that eager grasp was made.
The phantom parts, but parts to reunite
And reassume his place before her sight.   30

' Protesilaus, lo ! thy guide is gone !
 Confirm, I pray, the vision with thy voice :
This is our palace, yonder is thy throne ;
 Speak, and the floor thou tread'st on will rejoice.
Not to appall me have the gods bestowed
This precious boon and blest a sad abode.'

' Great Jove, Laodamia, doth not leave
 His gifts imperfect. Spectre though I be,
I am not sent to scare thee or deceive ;
 But in reward of thy fidelity.   40
And something also did my worth obtain ;
For fearless virtue bringeth boundless gain.

' Thou knowest, the Delphic oracle foretold
 That the first Greek who touched the Trojan strand
Should die ; but me the threat could not withhold.
 A generous cause a victim did demand ;
And forth I leapt upon the sandy plain,
A self-devoted chief—by Hector slain.'

' Supreme of heroes—bravest, noblest, best !
 Thy matchless courage I bewail no more,   50
Which then, when tens of thousands were depressed
 By doubt, propelled thee to the fatal shore ;
Thou found'st—and I forgive thee—here thou art—
A nobler counsellor than my poor heart.

' But thou, though capable of sternest deed,
    Wert kind as resolute and good as brave ;
And he whose power restores thee hath decreed
    Thou shouldst elude the malice of the grave :
Redundant are thy locks, thy lips as fair
As when their breath enriched Thessalian air.   60

' No spectre greets me—no vain shadow this ;
    Come, blooming hero, place thee by my side !
Give, on this well-known couch, one nuptial kiss
    To me this day a second time thy bride !'
Jove frowned in heaven ; the conscious Parcæ threw
Upon those roseate lips a Stygian hue.

' This visage tells thee that my doom is past :
    Know, virtue were not virtue if the joys
Of sense were able to return as fast
    And surely as they vanish.   Earth destroys   70
Those raptures duly, Erebus disdains ;
Calm pleasures there abide, majestic pains.

' Be taught, O faithful consort, to control
    Rebellious passion ! for the gods approve
The depth, and not the tumult, of the soul,
    A fervent, not ungovernable, love.
Thy transports moderate ; and meekly mourn
When I depart, for brief is my sojourn.'

' Ah, wherefore ?   Did not Hercules by force
    Wrest from the guardian monster of the tomb   80
Alcestis, a reanimated corse,
    Given back to dwell on earth in vernal bloom ?
Medea's spells dispersed the weight of years,
And Æson stood a youth 'mid youthful peers. -

'The gods to us are merciful, and they
  Yet further may relent ; for mightier far
Than strength of nerve and sinew, or the sway
  Of magic potent over sun and star,
Is love, though oft to agony distressed,
And though his favourite seat be feeble woman's breast.   90

' But if thou goest, I follow.'—' Peace !' he said.
  She looked upon him and was calmed and cheered ;
The ghastly colour from his lips had fled ;
  In his deportment, shape, and mien appeared
Elysian beauty, melancholy grace,
Brought from a pensive though a happy place.

He spake of love, such love as spirits feel
  In worlds whose course is equable and pure—
No fears to beat away, no strife to heal,
  The past unsighed for, and the future sure—   100
Spake of heroic arts in graver mood
Revived, with finer harmony pursued ;

Of all that is most beauteous, imaged there
  In happier beauty—more pellucid streams,
An ampler ether, a diviner air,
  And fields invested with purpureal gleams ;
Climes which the sun, who sheds the brightest day
Earth knows, is all unworthy to survey.

Yet there the soul shall enter which hath earned
  That privilege by virtue.   ' Ill,' said he,   110
'The end of man's existence I discerned,
  Who from ignoble games and revelry
Could draw, when we had parted, vain delight,
While tears were thy best pastime, day and night ;

'And while my youthful peers before my eyes—
  Each hero following his peculiar bent—
Prepared themselves for glorious enterprise
  By martial sports, or, seated in the tent,
Chieftains and kings in counsel were detained,
What time the fleet at Aulis lay enchained.   120

'The wished-for wind was given : I then revolved
  The oracle upon the silent sea,
And, if no worthier led the way, resolved
  That of a thousand vessels mine should be
The foremost prow in pressing to the strand,
Mine the first blood that tinged the Trojan sand.

'Yet bitter, ofttimes bitter, was the pang
  When of thy loss I thought, beloved wife !
On thee too fondly did my memory hang,
  And on the joys we shared in mortal life,   130
The paths which we have trod—these fountains, flowers,
My new-planned cities and unfinished towers.

'But should suspense permit the foe to cry,
  " Behold, they tremble ! haughty their array,
Yet of their number no one dares to die !"—
  In soul I swept the indignity away :
Old frailties then recurred ; but lofty thought,
In act embodied, my deliverance wrought.

'And thou, though strong in love, art all too weak
  In reason, in self-government too slow ;   140
I counsel thee by fortitude to seek
  Our blest reunion in the shades below.
The invisible world with thee hath sympathized ;
Be thy affections raised and solemnized.

Learn, by a mortal yearning, to ascend
  Towards a higher object.   Love was given,
Encouraged, sanctioned, chiefly for that end;
  For this the passion to excess was driven—
That self might be annulled, her bondage prove
The fetters of a dream, opposed to love.'   150

Aloud she shrieked, for Hermes reappears!
  Round the dear shade she would have clung—'t is vain;
The hours are past—too brief had they been years—
  And him no mortal effort can detain.
Swift, toward the realms that know not earthly day,
He through the portal takes his silent way,
And on the palace-floor a lifeless corse she lay.

Ah! judge her gently who so deeply loved—
  Her who in reason's spite, yet without crime,
Was in a trance of passion thus removed;   160
  Delivered from the galling yoke of time
And these frail elements, to gather flowers
Of blissful quiet 'mid unfading bowers.

Yet tears to human suffering are due;
And mortal hopes defeated and o'erthrown
Are mourned by man—and not by man alone,
As fondly he believes.   Upon the side
Of Hellespont—such faith was entertained—
A knot of spiry trees for ages grew
From out the tomb of him for whom she died;   170
And ever, when such stature they had gained
That Ilium's walls were subject to their view,
The trees' tall summits withered at the sight—
A constant interchange of growth and blight!

YARROW VISITED, September, 1814.

AND is this—Yarrow? *This* the stream
    Of which my fancy cherished
So faithfully a waking dream?
    An image that hath perished!
O that some minstrel's harp were near
    To utter notes of gladness,
And chase this silence from the air
    That fills my heart with sadness!

Yet why? a silvery current flows
    With uncontrolled meanderings;   10
Nor have these eyes by greener hills
    Been soothed in all my wanderings.
And through her depths Saint Mary's Lake
    Is visibly delighted;
For not a feature of those hills
    Is in the mirror slighted.

A blue sky bends o'er Yarrow vale,
    Save where that pearly whiteness
Is round the rising sun diffused,
    A tender hazy brightness;   20
Mild dawn of promise! that excludes
    All profitless dejection,
Though not unwilling here to admit
    A pensive recollection.

Where was it that the famous Flower
    Of Yarrow Vale lay bleeding?
His bed perchance was yon smooth mound
    On which the herd is feeding;

And haply from this crystal pool,
　　Now peaceful as the morning,   30
The water-wraith ascended thrice,
　　And gave his doleful warning.

Delicious is the lay that sings
　　The haunts of happy lovers,
The path that leads them to the grove,
　　The leafy grove that covers ;
And pity sanctifies the verse
　　That paints, by strength of sorrow,
The unconquerable strength of love—
　　Bear witness, rueful Yarrow !   40

But thou, that didst appear so fair
　　To fond imagination,
Dost rival in the light of day
　　Her delicate creation ;
Meek loveliness is round thee spread,
　　A softness still and holy,
The grace of forest charms decayed
　　And pastoral melancholy.

That region left, the vale unfolds
　　Rich groves of lofty stature,   50
With Yarrow winding through the pomp
　　Of cultivated nature ;
And, rising from those lofty groves,
　　Behold a ruin hoary !
The shattered front of Newark's towers,
　　Renowned in Border story.

Fair scenes for childhood's opening bloom,
　　For sportive youth to stray in,
For manhood to enjoy his strength,
　　And age to wear away in !   60

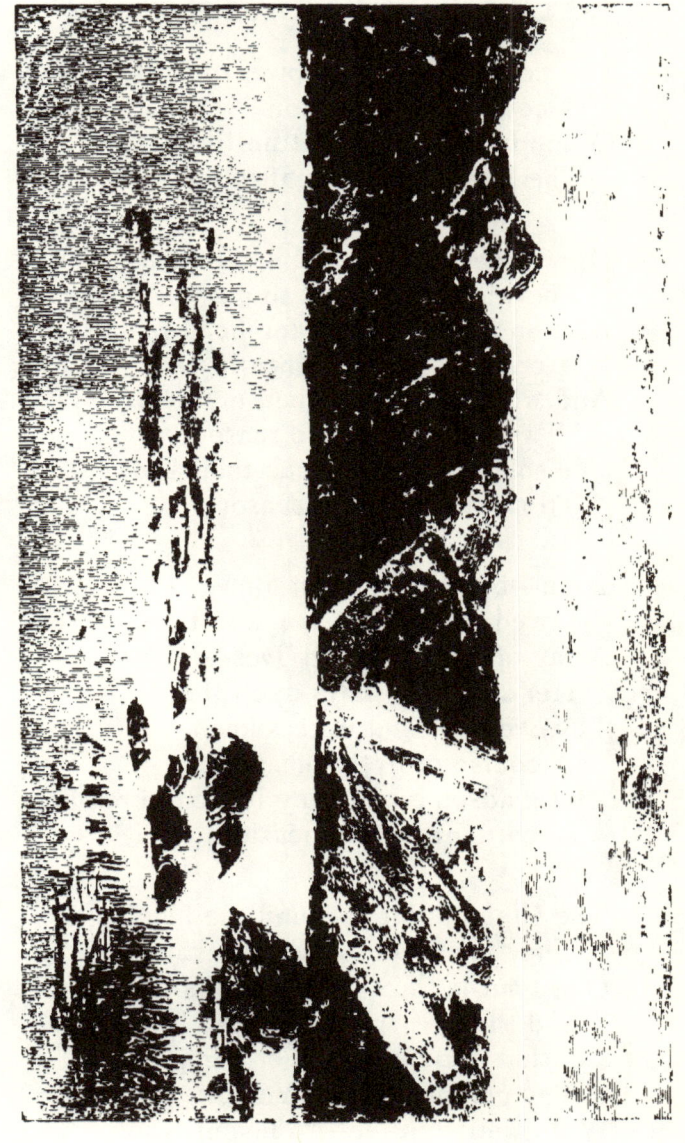

ULLESWATER.

Yon cottage seems a bower of bliss,
  A covert for protection
Of tender thoughts that nestle there,
  The brood of chaste affection.

How sweet, on this autumnal day,
  The wild-wood fruits to gather,
And on my true-love's forehead plant
  A crest of blooming heather !
And what if I enwreathed my own ?
  'T were no offence to reason ;   70
The sober hills thus deck their brows
  To meet the wintry season.

I see—but not by sight alone,
  Loved Yarrow, have I won thee ;
A ray of fancy still survives—
  Her sunshine plays upon thee !
Thy ever-youthful waters keep
  A course of lively pleasure ;
And gladsome notes my lips can breathe,
  Accordant to the measure.   80

The vapours linger round the heights—
  They melt, and soon must vanish ;
One hour is theirs, nor more is mine—
  Sad thought, which I would banish,
But that I know, where'er I go,
  Thy genuine image, Yarrow,
Will dwell with me—to heighten joy,
  And cheer my mind in sorrow.

TO B. R. HAYDON.

HIGH is our calling, friend! Creative art—
Whether the instrument of words she use
Or pencil pregnant with ethereal hues—
Demands the service of a mind and heart,
Though sensitive, yet in their weakest part
Heroically fashioned, to infuse
Faith in the whispers of the lonely Muse
While the whole world seems adverse to desert.
And O, when Nature sinks, as oft she may,
Through long-lived pressure of obscure distress,
Still to be strenuous for the bright reward
And in the soul admit of no decay,
Brook no continuance of weak-mindedness—
Great is the glory, for the strife is hard!

NOVEMBER 1.

How clear, how keen, how marvellously bright
The effluence from yon distant mountain's head,
Which, strewn with snow smooth as the sky can shed,
Shines like another sun—on mortal sight
Uprisen, as if to check approaching Night
And all her twinkling stars! Who now would tread,
If so he might, yon mountain's glittering head—
Terrestrial, but a surface by the flight
Of sad mortality's earth-sullying wing
Unswept, unstained? Nor shall the aërial powers

Dissolve that beauty, destined to endure,
White, radiant, spotless, exquisitely pure,
Through all vicissitudes, till genial Spring
Has filled the laughing vales with welcome flowers.

———

INSIDE OF KING'S COLLEGE CHAPEL, CAM-BRIDGE.

TAX not the royal saint with vain expense,
With ill-matched aims the architect who planned,
Albeit labouring for a scanty band
Of white-robed scholars only, this immense
And glorious work of fine intelligence!
Give all thou canst; high Heaven rejects the lore
Of nicely calculated less or more.
So deemed the man who fashioned for the sense
These lofty pillars, spread that branching roof,
Self-poised and scooped into ten thousand cells,
Where light and shade repose, where music dwells
Lingering and wandering on as loath to die;
Like thoughts whose very sweetness yieldeth proof
That they were born for immortality.

———

TO A SKYLARK.

ETHEREAL minstrel! pilgrim of the sky!
    Dost thou despise the earth where cares abound?
Or, while the wings aspire, are heart and eye
    Both with thy nest upon the dewy ground?—

Thy nest which thou canst drop into at will,
Those quivering wings composed, that music still!

Leave to the nightingale her shady wood ;
  A privacy of glorious light is thine,
Whence thou dost pour upon the world a flood
  Of harmony with instinct more divine—
Type of the wise who soar, but never roam,
True to the kindred points of heaven and home!

'SCORN NOT THE SONNET.'

SCORN not the sonnet ; critic, you have frowned,
Mindless of its just honours. With this key
Shakespeare unlocked his heart ; the melody
Of this small lute gave ease to Petrarch's wound ;
A thousand times this pipe did Tasso sound ;
Camoens soothed with it an exile's grief ;
The sonnet glittered a gay myrtle leaf
Amid the cypress with which Dante crowned
His visionary brow ; a glowworm lamp,
It cheered mild Spenser, called from fairy-land
To struggle through dark ways ; and when a damp
Fell round the path of Milton, in his hand
The thing became a trumpet, whence he blew
Soul-animating strains—alas, too few !

THE WISHING-GATE.

HOPE rules a land forever green :
All powers that serve the bright-eyed queen
   Are confident and gay ;
Clouds at her bidding disappear ;
Points she to aught? the bliss draws near,
   And fancy smooths the way.

Not such the land of wishes—there
Dwell fruitless day-dreams, lawless prayer,
   And thoughts with things at strife ;
Yet how forlorn, should *ye* depart,   10
Ye superstitions of the *heart*,
   How poor were human life !

When magic lore abjured its might,
Ye did not forfeit one dear right,
   One tender claim abate ;
Witness this symbol of your sway,
Surviving near the public way—
   The rustic Wishing-gate !

Inquire not if the fairy race
Shed kindly influence on the place   20
   Ere northward they retired ;
If here a warrior left a spell,
Panting for glory as he fell,
   Or here a saint expired.

Enough that all around is fair,
Composed with Nature's finest care

THE WISHING-GATE.

And in her fondest love—
Peace to embosom and content,
To overawe the turbulent,
    The selfish to reprove.   30

Yea, even the stranger from afar,
Reclining on this moss-grown bar,
    Unknowing and unknown,
The infection of the ground partakes,
Longing for his beloved, who makes
    All happiness her own.

Then why should conscious spirits fear
The mystic stirrings that are here,
    The ancient faith disclaim?
The local genius ne'er befriends   40
Desires whose course in folly ends,
    Whose just reward is shame.

Smile if thou wilt, but not in scorn,
If some, by ceaseless pains outworn,
    Here crave an easier lot;
If some have thirsted to renew
A broken vow, or bind a true
    With firmer, holier knot.

And not in vain, when thoughts are cast
Upon the irrevocable past,   50
    Some penitent sincere
May for a worthier future sigh,
While trickles from his downcast eye
    No unavailing tear.

The worldling, pining to be freed
From turmoil, who would turn or speed
    The currrent of his fate,

Might stop before this favoured scene
At Nature's call, nor blush to lean
   Upon the Wishing-gate.   60

The sage, who feels how blind, how weak
Is man, though loathe such help to *seek*,
   Yet passing here might pause,
And yearn for insight to allay
Misgiving, while the crimson day
   In quietness withdraws,

Or when the church-clock's knell profound
To Time's first step across the bound
   Of midnight makes reply—
Time pressing on with starry crest   70
To filial sleep upon the breast
   Of dread Eternity!

THE PRIMROSE OF THE ROCK.

A ROCK there is whose homely front
   The passing traveller slights;
Yet there the glowworms hang their lamps,
   Like stars, at various heights,
And one coy primrose to that rock
   The vernal breeze invites.

What hideous warfare hath been waged,
   What kingdoms overthrown,
Since first I spied that primrose-tuft
   And marked it for my own,   10
A lasting link in Nature's chain
   From highest heaven let down!

The flowers, still faithful to the stems,
   Their fellowship renew ;
The stems are faithful to the root,
   That worketh out of view ;
And to the rock the root adheres,
   In every fibre true.

Close clings to earth the living rock,
   Though threatening still to fall ;   20
The earth is constant to her sphere ;
   And God upholds them all :
So blooms this lonely plant, nor dreads
   Her annual funeral.

   *   *   *   *   *   *

Here closed the meditative strain ;
   But air breathed soft that day,
The hoary mountain-heights were cheered,
   The sunny vale looked gay,
And to the primrose of the rock
   I gave this after-lay.   30

I sang—Let myriads of bright flowers,
   Like thee, in field and grove
Revive unenvied.   Mightier far
   Than tremblings that reprove
Our vernal tendencies to hope,
   Is God's redeeming love ;

That love which changed—for wan disease,
   For sorrow that had bent
O'er hopeless dust, for withered age—
   Their moral element,   40
And turned the thistles of a curse
   To types beneficent.

Sin-blighted though we are, we too,
   The reasoning sons of men,
From one oblivious winter called,
   Shall rise and breathe again,
And in eternal summer lose
   Our threescore years and ten.

To humbleness of heart descends
   This prescience from on high,   50
The faith that elevates the just
   Before and when they die,
And makes each soul a separate heaven,
   A court for Deity.

YARROW REVISITED.

THE gallant youth, who may have gained,
   Or seeks, a 'winsome Marrow,'
Was but an infant in the lap
   When first I looked on Yarrow;
Once more, by Newark's castle-gate
   Long left without a warder,
I stood, looked, listened, and with thee,
   Great Minstrel of the Border!

Grave thoughts ruled wide on that sweet day,
   Their dignity installing   10
In gentle bosoms, while sere leaves
   Were on the bough or falling;
But breezes played and sunshine gleamed,
   The forest to embolden,
Reddened the fiery hues and shot
   Transparence through the golden.

For busy thoughts the stream flowed on
   In foamy agitation,
And slept in many a crystal pool
   For quiet contemplation.   20
No public and no private care
   The freeborn mind enthralling,
We made a day of happy hours,
   Our happy days recalling.

Brisk youth appeared, the morn of youth,
   With freaks of graceful folly—
Life's temperate noon, her sober eve,
   Her night not melancholy;
Past, present, future, all appeared
   In harmony united,   30
Like guests that meet, and some from far,
   By cordial love invited.

And if, as Yarrow, through the woods
   And down the meadow ranging,
Did meet us with unaltered face,
   Though we were changed and changing—
If *then* some natural shadows spread
   Our inward prospect over,
The soul's deep valley was not slow
   Its brightness to recover.   40

Eternal blessings on the Muse
   And her divine employment!
The blameless Muse, who trains her sons
   For hope and calm enjoyment,
Albeit sickness, lingering yet,
   Has o'er their pillow brooded,
And Care waylays their steps—a sprite
   Not easily eluded.

For thee, O Scott, compelled to change
   Green Eildon-hill and Cheviot   50
For warm Vesuvio's vine-clad slopes,
   And leave thy Tweed and Teviot
For mild Sorrento's breezy waves,
   May classic Fancy, linking
With native Fancy her fresh aid,
   Preserve thy heart from sinking!

O, while they minister to thee,
   Each vying with the other,
May Health return to mellow age
   With Strength, her venturous brother,   60
And Tiber, and each brook and rill
   Renowned in song and story,
With unimagined beauty shine,
   Nor lose one ray of glory!

For thou, upon a hundred streams,
   By tales of love and sorrow,
Of faithful love, undaunted truth,
   Hast shed the power of Yarrow;
And streams unknown, hills yet unseen,
   Wherever they invite thee   70
At parent Nature's grateful call,
   With gladness must requite thee.

A gracious welcome shall be thine,
   Such looks of love and honour
As thy own Yarrow gave to me
   When first I gazed upon her,
Beheld what I had feared to see,
   Unwilling to surrender
Dreams treasured up from early days,
   The holy and the tender.   80

And what, for this frail world, were all
    That mortals do or suffer,
Did no responsive harp, no pen,
    Memorial tribute offer?
Yea, what were mighty Nature's self?
    Her features, could they win us,
Unhelped by the poetic voice
    That hourly speaks within us?

Nor deem that localized romance
    Plays false with our affections,   90
Unsanctifies our tears—made sport
    For fanciful dejections.
Ah, no! the visions of the past
    Sustain the heart in feeling
Life as she is—our changeful life,
    With friends and kindred dealing,

Bear witness ye whose thoughts that day
    In Yarrow's groves were centred,
Who through the silent portal arch
    Of mouldering Newark entered,   100
And clomb the winding stair that once
    Too timidly was mounted
By the 'last minstrel'—not the last!—
    Ere he his tale recounted.

Flow on forever, Yarrow stream!
    Fulfil thy pensive duty,
Well pleased that future bards should chant
    For simple hearts thy beauty;
To dream-light dear while yet unseen,
    Dear to the common sunshine,   110
And dearer still, as now I feel,
    To memory's shadowy moonshine!

WINDERMERE FERRY.

ON THE DEPARTURE OF SIR WALTER SCOTT FROM ABBOTSFORD FOR NAPLES.

A TROUBLE, not of clouds or weeping rain,
Nor of the setting sun's pathetic light
Engendered, hangs o'er Eildon's triple height.
Spirits of power, assembled there, complain
For kindred power departing from their sight ;
While Tweed, best pleased in chanting a blithe strain,
Saddens his voice again and yet again.
Lift up your hearts, ye mourners ! for the might
Of the whole world's good wishes with him goes ;
Blessings and prayers, in nobler retinue
Than sceptred king or laurelled conqueror knows,
Follow this wondrous potentate.   Be true,
Ye winds of ocean and the midland sea,
Wafting your charge to soft Parthenope !

DEVOTIONAL INCITEMENTS.

> " Not to the earth confined,
> Ascend to heaven."

WHERE will they stop, those breathing powers,
The spirits of the new-born flowers ?
They wander with the breeze, they wind
Where'er the streams a passage find ;
Up from their native ground they rise
In mute aërial harmonies.
From humble violet, modest thyme,

Exhaled, the essential odours climb,
As if no space below the sky
Their subtle flight could satisfy.   10
Heaven will not tax our thoughts with pride
If like ambition be *their* guide.

Roused by this kindliest of May-showers,
The spirit-quickener of the flowers,
That with moist virtue softly cleaves
The buds and freshens the young leaves,
The birds pour forth their souls in notes
Of rapture from a thousand throats—
Here checked by too impetuous haste,
While there the music runs to waste,   20
With bounty more and more enlarged,
Till the whole air is overcharged.
Give ear, O man, to their appeal
And thirst for no inferior zeal,
Thou who canst *think* as well as feel!

Mount from the earth! aspire, aspire!
So pleads the town's cathedral choir
In strains that from their solemn height
Sink, to attain a loftier flight;
While incense from the altar breathes   30
Rich fragrance in embodied wreaths,
Or, flung from swinging censer, shrouds
The taper-lights and curls in clouds
Around angelic forms, the still
Creation of the painter's skill,
That on the service wait concealed
One moment, and the next revealed.
Cast off your bonds, awake, arise,
And for no transient ecstasies!
What else can mean the visual plea   40
Of still or moving imagery—
The iterated summons loud,

11

Not wasted on the attendant crowd,
Nor wholly lost upon the throng
Hurrying the busy streets along?
    Alas! the sanctities combined
By art to unsensualize the mind
Decay and languish, or, as creeds
And humours change, are spurned like weeds!
The priests are from their altars thrust,   50
Temples are levelled with the dust,
And solemn rites and awful forms
Founder amid fanatic storms.
Yet evermore, through years renewed
In undisturbed vicissitude
Of seasons balancing their flight
On the swift wings of day and night,
Kind Nature keeps a heavenly door
Wide open for the scattered poor.
Where flower-breathed incense to the skies   60
Is wafted in mute harmonies,
And ground fresh-cloven by the plough
Is fragrant with a humbler vow,
Where birds and brooks from leafy dells
Chime forth unwearied canticles,
And vapours magnify and spread
The glory of the sun's bright head—
Still constant in her worship, still
Conforming to the Eternal Will,
Whether men sow or reap the fields,   70
Divine monition Nature yields
That not by bread alone we live
Or what a hand of flesh can give,
That every day should leave some part
Free for a Sabbath of the heart:
So shall the seventh be truly blest,
From morn to eve with hallowed rest.

MOSSGIEL FARM.

'THERE,' said a stripling, pointing with meet pride
Towards a low roof with green trees half concealed,
'Is Mossgiel Farm; and that 's the very field
Where Burns ploughed up the daisy.' Far and wide
A plain below stretched seaward, while, descried
Above sea-clouds, the peaks of Arran rose;
And by that simple notice the repose
Of earth, sky, sea, and air was vivified.
Beneath ' the random bield of clod or stone '
Myriads of daisies have shone forth in flower
Near the lark's nest, and in their natural hour
Have passed away; less happy than the one
That, by the unwilling ploughshare, died to prove
The tender charm of poetry and love.

'MOST SWEET IT IS WITH UNUPLIFTED EYES.'

MOST sweet it is with unuplifted eyes
To pace the ground, if path be there or none,
While a fair region round the traveller lies
Which he forbears again to look upon;
Pleased rather with some soft ideal scene,
The work of fancy, or some happy tone
Of meditation, slipping in between
The beauty coming and the beauty gone.
If Thought and Love desert us, from that day
Let us break off all commerce with the Muse.
With Thought and Love companions of our way,
Whate'er the senses take or may refuse,
The mind's internal heaven shall shed her dews
Of inspiration on the humblest lay.

'A POET!—HE HATH PUT HIS HEART TO SCHOOL.'

A POET!—he hath put his heart to school,
Nor dares to move unpropped upon the staff
Which art hath lodged within his hand—must laugh
By precept only and shed tears by rule.
Thy art be nature; the live current quaff,
And let the groveller sip his stagnant pool,
In fear that else, when critics grave and cool
Have killed him, Scorn should write his epitaph.
How does the meadow-flower its bloom unfold?
Because the lovely little flower is free
Down to its root, and in that freedom bold;
And so the grandeur of the forest-tree
Comes not by casting in a formal mould,
But from its *own* divine vitality.

'GLAD SIGHT WHEREVER NEW WITH OLD.'

GLAD sight wherever new with old
   Is joined through some dear homeborn tie;
The life of all that we behold
   Depends upon that mystery.
Vain is the glory of the sky,
   The beauty vain of field and grove,
Unless, while with admiring eye
   We gaze, we also learn to love.

NOTES.

ABBREVIATIONS USED IN THE NOTES.

Cf. (*confer*), compare.
F. Q., Spenser's *Faërie Queene.*
Fol., following.
Id. (*idem*), the same.
K. or Knight, Prof. Wm. Knight's ed. of Wordsworth (Edinburgh, 1882-86).
Myers, Mr. F. W. H Myers's *Wordsworth* (see p. 10, foot-note).
New Eng. Dict., the Philological Society's *New English Dictionary*, edited by J.
A. H. Murray (Oxford, 1885).
T., Mr. H. H. Turner's *Selections from Wordsworth* (London, 1874)
W., Wordsworth.

Other abbreviations will be readily understood. The line-numbers in the references
to Shakespeare are those of the "Globe" edition, which vary from those of Rolfe's edition only in scenes that are wholly or partly in *prose.*

NOTE.—The quotations from Principal Shairp are from his *Studies in Poetry and
Philosophy* (1876) and his *Aspects of Poetry* (1881). These, with his *Poetic Interpretation of Nature* (1877), we heartily commend to teachers and students All three have
been reprinted in this country (Boston). In Stopford Brooke's *Theology in the English Poets* (London) nearly two hundred pages (93-286) are devoted to Wordsworth.
Mr. A. J. Symington's *William Wordsworth, a Biographical Sketch* (Glasgow, 1881)
may be added to the books mentioned on p. 10 (foot-note). The best complete edition
of the poet is Knight's, mentioned above, in eight octavo volumes ; and the next best is
that in one volume published by Macmillan & Co. (London and New York) in 1888.
The best *Selections from Wordsworth* are Matthew Arnold's (see p. 22, foot-note) and
the one edited by Knight and other members of the English Wordsworth Society (London, 1881) ; both being on a more extended scale than the present volume. The *Wordsworthiana*, edited by Knight (Macmillan, 1889), is an admirable selection from the
papers read to the Wordsworth Society, of which Mr. Hutton's (p. 167 fol. above) may
serve as a sample.

THE WORDSWORTH GRAVES, GRASMERE CHURCHYARD.

NOTES.

INTRODUCTION.

"ON WORDSWORTH'S TWO STYLES," BY MR. R. H. HUTTON.*—
"The essential feature of Wordsworth's poetry has been described by
the greatest of our living critics in language that none of our Society is
at all likely to forget. After speaking of Goethe's experience of the
Iron Age, Matthew Arnold says of Wordsworth:

> ' He too upon a wintry clime
> Had fallen—on this iron time
> Of doubts, disputes, distractions, fears.
> He found us when the age had bound
> Our souls in its benumbing round ;
> He spoke and loosed our heart in tears.
> He laid us as we lay at birth
> On the cool flowery lap of earth,

---

* Read to the Wordsworth Society, May, 1882, and printed in *Wordsworthiana*, p.
63 fol.

> Smiles broke from us and we had ease ;
> The hills were round us, and the breeze
> Went o'er the sunlit fields again ;
> Our foreheads felt the wind and rain.
> Our youth returned; for there was shed
> On spirits that had long been dead,
> Spirits dried up and closely furled,
> The freshness of the early world.
> Ah ! since dark days still bring to light
> Man's prudence and man's fiery might,
> Time may restore us in his course
> Goethe's sage mind and Byron's force ;
> But where will Europe's latter hour
> Again find Wordsworth's healing power?
> Others will teach us how to dare,
> And against fear our breast to steel :
> Others will strengthen us to bear ;
> But who, ah ! who will make us feel?
> The cloud of mortal destiny,
> Others will front it fearlessly ;
> But who, like him, will put it by?'

I think this is rightly chosen as the characteristic of Wordsworth's poetry, that he puts by for us the ' cloud of mortal destiny,' that he restores us the ' freshness of the early world ;' that he gives us back the magic circle of the hills, makes us feel the breath of the wind and the coolness of the rain upon our foreheads; and touches both the vigour of youth and the peace of age with more of that serene lustre which dew gives to the flowers than any other poet. But the same great critic has assured us that, properly speaking, Wordsworth has no style, ' no assured poetic style of his own;' and this though he freely admits that ' it is style, and the elevation given by style, which chiefly makes the effectiveness of *Laodamia.*' For my part I should have said that as to Wordsworth's blank verse Mr. Arnold is right; that in his blank verse Wordsworth is so dependent on his matter that he runs through almost all styles, good and bad. But in his rhymed verse I should have preferred to say—though the admission may, perhaps, be used on behalf of Mr. Arnold's drift— that Wordsworth had two distinct styles—the style of his youth and the style of his age—the elastic style of fresh energy, born of his long devotion to Nature's own rhythms, and the style of gracious and stately feeling, born of his benignity, of his deepset, calm sympathy with human feeling—the style of *The Solitary Reaper*, and the style of *Devotional Incitements*. Surely the style of the verse,

> ' Alone she cuts and binds the grain,
> And sings a melancholy strain ;
> O, listen, for the vale profound
> Is overflowing with the sound !'

is Wordsworth's, in as true a sense as the style of ' After life's fitful fever he sleeps well,' is Shakespeare's. Or again, is there not the personal stamp of Wordsworth indelibly imprinted on every line in the *Song at the Feast of Brougham Castle?*

> ' No thoughts hath he but thoughts that pass
> Light as the wind along the grass.
> Can this be he who hither came
> In secret, like a smothered flame?'

Less personal, certainly less indelibly branded with Wordsworth's hand, is what I call the later style. Still, I think such lines as these, in the *Devotional Incitements,* describing the comparatively slight power of Art, when compared with Nature, to excite reverence, have on them an indelible impress of Wordsworth's developed genius, in its gracious, pure, and serene solemnity:

> ' The priests are from their altars thrust ;
> Temples are levelled with the dust ;
> And solemn rites and awful forms
> Founder amid fanatic storms.
> Yet evermore, through years renewed
> In undisturbed vicissitude
> Of seasons balancing their flight
> On the swift wings of day and night,
> Kind Nature keeps a heavenly door
> Wide open for the scattered poor.'

" The most characteristic earlier and the most characteristic later style are alike in the limpid coolness of their effect—the effect in the earlier style of bubbling water, in the later of morning dew. Both alike lay the dust, and take us out of the fret of life, and restore the truth to feeling, and cast over the vision of the universe

> ' The image of a poet's heart,
> How bright, how solemn, how serene !'

But the earlier and the later styles, even in their best specimens, do this in very different ways, while the inferior specimens of each are marked by very different faults. As models of the two styles at their best, I would take, for instance, *The Daffodils* for the earlier, and *The Primrose of the Rock* for the later; *Yarrow Unvisited* for the earlier, and *Yarrow Revisited* for the later; *The Leech-gatherer* (or as Wordsworth rather cumbrously called it, *Resolution and Independence*) for the earlier, and *Laodamia* for the later style. The chief differences between the two styles seem to me these: That objective fact, especially when appealing to the sense of vision, sometimes utterly bald and trivial, though often very commanding in its effects, plays so much larger a part in the earlier than the later ; that the earlier, when it reaches its mark at all, has a pure elasticity, a passionless buoyancy (passionless, I mean, in the sense of being devoid of the hotter passions) in it, almost unique in poetry; and lastly, that in the greater of the earlier pieces emotion is uniformly suggested rather than expressed; or, if I may be allowed the paradox, expressed by reticence, by the jealous parsimony of a half-voluntary, half-involuntary reserve. In the later style, on the other hand, objective fact is much less prominent; bald moralities tend to take the place of bald realities; and though the buoyancy is much diminished, emotion is much more freely, frankly, and tenderly expressed, so that there is often in it a richness and mellowness of effect quite foreign to Wordsworth's earlier mood. The ruggedness of the earlier style is what one may call one of knots and flinty protuberances; there is an occasional bleakness about it; the passion with which passion is kept down, though often exalted, is sometimes hard; there is a scorn of sweetness, an excess of simplicity, which frequently touches *simplesse;* and though the depth of feeling which is dammed up makes its surging voice heard in the happier instances, yet in the less happy instances the success of the operation is only too great, and leaves us oppressed with a sense of unexpected blankness.

"In the later style, all this is changed. The keenness of sheer objective vision is still felt, but is less dominant; while emotion, no longer restrained, flows naturally, and with a sweet and tender lustre shining upon it, into musical expression. I may illustrate the difference between the two styles, so far as regards the degrees of their direct expressiveness, by a characteristic change which Wordsworth made in his later editions in the beautiful poem entitled *The Fountain.* The poet, it will be remembered, there remonstrates with the schoolmaster, whom he calls Matthew, for speaking of himself as unloved in his old age :

> ' Now both himself and me he wrongs,
>   The man who thus complains!
> I live and sing my idle songs
>   Upon these happy plains;
> And, Matthew, for thy children dead,
>   I 'll be a son to thee."
> At this he grasped his hands, and said,
>   "Alas, that cannot be!"' '

In the later editions, Wordsworth altered this to

> ' At this he grasped my hand, and said,
>   "Alas, that cannot be!"' '

The earlier reading looks like hard fact, and no doubt sounds a little rough and abrupt. But I feel pretty sure, not only that the earlier version expressed the truth as it was present to Wordsworth's inner eye when he wrote the poem, but that it agreed better with the mood of those earlier years, when the old man's wringing of his own hands, in a sort of passion of protest against the notion that any one could take the place of his lost child, would have seemed much more natural and dignified to Wordsworth than the mere kindly expression of grateful feeling for which he subsequently exchanged it.

"Now I will go a little into detail. Contrast the power, which is very marked in both cases, of the poem on *The Daffodils*, with that on *The Primrose of the Rock.* You all know the wonderful buoyancy of that poem on the daffodils—the reticent passion with which the poet's delight is expressed, not by dwelling on feeling, but by selecting as a fit comparison to that ' crowd ' and ' host ' of golden daffodils the impression produced on the eye by the continuousness of ' the stars that shine and sparkle in the Milky Way,' the effect of wind, and of the exultation which wind produces, in the lines,

> ' Ten thousand saw I at a glance,
>   Tossing their heads in sprightly dance ;'

and in the rivalry suggested between them and the waves:

> ' The waves beside them danced, but they
>   Outdid the sparkling waves in glee.'

You all know the exquisite simplicity of the conclusion, when the poet tells us that, as often as they recur to his mind, and

—'flash upon that inward eye
Which is the bliss of solitude,'

his heart 'with pleasure fills, and dances with the daffodils.'

" The great beauty of that poem is its wonderful buoyancy, its purely objective way of conveying that buoyancy, and the extraordinary vividness with which 'the lonely rapture of lonely minds' is stamped upon the whole poem, which is dated 1804. Now turn to *The Primrose of the Rock*, which was written twenty-seven years later, in 1831. We find the style altogether more ideal—reality counts for less, symbol for more. There is far less elasticity, far less exultant buoyancy here, and yet a grander and more stately movement. The *reserve* of power has almost disappeared; but there is a graciousness absent before, and the noble strength of the last verse is most gentle strength:

' A rock there is whose homely front
    The passing traveller slights;
Yet there the glow-worms hang their lamps,
    Like stars, at various heights;
And one coy primrose to that rock
    The vernal breeze invites.

' What hideous warfare hath been waged,
    What kingdoms overthrown,
Since first I spied that primrose-tuft
    And marked it for my own:
A lasting link in Nature's chain,
    From highest heaven let down!

' The flowers, still faithful to the stems,
    Their fellowship renew;
The stems are faithful to the root,
    That worketh out of view;
And to the rock the root adheres
    In every fibre true.

' Close clings to earth the living rock,
    Though threatening still to fall;
The earth is constant to her sphere,
    And God upholds them all:
So blooms this lonely plant, nor dreads
    Her annual funeral.'

" It will be observed at once that in *The Daffodils* there is no attempt to explain the delight which the gay spectacle raised in the poet's heart. He exults in the spectacle itself, and reproduces it continually in memory. The wind in his style blows as the wind blows in *The Daffodils*, with a sort of physical rapture. In the later poem the symbol is everything. The mind pours itself forth fully in reflective gratitude, as it glances at the moral overthrow which the humble primrose of the rock—and many things of human mould as humble and faithful as the primrose of the rock—has outlived. In point of mere expression, I should call the later poem the more perfect of the two. The enjoyment of the first lies in the intensity of the feeling which it somehow indicates without expressing, of which it merely hints the force by its eager and springy movement.

" Now, take the earliest and latest *Yarrow*, and note the same differ-

ence.   How swift and bare and rapid, like the stream itself, as Wordsworth chooses to describe it—

> ‘ A river bare
> That glides the dark hills under ’—

is the verse in which he depreciates the reality, in order to enhance the
treasure of an unverified vision!   Yarrow is represented as a fit home
chiefly for the country-people who go to market at Selkirk, and for the
wild birds and ground game which fly and burrow beside it:

> ‘ Let Yarrow folk frae Selkirk Town,
>   Who have been buying, selling,
> Go back to Yarrow—’t is their own—
>   Each maiden to her dwelling.
> On Yarrow’s banks let herons feed,
>   Hares couch, and rabbits burrow;
> But we will downward with the Tweed,
>   Nor turn aside to Yarrow.’

The charm of that is the charm of a perfectly bare representation of a
perfectly simple scene, enhanced by the suggestion which lurks everywhere that the common facts of life are pretty certain to seem common,
unless, indeed, you bring an imagination strong enough to transfigure
them; while if you do, the poet insists that the true magic is in you, and
not in the scene, since it is independent of the actual vision on which
the mind seems to feed.   The beauty of the verse is almost all confined
to the thought itself; the only touch of extraneous beauty is the careless suggestion that ‘ the swan on still Saint Mary’s Lake ’ may, if it
pleases, ‘ float double, swan and shadow,’ without tempting them aside
to see it; and even that seems put in only to suggest, as it were, how
greatly the power of vividly imagining even such a sight as this exceeds
in significance the power which the mere eyes possess of discerning loveliness even where they have taken in the forms and colour which ought
to suggest it.   The whole beauty of the verses is in their bareness.   The
poem may be said to have for its very subject the economy of imaginative force, the wantonness of poetic prodigality, the duty of retaining in
the heart reserves of potential and meditative joy, on which you refuse
to draw all you might draw of actual delight:

> ‘ Be Yarrow stream unseen, unknown!
>   It must, or we shall rue it;
> We have a vision of our own;
>   Ah! why should we undo it?’

And the style corresponds to the thought; it is the style of one who exults in holding over, and being strong and buoyant enough to hold over,
a promised imaginative joy.   A certain ascetic radiance—if the paradox
be permissible—a manly jubilation in being rich enough to sacrifice an
expected delight, makes the style sinewy, rapid, youthful, and yet careful in its youthfulness, as jealous of redundancy as it is firm and elastic.
This was written in 1803.   Turn to *Yarrow Revisited*, which was written twenty-eight years later, in 1831.   The rhythm is the same, but how
different the movement; how much sweeter and slower, how many more
the syllables on which you must dwell, sometimes with what the ear admits to be an over-emphasis; how much richer the music, when it is mu-

sic; how much more hesitating, not to say vacillating, the reflection; and how the versification itself renders all this, with its sedate pauses—pauses, to use another poet's fine expression, ' as if Memory had wept '—its amplitude of tender feeling, its lingerings over sweet colours, its anxious desire to find compensations for the buoyancy of youth in wise reflection!—

> ' Once more by Newark's castle-gate
>   Long left without a warder,
> I stood, looked, listened, and with thee,
>   Great Minstrel of the Border!
>
> ' Grave thoughts ruled wide 'on that sweet day,
>   Their dignity installing
> In gentle bosoms, while sere leaves
>   Were on the bough or falling;
> But breezes played and sunshine gleamed,
>   The forest to embolden,
> Reddened tne fiery hues and shot
>   Transparence through the golden.
>
> ' For busy thoughts the stream flowed on
>   In foamy agitation,
> And slept in many a crystal pool
>   For quiet contemplation.
> No public and no private care
>   The freeborn mind enthralling,
> We made a day of happy hours,
>   Our happy days recalling.
>
> * * * * * *
>
> ' And if, as Yarrow, through the woods
>   And down the meadow ranging,
> Did meet us with unaltered face,
>   Though we were changed and changing—
> If *then* some natural shadows spread
>   Our inward prospect over,
> The soul's deep valley was not slow
>   Its brightness to recover.'

The expression there is richer, freer, more mellow; but the reserve force is spent; all the wealth of the moment—and perhaps something more than the wealth of the moment, something which was not wealth, though mistaken for it—was poured out. One cannot but feel now and again that, as Sir Walter said of his aged harper,

> ' His trembling hand had lost the ease
> Which marks security to please.
> And scenes long past of joy and pain
> Came wildering o'er his aged brain.'

"Mr. Arnold places almost all the really first-rate work of Wordsworth in the decade between the years 1798 and 1808. I think he is right here. But I should put Wordsworth's highest perfection of style much nearer the later date than the earlier; at least if, as I hold, the *Song at the Feast of Brougham Castle* touches the very highest point which he ever reached. *The Leech-gatherer* was written in the same year, though its workmanship is not nearly so perfect. Let me contrast its style with that of *Laodamia*, of which the subject is closely analogous, and which was written only seven years later, in 1814; though these

seven years mark, as it appears to me, a very great transformation of
style. Both poems treat of Wordsworth's favourite theme—the strength
which the human heart has, or ought to have, to contain itself in adverse
circumstances, and the spurious character of that claim of mere emotion
to command us by which we are so often led astray. *The Leech-gath-*
erer has much less of buoyancy than the earlier poems, and something
here and there of the stateliness of the later style, especially in the
noble verse:

> ' I thought of Chatterton, the marvellous boy,
>   The sleepless soul that perished in his pride;
> Of him who walked in glory and in joy,
>   Following his plough, along the mountain-side:
> By our own spirits are we deified:
> We poets in our youth begin in gladness,
> But thereof comes in the end despondency and madness.'

But on the whole, the poem is certainly marked by that emphatic visual
imagination, that delight in the power of the eye, that strength of reserve, that occasional stiffness of feeling, and that immense rapture of
reverie, which characterize the earlier period, though it wants the more
rapid and buoyant movement of that period. Take the wonderful description of *The Leech-gatherer* himself:

> ' Himself he propped—his body, limbs, and face—
>   Upon a long gray staff of shaven wood:
> And still, as I drew near with gentle pace,
>   Upon the margin of that moorish flood,
> Motionless as a cloud, the old man stood;
> That heareth not the loud winds when they call,
> And moveth all together, if it move at all.'

Or take the description of the reverie into which the old man's words
threw Wordsworth:

> ' The old man still stood talking by my side,
>   But now his voice to me was like a stream
> Scarce heard, nor word from word could I divide;
>   And the whole body of the man did seem
> Like one whom I had met with in a dream,
> Or like a man from some far region sent,
> To give me human strength by apt admonishment.'

" In turning to *Laodamia,* we see that a great change of style—a great
relaxation of the high tension of the earlier power—and with it a great
increase in grace and sweetness has come. When Protesilaus announces
that his death was due to his having offered up his own life for the success of the Greek host, by leaping first to the strand where it was decreed that the first comer should perish, Laodamia replies:

> ' " Supreme of heroes—bravest, noblest, best!
>   Thy matchless courage I bewail no more,
> Which then, when tens of thousands were deprest
>   By doubt, propelled thee to the fatal shore;
> Thou found'st, and I forgive thee—here thou art—
> A nobler counsellor than my poor heart.

> ' " But thou, though capable of sternest deed,
>   Wert kind as resolute, and good as brave;
> And he whose power restores thee hath decreed
>   That thou shouldst cheat the malice of the grave:

Redundant are thy locks, thy lips as fair
As when their breath enriched Thessalian air.

"No spectre greets me—no vain shadow this;
  Come, blooming hero, place thee by my side!
Give, on this well-known couch, one nuptial kiss
  To me, this day a second time thy bride!"
Jove frowned in heaven; the conscious Parcæ threw
Upon those roseate lips a Stygian hue.

' "This visage tells thee that my doom is past:
  Know, virtue were not virtue, if the joys
Of sense were able to return as fast
  And surely as they vanish. Earth destroys
Those raptures duly, Erebus disdains;
Calm pleasures there abide, majestic pains.

' "Be taught, O faithful consort, to control
  Rebellious passion; for the gods approve
The depth, and not the tumult, of the soul,
  A fervent, not ungovernable, love.
Thy transports moderate; and meekly mourn
When I depart, for brief is my sojourn."'

There is certainly an air of classic majesty and a richness of colour about this which contrasts curiously with the strong sketch of the lonely leech-gatherer, though there seems to me a fitness in the fact that the style of the poem which paints the humble self-reliance of desolate fortitude is for the most part cast in the mould of a bare and almost bleak dignity.

"But I must come to an end. The later style has, I think, this advantage over the earlier, that where its subject is equally fine—which, as I admit, it often is not—the workmanship is far more complete, often almost of crystal beauty, and without the blots, the baldness, the deadwood, which almost all Wordsworth's earlier works exhibit. Where, for instance, in all the range of poetry, shall we find a more crystal piece of workmanship than the sonnet—written, I think, as late as 1827, and addressed to Lady Beaumont in her seventieth year—with which I may conclude this paper:

' Such age how beautiful! O lady bright,
Whose mortal lineaments seem all refined
By favouring nature and a saintly mind
To something purer and more exquisite
Than flesh and blood—whene'er thou meet'st my sight,
When I behold thy blanched unwithered cheek,
Thy temples fringed with locks of gleaming white,
And head that droops because the soul is meek,
Thee with the welcome snowdrop I compare,
That child of winter, prompting thoughts that climb
From desolation toward the genial prime,
Or with the moon conquering earth's misty air,
And filling more and more with crystal light
As pensive evening deepens into night.'"

ST. OSWALD'S CHURCH, GRASMERE.

EXTRACT

FROM THE CONCLUSION OF A POEM COMPOSED IN ANTICIPATION OF
LEAVING SCHOOL.

THIS was written in 1786, and first printed in 1815. The following
note concerning it is from those dictated by Wordsworth in 1843, at the
request of his friend, Miss Isabella Fenwick, giving the circumstances
under which many of his poems were composed:

"Written at Hawkshead. The beautiful image with which this
poem concludes suggested itself to me while I was resting in a boat along
with my companions under the shade of a magnificent row of sycamores,
which then extended their branches from the shore of the promontory
upon which stands the ancient, and at that time the more picturesque, Hall
of Coniston, the seat of the Le Flemings from very early times. The
poem of which it was the conclusion was of many hundred lines, and
contained thoughts and images most of which have been dispersed
through my other writings."

3-5. *That, wheresoe'er*, etc. A MS. copy mentioned by Knight
reads:

> "That when the close of life draws near,*
> And I must quit this earthly sphere,
> If in that hour a tender tie," etc.

9-14. *Thus, while the sun*, etc. The text is that of the ed. of 1845,
which we have followed except in the occasional instances mentioned in
these notes. The ed. of 1815 reads:

> "Thus when the sun, prepared for rest,
> Hath gained the precincts of the west,
> Though his departing radiance fail
> To illuminate the hollow vale," etc.

The ed. of 1832 has:

> "Thus from the precincts of the west,
> The sun, when sinking down to rest," etc.

The ed. of 1836 changes *when* in this latter to "while." In 1820 the
last line was changed to "On the dear mountain-tops where first he
rose," but the reading of 1815 (as in the text) was restored in 1845. It
is strange that the poet should have made any changes in this poem or
the next.

WRITTEN IN VERY EARLY YOUTH.

PROBABLY written in 1786, and first printed in 1807.

4. *Is cropping audibly*, etc. The ed. of 1807 has "Is up and cropping
yet his later meal." In 8 below, it has "seems" for *comes*.

---

* Knight has "dear," which is either his misprint or a slip of the pen in the MS.

THE REVERIE OF POOR SUSAN.

WRITTEN in 1797, and published in 1800. Wordsworth says in his MS. notes: "This arose out of my observation of the affecting music of these birds hanging in this way in the London streets during the freshness and stillness of the Spring morning."

Myers (p. 16) remarks: "Wordsworth's limitations were inseparably connected with his strength. And just as the flat scenery of Cambridgeshire had only served to intensify his love for such elements of beauty and grandeur as still were present in sky and fen, even so the bewilderment of London taught him to recognize with an intenser joy such fragments of things rustic, such aspects of things eternal, as were to be found amidst that rush and roar. To the frailer spirit of Hartley Coleridge the weight of London might seem a load impossible to shake off. 'And what hath Nature,' he plaintively asked—

'And what hath Nature but the blank void sky
And the thronged river toiling to the main?'

But Wordsworth saw more than this. He became, as one may say, the poet not of London considered as London, but of London considered as a part of the country. . . . Among the poems describing these sudden shocks of vision and memory none is more exquisite than the *Reverie of Poor Susan*. The picture is one of those which come home to many a country heart with one of those sudden 'revulsions into the natural' which philosophers assert to be the essence of human joy. But noblest and best known of all these poems is the *Sonnet on Westminster Bridge*, 'Earth hath not anything to show more fair;' in which Nature has reasserted her dominion over the works of all the multitude of men; and in the early clearness the poet beholds the great city—as Sterling imagined it on his dying bed—'not as full of noise and dust and confusion, but as something silent, grand, and everlasting.' And even in later life, when Wordsworth was often in London, and was welcome in any society, he never lost this external manner of regarding it. He was always of the same mind as the group of listeners in his *Power of Music*:

'Now, Coaches and Chariots! roar on like a stream!
Here are twenty souls happy as souls in a dream:
They are deaf to your murmurs, they care not for you,
Nor what ye are flying, nor what ye pursue.'"

The following stanza is appended to the poem in the ed. of 1800:

"Poor outcast! return—to receive thee once more
The house of the father will open its door.
And thou* once again, in thy plain russet gown,
May'st hear the thrush sing from a tree of its own."

1. *Wood Street.* There are at least four streets of this name in London, but the one meant here is evidently that which runs from Cheap-

---

* Knight, in his collation of the various readings, makes this read "then ;" but, if it reads thus in the ed. of 1800, it is obviously a misprint for "thou."

side northward. *Lothbury* (7) is a street behind the Bank of England, not far away.

"WE ARE SEVEN."

THE history of this poem (first printed in the *Lyrical Ballads*, 1798) is given by Wordsworth as follows:

"Written at Alfoxden in the spring of 1798, under circumstances somewhat remarkable. The little girl who is the heroine I met within the area of Goodrich Castle in the year 1793. Having left the Isle of Wight and crossed Salisbury Plain . . . I proceeded by Bristol up the Wye, and so on to North Wales, to the Vale of Clwydd, where I spent my summer under the roof of the father of my friend, Robert Jones. In reference to this poem I will here mention one of the most remarkable facts in my own poetic history and that of Mr. Coleridge. In the spring of the year 1798, he, my sister, and myself started from Alfoxden, pretty late in the afternoon, with a view to visit Lenton and the Valley of Stones near it; and as our united funds were very small, we agreed to defray the expense of the tour by writing a poem, to be sent to the New Monthly Magazine set up by Phillips the bookseller, and edited by Dr. Aikin. Accordingly we set off and proceeded along the Quantock Hills towards Watchet, and in the course of this walk was planned the poem of the *Ancient Mariner*, founded on a dream, as Mr. Coleridge said, of his friend, Mr. Cruikshank. . . . As we endeavoured to proceed conjointly (I speak of the same evening) our respective manners proved so widely different that it would have been quite presumptuous in me to do anything but separate from an undertaking upon which I could only have been a clog. We returned after a few days from a delightful tour, of which I have many pleasant, and some of them droll enough, recollections. We returned by Dulverton to Alfoxden. The *Ancient Mariner* grew and grew till it became too important for our first object, which was limited to our expectation of five pounds, and we began to talk of a volume, which was to consist, as Mr. Coleridge has told the world, of poems chiefly on supernatual subjects taken from common life, but looked at, as much as might be, through an imaginative medium. Accordingly I wrote *The Idiot Boy*, '*Her eyes are wild*,' etc., '*We are Seven*,' *The Thorn*, and some others. To return to '*We are Seven*,' the piece that called forth this note, I composed it while walking in the grove at Alfoxden. My friends will not deem it too trifling to relate that while walking to and fro I composed the last stanza first, having begun with the last line. When it was all but finished, I came in and recited it to Mr. Coleridge and my sister, and said, 'A prefatory stanza must be added, and I should sit down to our little tea-meal with greater pleasure if my task were finished.' I mentioned in substance what I wished to be expressed, and Coleridge immediately threw off the stanza thus:

'A little child, dear brother Jem,' etc.

I objected to the rhyme, 'dear brother Jem,' as being ludicrous, but we all enjoyed the joke of hitching in our friend, James T——'s name, who was familiarly called Jem. He was the brother of the dramatist, and this reminds me of an anecdote which it may be worth while here to notice. The said Jem got a sight of the *Lyrical Ballads* as it was going through the press at Bristol, during which time I was residing in that city. One evening he came to me with a grave face, and said, 'Wordsworth, I have seen the volume that Coleridge and you are about to publish. There is one poem in it which I earnestly entreat you will cancel, for, if published, it will make you everlastingly ridiculous.' I answered that I felt much obliged by the interest he took in my good name as a writer, and begged to know what was the unfortunate piece he alluded to. He said, 'It is called "*We are Seven*."' 'Nay!' said I, 'that shall take its chance, however,' and he left me in despair. I have only to add that in the spring of 1841 I revisited Goodrich Castle, not having seen that part of the Wye since I met the little girl there in 1793. It would have given me greater pleasure to have found in the neighbouring hamlet traces of one who had interested me so much; but that was impossible, as unfortunately I did not even know her name. The ruin, from its position and features, is a most impressive object. I could not but deeply regret that its solemnity was impaired by a fantastic new castle set up on a projection of the same ridge, as if to show how far modern art can go in surpassing all that could be done by antiquity and nature with their united graces, remembrances, and associations."

1. *A simple child.* According to Knight, the ed. of 1798 has "A simple child, dear brother Jim," not "Jem," as in Wordsworth's MS. note.

19. *Conway.* The town of that name in North Wales.

44. *And sing a song to them.* The reading of 1836, that of 1798 being "I sit and sing to them."

54. *And when the grass was dry.* The ed. of 1798 has "And all the summer day;" changed in 1827 as in the text.

63. *Quick was the little maid's reply.* The reading of 1798 (changed in 1836) is "The little maiden did reply."

LINES WRITTEN IN EARLY SPRING.

WRITTEN and published in 1798. Wordsworth says: "Actually composed while I was sitting by the side of the brook that runs down from the Comb, in which stands the village of Alford, through the grounds of Alfoxden. It was a chosen resort of mine. The brook fell down a sloping rock so as to make a waterfall considerable for that country, and across the pool below had fallen a tree, an ash if I rightly remember, from which rose, perpendicularly, boughs in search of the light intercepted by the deep shade above. The boughs bore leaves of green that for want of sunshine had faded into almost lily-white; and from the underside of this natural sylvan bridge depended long and beautiful tresses of ivy which waved gently in the breeze that might, poetically speaking, be called the breath of the waterfall. This motion varied of course in proportion to the power of water in the brook. When, with dear friends, I revisited this spot, after an interval of more than forty years, this interesting feature of the scene was gone. To the owner of the place I could not but regret that the beauty of this retired part of the grounds had not tempted him to make it more accessible by a path, not broad or obtrusive, but sufficient for persons who love such scenes to creep along without difficulty."

9. *That green bower.* The ed. of 1798 has "sweet" for *green*, which dates from 1836.

15. *The least motion which they made.* Matthew Arnold, in his *Selections* (English ed.), has "that they made," which is better, but it is not given in Knight's collation. Cf. note on *Complaint of Forsaken Indian Woman*, 4.

21, 22. *If this belief*, etc. The reading of 1798 is:

> " If I these thoughts may not prevent,
> If such be of my creed the plan," etc.

In 1820 the present reading was adopted, except that line 21 had "is," changed to *be* in 1827.

TO MY SISTER.

WRITTEN and printed in 1798. The poet gives its history as follows: "Composed in front of Alfoxden House. My little boy-messenger on this occasion was the son of Basil Montagu. The larch mentioned in the first stanza was standing when I revisited the place in May, 1841, more than forty years after. I was disappointed that it had not improved in appearance as to size, nor had it acquired anything of the majesty of age, which, even though less perhaps than any other tree, the larch sometimes does. A few score yards from this tree, grew, when we inhabited Alfoxden, one of the most remarkable beech-trees ever seen. The ground sloped both towards and from it. It was of immense size, and threw out arms that struck into the soil, like those of the banyan-tree, and rose again from it. Two of the branches thus inserted themselves twice, which gave to each the appearance of a serpent moving along by gathering itself up in folds. One of the large boughs of this tree had been torn off by the wind before we left Alfoxden, but five remained. In 1841 we could barely find the spot where the tree had stood. So remarkable a production of nature could not have been wilfully destroyed."

26. *Than years of toiling reason.* The first reading (changed in 1836) was "Than fifty years of reason."

29. *Our hearts will make.* The ed. of 1798 has "may" for *will;* changed in 1826.

EXPOSTULATION AND REPLY.

WORDSWORTH says: "This poem is a favourite among the Quakers, as I have learnt on many occasions. It was composed in front of the house at Alfoxden, in the spring of 1798." It was printed the same year in the *Lyrical Ballads*, and is one of the very few poems in which the author made no alterations.

13. *Esthwaite lake.* A lakelet, about two miles long and a third of a mile wide, west of Windermere and south of the village of Hawkshead, where Wordsworth went to school (see p. 16 above).

THE TABLES TURNED.

WRITTEN and published in 1798.

1–4. *Up! up! my friend*, etc. In the ed. of 1798 the lines are arranged thus:

> "Up! up! my friend, and clear your looks;
> Why all this toil and trouble?
> Up! up! my friend, and quit your books;
> Or surely you'll grow double."

13. *Throstle.* A diminutive of *thrush*. Cf. Shakespeare, *M. of V.* i. 2. 65: "if a throstle sing," etc.

14. *He too is no mean preacher.* The original reading (changed in 1815) was "And he is no mean preacher."

THE COMPLAINT OF A FORSAKEN INDIAN WOMAN.

WRITTEN and published in 1798, with the following prefatory note:

"When a Northern Indian, from sickness, is unable to continue his journey with his companions, he is left behind, covered over with deerskins, and is supplied with water, food, and fuel if the situation of the place will afford it. He is informed of the track which his companions intend to pursue; and if he is unable to follow or overtake them, he perishes alone in the desert, unless he should have the good fortune to fall in with some other tribes of Indians. The females are equally, or still more, exposed to the same fate. See that very interesting work, Hearne's *Journey from Hudson's Bay to the Northern Ocean.* In the high northern latitudes, as the same writer informs us, when the Northern Lights vary in their position in the air, they make a rustling and a crackling noise, as alluded to in the following poem."

4. *The stars, they were among my dreams.* The reading in Matthew Arnold's *Selections* is "The stars were mingled with my dreams." This is better, but it is not given in Knight's collation of the texts, and we

suspect it to be Arnold's own emendation. In 30 below he has "My friends;" not mentioned by Knight, and perhaps a misprint due to the *My friends* just above. See on *Lines Written in Early Spring*, 15.

6. *I heard, I saw, the flashes drive.* The ed. of 1798 has "I saw the crackling flashes drive," which was changed in 1820 to "I heard and saw the flashes drive," and in 1827 to the reading in the text.

23, 24. *Too soon I yielded to despair*, etc. The original reading (changed in 1815) was:

> " Too soon despair o'er me prevailed,
> Too soon my heartless spirit failed."

36. *A most strange working.* The ed. of 1798 has "something" for *working;* changed in 1815.

40. *A helpless child.* Originally "a little child;" changed in 1815.

61–70. *Young as I am*, etc. This stanza is omitted in the eds. from 1815 to 1832, and also in Arnold's and Knight's *Selections*. To our thinking, the poem ends more effectively without it. The ed. of 1798 has in line 61: "My journey will be shortly run;" and in 69, 70:

> " I feel my body die away,
> I shall not live another day."

The present text dates from 1836.

The rhyme of *know* and *no* (64, 65) is to be noted. In Italian poetry, as in Spanish and Portuguese, words identical in sound may be rhymed if they differ in sense. Chaucer, Spenser, and Milton indulge in the same license, as do some of our more recent poets—Tennyson and Lowell, for example. Cf. the rhyme of *complains* and *plains* in *The Fountain*, 58, 60.

LINES

COMPOSED A FEW MILES ABOVE TINTERN ABBEY, ON REVISITING THE BANKS OF THE WYE DURING A TOUR. JULY 31, 1798.

WORDSWORTH says: "No poem of mine was composed under circumstances more pleasant for me to remember than this. I began it upon leaving Tintern, after crossing the Wye, and concluded it just as I was entering Bristol in the evening, after a ramble of four or five days, with my sister. Not a line of it was altered, and not any part of it written down till I reached Bristol. It was published almost immediately after in the little volume of which so much has been said in these Notes."*

Myers (p. 33) remarks: "The *Lines written above Tintern Abbey* have become, as it were, the *locus classicus*, or consecrated formulary of the Wordsworthian faith. They say in brief what it is the work of the poet's biographer to say in detail." Again (p. 129) he says: "So congruous in all ages are the aspirations and the hopes of men that it would

---

* The *Lyrical Ballads*, 1798.

be rash indeed to attempt to assign the moment when any spiritual truth rises for the first time on human consciousness. But thus much, I think, may be fairly said, that the maxims of Wordsworth's form of natural religion were uttered before Wordsworth only in the sense in which the maxims of Christianity were uttered before Christ. To compare small things with great—or, rather, to compare great things with things vastly greater—the essential spirit of the *Lines near Tintern Abbey* was for practical purposes as new to mankind as the essential spirit of the Sermon on the Mount. Not the isolated expression of moral ideas, but their fusion into a whole in one memorable personality, is that which connects them forever with a single name. Therefore it is that Wordsworth is venerated; because to so many men—indifferent, it may be, to literary or poetical effects, as such—he has shown by the subtle intensity of his own emotion how the contemplation of Nature can be made a revealing agency, like Love or Prayer—an opening, if indeed there be any opening, into the transcendent world."

T. states "the connection of thought" in the poem as follows:

"After five long years the poet once more looks upon the sylvan Wye. Nor, during that absence among far other scenes, has the memory of a spot so beautiful and quiet ever left him. Nay more, it may be that to the unconscious influence of those beauteous forms he owes the highest of his poetic moods—that mood in which the soul transcends the world of sense, and views the world of being and the mysterious harmony of the universe. He believes that this is so; at least he knows how often the memory of this quiet beauty has cheered the dreariness of life and soothed its fever.

"And now he once more stands beside the real scene of his dreams, and his present sensations mingle with his past, not without a painful feeling that the past has in a measure faded and belongs to his former self, yet feeling that the joy of the present moment will recur through years to come.

"For although he is no longer his former self, no longer feels the same all-sufficing passion for the mere external forms and colours of Nature, is no longer filled with the same gladness of mere animal life, yet Nature has not forsaken, but only fulfilled her kindly purpose towards her worshipper. Taught by her, he has reached a more serene and higher region; higher because more human in its interest, more thoughtful in its nature, more moral in its object.

"And even if he had not reached this higher mood, none the less by sympathy with his sister could he feel the full joys of his former self. That she should now be as he was then is his wish and prayer; for doubtless she too will be led by Nature, who never leaves her task incomplete, to the higher and more tranquil mood which is the ripe fruit of former flowers. And so, whatever sorrows might befall her in after times, both he and she could with joy remember that Nature by such scenes and by his aid had wrought in her an unfailing source of comfort."

3. *These waters*, etc. The valley of the Wye between Monmouth and Chepstow (where it joins the Severn) is famous for its beauty. As

Wordsworth notes, "the river is not affected by the tides a few miles above Tintern." T. quotes Tennyson, *In Memoriam :*

> "There twice a day the Severn fills,
> The salt sea-water passes by,
> And hushes half the babbling Wye,
> And makes a silence in the hills.
> *   *   *   *   *
> The tide flows down, the wave again
> Is vocal in its wooded walls."

4. *With a sweet inland murmur.* The reading of 1798. In 1845 *sweet* was changed to "soft."

13-15. *Are clad . . . landscape.* The reading of 1802. That of 1798 was :

> "Among the woods and copses lose themselves,
> Nor with their green and simple hue disturb
> The wild green landscape. Once again I see," etc.

The ed. of 1845 reads:

> "Are clad in one green hue, and lose themselves
> 'Mid groves and copses. Once again I see," etc.

19. *Sent up in silence,* etc. "The silence is made noticeable by the human life implied by the smoke, but of which there is no other sign" (T.).
After this line the ed. of 1798 had the line, "And the low copses—coming from the trees," etc.

23, 24. *These beauteous forms,* etc. The first reading (changed in 1827) was:

> "Though absent long,
> These forms of beauty have not been to me," etc.

29-31. *Felt in the blood,* etc. T. compares *The Fountain,* 29-32 and *I wandered lonely,* 19-24.

33. *As have no slight or trivial influence.* The ed. of 1798 has "As may have had no trivial influence;" changed in 1820.

48. *While with an eye,* etc. "The feeling that 'this unintelligible world' is yet the work of a spirit 'working harmoniously through the all,' and the intense joy produced by the energy of the poet's highest powers freed from the bonds of sense, give, in the first place, a quiet undisturbed by doubt or by the 'passing shows of being,' and secondly, and as a consequence, a perception of the highest and truest life " (T.).

54. *The fever of the world.* Cf. *Macbeth,* iii. 2. 23: "life's fitful fever."

55. *Hung upon.* Weighed down, oppressed.

62. *The picture of the mind.* The memory of his former visit to the place.

85. *Aching joys.* T. compares Shelley:

> "Till joy forget itself again,
> And too intense is turned to pain."

87. *Other gifts have followed,* etc. Cf. *Ode on Immortality,* 175-180.

107. *Of eye and ear,* etc. " This line has a close resemblance to an

admirable line of Young's, the exact expression of which I do not recollect " (W.). We do not know that any editor or commentator has recognized the line referred to.

110. *The anchor of my purest thoughts.* "It is by means of the knowledge of nature, rendered possible by the senses, that the soul can best hold fast in faith to her noblest conceptions " (T.).

114. *Genial.* Sympathetic; recalling with renewed pleasure the impressions of his former visit.

116. *My dearest friend.* His sister Dorothy.

135. *Therefore*, etc. "Since Nature will not fail to crown the first dizzy raptures of her worshipper with her second and higher gift " (T.).

140. *A sober pleasure.* For the antithesis, cf. Milton, *Comus*, 260:

> " Yet they in pleasing slumber lull'd the sense
> And in sweet madness robbed it of itself;
> But such a sacred and home-felt delight,
> Such sober certainty of waking bliss,
> I never heard till now."

144. *If solitude, or fear, or pain*, etc. "What prophetic pathos do these words assume when we remember how long and mournfully, ere life ended, those wild eyes were darkened !" (Shairp). Cf. Myers (p. 28): "'The shooting lights of her wild eyes' reflected to the full the strain of imaginative emotion which was mingled in the poet's nature with that spirit of steadfast and conservative virtue which has already given to the family a Master of Trinity, two bishops, and other divines and scholars of weight and consideration. In the poet himself the conservative and ecclesiastical tendencies of his character became more and more apparent as advancing years stiffened the movements of the mind. In his sister the ardent element was less restrained; it showed itself in a most innocent direction, but it brought with it a heavy punishment. Her passion for nature and her affection for her brother led her into mountain rambles which were beyond her strength, and her last years were spent in a condition of physical and mental decay."

"SHE DWELT AMONG THE UNTRODDEN WAYS."

WRITTEN in Germany in 1799, and first printed in 1800. No changes have been made in the text.

Myers (p. 33), referring to the poet's sojourn at Goslar (see p. 15 above), remarks: "Here it was that the memory of some emotion prompted the lines on *Lucy*. Of the history of that emotion he has told us nothing; I forbear, therefore, to inquire concerning it, or even to speculate. That it was to the poet's honour, I do not doubt; but who ever learned such secrets rightly? or who should wish to learn? It is best to leave the sanctuary of all hearts inviolate, and to respect the reserve not only of the living but of the dead. Of these poems, almost alone, Wordsworth in his autobiographical notes has said nothing whatever.

One of them he suppressed for years,* and printed only in a later volume. One can, indeed, well imagine that there may be poems which a man may be willing to give to the world only in the hope that their pathos will be, as it were, protected by its own intensity, and that those who are worthiest to comprehend will be least disposed to discuss them."

George Brimley refers to this poem as "tender and graceful, sad, holy, and beautiful as a Madonna."

2. *Beside the springs of Dove.* This beautiful stream, dear to anglers and poets, has its source near Buxton in Derbyshire, and flows southward into the Trent. Charles Cotton sings of it thus:

> "O my beloved nymph, fair Dove,
> Princess of rivers, how I love
> Upon thy flowery banks to lie," etc.

See Walton's *Complete Angler* for many other allusions to its charms.

"I TRAVELLED AMONG UNKNOWN MEN."

WRITTEN in Germany in 1799, but not published until 1807.

15, 16. *And thine too is,* etc. The ed. of 1807 has "is too" and "Which" for *That.* The latter change was made in 1815, the former in 1836.

Sara Coleridge says of this stanza : "A friend, a true poet himself, to whom I owe some new insight into the merits of Mr. Wordsworth's poetry, and who showed me, to my surprise, that there were nooks in that rich and varied region some of the shy treasures of which I was not perfectly acquainted with, first made me feel the great beauty of this stanza ; in which the poet, as it were, *spreads day and night* over the object of his affections, and seems, under the influence of his passionate feeling, to think of England, whether in light or darkness, only as her play-place and verdant home."

"THREE YEARS SHE GREW IN SUN AND SHOWER."

WRITTEN in Germany in 1799, and published in 1800. The only change in the text (made in 1802) is in line 23, which originally read "A beauty that shall mould her form."

Hon. Roden Noel, in a paper read before the Wordsworth Society in 1884, remarks : "In that loveliest of lyrics, *Three years she grew,* we have the picture of Lucy, to whom Nature was 'law and impulse,' an

---

* The reference is to *I Travelled among Unknown Men.*

overseeing power to kindle or restrain,' to whom the cloud lent state and the willow grace, into whose face from the rivulets passed ' beauty born of murmuring sound,' to whom belonged ' the silence and the calm of mute insensate things.' "

Mr. W. A. Heard, in a paper read to the same society the same year, says: "Wordsworth does not separate the physical and the spiritual: nothing is solely physical in its effect, everything has a spiritual result. This combination of physical and spiritual teaching in nature is the idea embodied in *Three years she grew.* One stanza is specially apposite: ' And she shall lean her ear,' etc. This is not only true poetry, but it has a Platonic felicitousness of language as the expression of a philosophy."

George Brimley calls the poem "the most exquisite description ever written of an English country girl, half child, half woman, with the wildness and witchery of a sylphide, the grace of a duchess, and the purity of an angel."

11. *Shall feel an overseeing power*, etc.   T compares *Tintern Abbey*, 108 fol.

20. *For her the willow bend.*   Lending her its lithe grace.

"A SLUMBER DID MY SPIRIT SEAL."

WRITTEN in 1799, published in 1800. "A poem impassioned beyond the comprehension of those who fancy that Wordsworth lacks passion, merely because in him passion is neither declamatory nor, latently, sensual" (Aubrey de Vere).

7. *Rolled round in earth's diurnal course*, etc   Cf. Shakespeare, *Tempest*, i. 2. 396 :

> " Full fathom five thy father lies ;
> Of his bones are coral made ;
> Those are pearls that were his eyes :
> Nothing of him that doth fade
> But doth suffer a sea-change
> Into something rich and strange."

See also Bryant, *Thanatopsis :*

> " Earth that nourished thee shall claim
> Thy growth to be resolved to earth again ;
> And, lost each human trace, surrendering up
> Thine individual being, shalt thou go
> To mix forever with the elements—
> To be a brother to the insensible rock.
> And to the sluggish clod which the rude swain
> Turns with his share and treads upon."

To the same purport, but in a different vein, are Hamlet's speculations on " the noble dust of Alexander " (v. I. 224 fol.).

MATTHEW.

WRITTEN in 1799, published in 1800. The only textual change is the substitution of *dew* (1815) for the original "oil" in line 24. The following note was prefixed to the poem :

"In the School of ——— is a tablet, on which are inscribed, in gilt letters, the names of the several persons who have been Schoolmasters there since the foundation of the school, with the time at which they entered upon and quitted their office. Opposite to one of those names the author wrote the following lines."

In the later MS. notes we find this :

"Such a tablet as is here spoken of continued to be preserved in Hawkshead School, though the inscriptions were not brought down to our time. This and other poems connected with Matthew would not gain by a literal detail of facts. Like the Wanderer in *The Excursion*, this Schoolmaster was made up of several, both of his class and men of other occupations. I do not ask pardon for what there is of untruth in such verses, considered strictly as matters of fact. It is enough if, being true and consistent in spirit, they move and teach in a manner not unworthy of a poet's calling."

2. *Hath tempered so her clay.* For the technical *temper* (=moisten, for moulding), cf. *Lear*, i. 4. 326 :

> "Old fond eyes,
> Beweep this cause again, I 'll pluck ye out,
> And cast you, with the waters that you lose,
> To temper clay."

THE FOUNTAIN.

WRITTEN in 1799, published in 1800.

9. "*Now, Matthew*," etc. The original reading (changed in 1820) was, "Now, Matthew, let us try to match," etc.

10. *This water's pleasant tune.* Cf. Coleridge, *Ancient Mariner :*

> "A noise like of a hidden brook
> In the leafy month of June,
> That to the sleeping-woods all night
> Singeth a quiet tune."

21. *Down to the vale*, etc. The reading of 1800, changed for the worse in 1836 to "No check, no stay, this streamlet fears."

35. *Mourns less*, etc. "He wrings from the temporary sadness fresh conviction that the ebbing away, both in spirit and appearance, of the brightest past, sad as it must ever be, is not so sad a thing as the weak yearning which, in departing, it often leaves stranded on the soul

to cling to the appearance when the spirit is irrevocably gone " (Hutton).

37. 38. *The blackbird*, etc. We follow the ed. of 1800 rather than that of 1836, which reads :

> " The blackbird amid leafy trees,
> The lark above the hill."

45. *But we are pressed by heavy laws.* Which compel us to do what we have done or what others will expect of us.

59. *I live.* The pronoun is of course emphatic.

60. *Plains.* For the rhyme, see on *Complaint of Forsaken Indian Woman*, 61-70.

63. *At this he grasped my hand.* For the original reading (changed in 1815), see p. 170 above.

THE TWO APRIL MORNINGS.

WRITTEN in 1799, published in 1800.

25-28. *And just above*, etc. The reading of 1802, that of 1800 being as follows .

> " And on that slope of springing corn
> The selfsame crimson hue
> Fell from the sky that April morn,
> The same which now I view."

29-31 *With rod and line*, etc. The ed. of 1800 reads :

> " With rod and line my silent sport
> I plied by Derwent's wave,
> And, coming to the church, stopped short," etc.

In 1815 the first two lines were altered as in the text, and in 1836 the third line was made " And, to the churchyard come, stopped short."

60. *Wilding.* Wild apple, or crab-apple. Cf. Spenser, *F. Q.* iii. 7. 17 :

> " Oft from the forrest wildings he did bring,
> Whose sides empurpled were with smyling red."

HART-LEAP WELL.

WRITTEN and published in 1800, with the following prefatory note :

" Hart-Leap Well is a small spring of water, about five miles from Richmond in Yorkshire, and near the side of the road that leads from Richmond to Askrigg. Its name is derived from a remarkable Chase, the memory of which is preserved by the monuments spoken of in the second part of the following poem, which monuments do now exist as I have there described them."

The following is from the later MS. notes :

" Written at Town-end, Grasmere. The first eight stanzas were composed extempore one winter evening in the cottage ; when, after having tired myself with labouring at an awkward passage in *The Brothers*, I started with a sudden impulse to this to get rid of the other, and finished it in a day or two. My sister and I had passed the place a few weeks before in our wild winter journey from Sockburn on the banks of the Tees to Grasmere. A peasant whom we met near the spot told us the story so far as concerned the name of the well and the hart, and pointed out the stones. Both the stones and the well are objects that may easily be missed; the tradition by this time may be extinct in the neighborhood : the man who related it to us was very old."

3, 4. *He turned aside*, etc. This is the reading of 1800. That of 1836 is as follows :

> " And now, as he approached a vassal's door,
> ' Bring forth another horse !' he cried aloud."

21. *He cheered and chid.* The ed. of 1800 has "chid and cheered ," changed in 1827. The present order is more natural.

27. *This chase*, etc. The reading of 1802, the earlier being . " This race it looks not like an earthly race."

35. *Cracked his whip.* The early reading was "smacked his whip;" changed in 1820.

38. *Glorious feat.* The ed. of 1800 has "glorious fact," and in 40 " All foaming like a mountain cataract;" changed in 1820.

46. *Never had living man*, etc. The reading of 1820, that of 1800 being, " Was never man in such a joyful case," with " place " as the rhyme.

49. *Climbing.* Originally "turning;" changed in 1802.

50. *Four roods.* The ed. of 1800 has " Nine roods," changed in 1845. The poet appears to have decided that 148½ feet was too much for the three leaps of the hart.

51. *Three several hoof-marks*, etc. The ed. of 1800 reads, " Three several marks which with his hoofs the beast " (changed in 1802); and the next line had " verdant " for *grassy* until 1820.

54. *Human eyes.* Originally " living eyes;" changed in 1836.

65. *Gallant stag.* Until 1827 the reading was " gallant brute."

70. *Paramour.* Lady-love, mistress, originally not used in a bad sense. Cf. Spenser, *Shep. Kal.* April, 139.

> " Bring Coronations, and Sops in wine,
> Worne of Paramours. '

75. *Swale.* A river in Yorkshire which unites with the *Ure* to form the Ouse.

80. *And far and wide*, etc. The ed. of 1800 has " The fame whereof through many a land did ring;" changed in 1815.

82. *The living well.* For the use of *living*, cf. *John*, iv. 10.

90. *Led his wondering paramour.* Till 1820 the reading was " journeyed with his paramour."

98. *To freeze the blood.* The ed. of 1800 has "curl" for *freeze*, substituted in 1802.

101. *Hawes . . . Richmond.* Towns in Yorkshire.

113. *The hill.* It was "hills" until 1815.

150. *The fountain.* The first reading was "this fountain;" changed in 1832.

153. *The scented thorn.* The original reading; changed in 1836 to "the flowering thorn."

157. *Now here is.* Until 1827 the reading was "But now here 's."

THE SPARROW'S NEST.

WRITTEN in 1801, published in 1807. The poet's MS. note says: "Written in the orchard, Town-end, Grasmere. At the end of the garden of my father's house at Cockermouth was a high terrace that commanded a fine view of the river Derwent and Cockermouth Castle. This was our favourite play-ground. The terrace-wall, a low one, was covered with closely-clipt privet and roses, which gave an almost impervious shelter to birds that built their nests there. The latter of these stanzas alludes to one of those pests."

1-4. *Behold . . . delight.* The reading of 1807 (changed in 1815) was as follows:

> "Look, five blue eggs are gleaming there!
> Few visions have I seen more fair,
> Nor many prospects of delight
> More pleasing than that simple sight!"

9. *My sister Emmeline.* It was his only sister Dorothy.

11, 12. *She looked at it,* etc. The original reading, not improved by the change in 1845 to

> "She looked at it as if she feared it,
> Still wishing, dreading to be near it."

15. *The blessing of my later years.* This his sister really was to him. See Myers, chap. iii., or Shairp's *Studies in Poetry,* p. 28 fol.

TO A BUTTERFLY.

WRITTEN in 1802, published in 1807. Wordsworth says of it : "Written in the orchard, Town-end, Grasmere. My sister and I were parted immediately after the death of our mother, who died in 1778, both being very young."

Dorothy, in her *Journal,* says : "While we were at breakfast W. wrote the poem to a Butterfly. The thought came upon him as we were talking about the pleasure we both always felt at the sight of a butterfly. I told him that I used to chase them a little, but that I was afraid of brushing the dust off their wings and did not catch them."

"MY HEART LEAPS UP WHEN I BEHOLD."

ACCORDING to Dorothy Wordsworth's *Journal*, this was written March 26, 1802, at Town-end, Grasmere. It was first published in 1807.

Coleridge, in *The Friend*, remarks: " I am informed that these lines have been cited as a specimen of despicable puerility. So much the worse for the citer; not willingly in *his* presence would I behold the sun setting behind our mountains. . . . But let the dead bury their dead ! The poet sang for the living."

The last three lines of the poem were originally prefixed as a motto to the *Ode on Immortality*.

TO A BUTTERFLY.

WRITTEN April 20, 1802, in the orchard at Town-end, and published in 1807.

12, 13. *Here rest your wings*, etc. The first reading (changed in 1815) was :

> " Stop here whenever you are weary,
> And rest as in a sanctuary!"

Sanctuary is here used in the sense of an asylum or place of refuge in which a person was privileged from persecution or arrest. Cf. *Richard III.*, iii. 1. 27 :

> " The queen your mother and your brother York
> Have taken sanctuary;"

that is, in the Sanctuary at Westminster, which was within the precincts of the Abbey. See also Browning, *Ring and Book*, i. 1394 : " Took sanctuary within the holier blue," etc.

TO THE SMALL CELANDINE.

WRITTEN at Town-end, April 30, 1802, and published in 1807. In a prefatory note the poet says: " It is remarkable that this flower, coming out so early in the spring as it does, and so bright and beautiful, and

13

in such profusion, should not have been noticed earlier in English verse. What adds much to the interest that attends it is its habit of shutting itself up and opening out, according to the degree of light and temperature of the air."

The flower is the *Ficaria ranunculoides*, and another popular name for it in England is the *pilewort*. It is also known as the *swallow-wort*, not, says Gerard in his *Herbal*, "because it first springeth at the coming in of the swallows, or dieth when they go away, for it may be found all the year, but because some hold opinion that with this herbe the dams restore eyesight to their young ones when their eye be put out."

16. *Like a sage astronomer.*   Until 1836 *sage* was "great."

27. *Her nest.*   Originally "its nest;" changed in 1832.

58. *Ill-requited upon earth.*   The reading up to 1836 was "Scorned and slighted upon earth."

61, 62. *Serving at my heart's command*, etc.   Originally (till 1836) the reading was:

> "Singing at my heart's command,
>   In the lanes my thoughts pursuing."

Pursuing was an imperfect rhyme to *ensuing*, or what is called an "identical" rhyme.

TO THE SAME FLOWER.

WRITTEN May 1, 1802; published in 1807.

14. *When the rising sun he painted.*   The *Sun* and *Rising Sun* are common names for inns in England.

20. *Kerchief-plots.*   That is, no larger than a kerchief.

38. *Thy sheltering hold.*   "Thy sheltered hold" until 1832.

39. *Liveliest of the vernal train.*   This reading dates back only to 1846, the earlier one being "Bright as any of the train."

50. *"Beneath our shoon."*   Cf. Milton, *Comus*, 634:

> "Unknown, and like esteem'd, and the dull swain
> Treads on it daily with his clouted shoon."

For *shoon*, see also *Joshua*, ix. 5.

51, 52. *Let the bold discoverer thrid*, etc.   A much-tinkered couplet. The ed. of 1807 has

> "Let, as old Magellan did,
>   Others roam about the sea;"

that of 1820:

> "Let, with bold adventurers' skill,*
>   Others thrid the polar sea;"

and that of 1827:

> "Let the bold adventurer thrid
>   In his bark the polar sea."

The present reading dates from 1846.   *Thrid* is an old form of *thread*.

---

* We suspect that the rhyming line was "Rear a pyramid who will;" but Knight (on whom we are dependent for most of these *variæ lectiones*) gives no such reading.

THE LEECH-GATHERER,
Or, Resolution and Independence.

WRITTEN at Town-end, May 7, 1802, and printed in 1807. A prefatory note says: "This old man I met a few hundred yards from my cottage; and the account of him is taken from his own mouth."

See Mr. Hutton's comments on the style of the poem (p. 174 above). Coleridge remarks that "This fine poem is especially characteristic of the author: there is scarce a defect or excellence in his writings of which it would not present a specimen."

Wordsworth himself, referring to the poem, says: "I describe myself as having been exalted to the highest pitch of delight by the joyousness and beauty of Nature; and then as depressed, even in the midst of those beautiful objects, to the lowest dejection and despair. A young poet in the midst of the happiness of Nature is described as overwhelmed by the thoughts of the miserable reverses which have befallen the happiest of all men, namely, poets. I think of this till I am so deeply impressed with it that I consider the manner in which I am rescued from my dejection and despair almost as an interposition of Providence. A person reading the poem with feelings like mine will have been awed and controlled, expecting something spiritual or supernatural. What is brought forward? A lonely place, 'a pond, by which an old man *was*, far from all house or home:'* not *stood*, nor *sat*, but *was*—the figure presented in the most naked simplicity possible. The feeling of spirituality or supernaturalness is again referred to as being strong in my mind in this passage. How came he here? thought I, or what can he be doing? I then describe him, whether ill or well is not for me to judge with perfect confidence; but this I *can* confidently affirm, that though I believe God has given me a strong imagination, I cannot conceive a figure more impressive than that of an old man like this, the survivor of a wife and ten children, travelling alone among the mountains and all lonely places, carrying with him his own fortitude, and the necessities which an unjust state of society has laid upon him. You speak of his speech as tedious. Everything is tedious when one does not read with the feelings of the author. . . . It is in the character of the old man to tell his story, which an impatient reader must feel tedious. But, good heavens! such a figure, in such a place; a pious, self-respecting, miserably infirm and pleased old man, telling such a tale!"

Myers, quoting the above (p. 138), adds: "The naïve earnestness of this passage suggests to us how constantly recurrent in Wordsworth's mind were the two trains of ideas which form the substance of the poem; the interaction, namely (if so it may be termed), of the moods of Nature with the moods of the human mind; and the dignity and interest of man as man, depicted with no complex background of social or political life,

---

* One would infer that this was a quotation from the poem, but it does not appear in any published form of it.

but set amid the primary affections and sorrows, and the wild aspects of
the external world."

13. *That, glittering.*   The reading till 1827 was "which, glittering."

29. *Warbling in the sky.*   Originally "singing in the sky;" changed
in 1820.

43. *Chatterton, the marvellous boy.*   Thomas Chatterton, born in 1752,
whose forgeries of old English poetry deceived for a time the scholars
and critics, and who died by his own hand in 1770.

44. *His pride.*   Until 1815 it was "its pride."

45. *Him who walked in glory*, etc.   The allusion to Burns is obvious.

46. *Following his plough*, etc.   Originally "Behind his plough, upon
the mountain-side;" changed in 1820.

53, 54. *When I with these untoward thoughts*, etc.   Until 1820, the
reading was :

> " When up and down my fancy thus was driven,
>   And I with these untoward thoughts had striven."

After this stanza the following was added in the eds. of 1807 and 1815:

> " My course I stopped as soon as I espied
>   The old man in that naked wilderness;
>   Close by a pond, upon the further side,
>   He stood alone ; a minute's space I guess
>   I watched him, he continuing motionless :
>   To the pool's further margin then I drew,
>   He being all the while before me full in view."

57. *As a huge stone*, etc.   Wordsworth, in his preface to the ed. of
1815, commenting upon imagination "employed upon images in a conjunction by which they modify each other," remarks : " Take these images separately, and how unaffecting the picture compared with that
produced by their being thus connected with, and opposed to, each
other !

> ' As a huge stone is sometimes seen to lie
>   Couched on the bald top of an eminence,
>   Wonder to all who do the same espy
>   By what means it could thither come, and whence,
>   So that it seems a thing endued with sense,
>   Like a sea-beast crawled forth, which on a shelf
>   Of rock or sand reposeth, there to sun himself.
>
> Such seemed this man ; not all alive or dead,
> Nor all asleep, in his extreme old age.
>
> .   .   .   .   .   .
>
> Motionless as a cloud the old man stood,
> That heareth not the loud winds when they call,
> And moveth altogether if it move at all.'

In these images, the conferring, the abstracting, and the modifying powers of the Imagination, immediately and mediately acting, are all brought
into conjunction.   The stone is endowed with something of the power
of life to approximate it to the sea-beast; and the sea-beast stripped of
some of its vital qualities to assimilate it to the stone; which intermedi-
ate image is thus treated for the purpose of bringing the original image,
that of the stone, to a nearer resemblance to the figure and condition of
the aged man, who is divested of so much of the indications of life and

motion as to bring him to the point where the two objects unite and co-alesce in just comparison.   After what has been said, the image of the cloud need not be commented upon."

67. *Life's pilgrimage.*   It was " their pilgrimage " until 1827.

71. *Limbs, body, and pale face.*   The reading of 1836, the earlier be-ing " his body, limbs, and face."

74. *Upon the margin*, etc.   The first reading (changed in 1820) was " Beside the little pond or moorish flood."

82. *And now a stranger's privilege I took.*   Until 1820 the line was " And now such freedom as I could I took."

88. *What occupation do you there pursue?*   The reading until 1820 was " What kind of work is that which you pursue ?"

90, 91. *Ere he replied*, etc.   The ed. of 1807 has :

> " He answered me with pleasure and surprise :
> And there was, while he spoke, a fire about his eyes."

That of 1820 reads :

> " He answered, while a flash of mild surprise
> Broke from the sable orbs of his yet vivid eyes."

In 1836 the present reading was adopted.

99. *He told, that to these waters*, etc.   Until 1827 it was " He told me that he to this pond had come."

104. *Housing.*   Finding a lodging.

112. *By apt admonishment.*   The first reading was " and strong ad-monishment."   In 1820 *and* was changed to *by*, and in 1827 *strong* to *apt*.

117. *Perplexed and longing to be comforted.*   At first " And now, not knowing what the old man said;" changed in 1815 to " But now per-plexed by what the old man said ;" and in 1820 as in the text.

120-126. *He with a smile*, etc.   A poor stanza, which Coleridge con-trasts with those that precede and follow it.

123. *The pools.*   It was " the ponds " until 1827.

UPON WESTMINSTER BRIDGE.

WORDSWORTH, in the ed. of 1807, where this sonnet was first printed, gives the date of composition as " September 3, 1802," adding " written on the roof of a coach, on my way to France;" but, according to his sis-ter's diary, it was on the 30th of July, 1802, that they left London for Dover, *en route* for Calais.   The following is the entry: "*July* 30.— Left London between five and six o'clock of the morning outside the Dover coach.   A beautiful morning.   The city, St. Paul's, with the river—a multitude of little boats, made a beautiful sight as we crossed Westminster Bridge; the houses not overhung by their clouds of smoke, and were spread out endlessly; yet the sun shone so brightly, with such a pure light, that there was something like the purity of one of Nature's own grand spectacles."

Lord Coleridge, at a meeting of the Wordsworth Society, in 1882, told how Bishop Thirlwall, after being kept till past daybreak in the House of Lords, being asked if he did not feel much exhausted, replied, "Yes, perhaps so; but I was more than repaid by walking out upon Westminster Bridge after the division, seeing London in the morning light as Wordsworth saw it, and repeating to myself his noble sonnet as I walked home."

At the same meeting a letter was read from Mr. Robert Spence Watson, in which he says: "Many years ago, I think it was in 1859, I chanced to be passing (in a pained and distressed state of mind, occasioned by the death of a friend) over Waterloo Bridge * at half-past three in the morning. It was broad daylight, and I was alone. Never when alone in the remotest recesses of the Alps, with nothing around me but the mountains, or upon the plains of Africa, alone with the wonderful glory of the Southern night, have I seen anything to approach the solemnity—the soothing solemnity—of the city, sleeping under the early sun. 'Earth hath not anything to show more fair.' How simply, yet how perfectly, Wordsworth has interpreted it. It was a happy thing for us that the Dover coach left at so untimely an hour in the morning. It was this sonnet, I think, that first opened my eyes to Wordsworth's greatness as a poet. Perhaps nothing that he has written shows more strikingly that vast sympathy which is his peculiar dower."

Caroline Fox, in her *Memories of Old Friends*, says: "Mamma spoke of the beauty of Rydal, and asked whether it did not rather spoil him [Wordsworth] for common scenery. 'O, no!' he said, 'it rather opens my eyes to see the beauty there is in all; God is everywhere, and thus nothing is common or devoid of beauty. No, ma'am, it is the *feeling* that instructs the *seeing*. Wherever there is a heart to feel, there is also an eye to see; even in a city you have light and shade, reflections, probably views of the water and trees, and a blue sky above you, and can you want for beauty with all these? People often pity me while residing in a city, but they need not, for I can enjoy its characteristic beauties as well as any.'"

See also the quotation from Myers in notes on *Poor Susan*, p. 178 above.

4. *Like a garment.* T. quotes *Psalm* civ. 2.

"IT IS A BEAUTEOUS EVENING."

WRITTEN on the beach near Calais, August, 1802; published in 1807.

1. *It is a beauteous evening, calm and free.* The reading of 1807, to which the poet returned in 1846, after changing it in 1836 to "Air sleeps, — from strife or stir the clouds are free," and in 1842 to "A fairer face of evening cannot be."

2. *As a nun.* Cf. Milton, *Comus*, 189:

---

* Waterloo Bridge crosses the Thames some distance below Westminster, which is close to the Houses of Parliament.

> " When the gray-hooded Even,
> Like a sad votarist in palmer's weed."

5. *The gentleness of heaven is on the sea.* The reading of 1807, changed for the worse in 1836 to "broods o'er the sea."

6. *Listen!* Changed in 1836 to "But list!" and restored in 1842.

9. *Dear child! dear girl!* His sister. See on *Tintern Abbey*, 116, 144, and *The Sparrow's Nest*, 15.

ON THE EXTINCTION OF THE VENETIAN REPUBLIC.

Of the same date as the preceding sonnet.

1. *Once did she hold the gorgeous East in fee.* At the close of the Fourth Crusade, in 1202, the Venetians, who had been united with the French in the expedition, became possessors of the Morea, part of Thessaly, the Cyclades, some of the Byzantine cities, and the coasts of the Hellespont, with three eighths of Constantinople.

2. *The safeguard of the West.* "This may refer to the prominent part which Venice took in the Crusade, or to the development of her naval power, which made her mistress of the Mediterranean for many years, and an effective bulwark against invasions from the East" (K.). Cf. Byron, *Childe Harold*, iv. 14:

> " Though making many slaves, herself still free,
> And Europe's bulwark 'gainst the Ottomite."

4. *The eldest child of Liberty.* Venice was founded by refugees from the mainland when Italy was invaded by Attila. "In the midst of the waters, free, indigent, laborious, and inaccessible, they gradually coalesced into a republic" (Gibbon).

6. *No guile seduced.* That is, *whom* (or *which*) no guile seduced, etc. The semicolon at the end of the preceding line in all the editions disguises the construction, as we understand it.

8. *She must espouse the everlasting sea.* Referring to the ceremony of "wedding the Adriatic," performed on Ascension Day, when the Doge threw a ring into the sea from the state-galley *Bucentaur* (or *Bucentoro*) in token of the maritime supremacy of the Republic. Cf. *Childe Harold*, iv. 11:

> " The spouseless Adriatic mourns her lord;
> And, annual marriage now no more renewed,
> The Bucentaur lies rotting unrestored,
> Neglected garment of her widowhood!"

The Venetian Republic became extinct in 1797, about five years before this sonnet was written. By the treaty of Campo Formio, its territories were divided between the Emperor Francis and Napoleon.

> " Venice, lost and won,
> Her thirteen hundred years of freedom done,
> Sinks, like a seaweed, into whence she rose!"

TO TOUSSAINT L'OUVERTURE.

WRITTEN in August, 1802, published in 1807.

François Dominique Toussaint was born at Buda in San Domingo in 1743. His father and mother were both African slaves. He was a Royalist in political sympathies until 1794, when the action of the French Convention giving liberty to the slaves won him to the side of the Republic. He was made a general of division by Laveux, and wrested the whole northern part of the island from the English. In admiration of his achievements Laveux exclaimed, " Mais cet homme fait ouverture partout " (This man opens the way everywhere); and from that time he was called Toussaint L'Ouverture. In 1796 he was appointed commander-in-chief of the French army of San Domingo, and both the British and the Spanish surrendered everything to him. He became governor of the island, which prospered under his rule. In 1801, when Napoleon re-established slavery in San Domingo, Toussaint professed obedience to the decree, but showed that he intended to resist it. A powerful fleet was sent from France to enforce it, and Toussaint was proclaimed an outlaw. After a desperate resistance he was finally led to surrender by pledges on the part of the French that the liberty of his people would be secured; but these pledges were basely violated, and Toussaint himself was arrested, and in June, 1802, sent to Paris, where he died after ten months' imprisonment. He had been two months in prison when this sonnet was written.*

2–4. *Whether the listening rustic*, etc. The reading of 1807 was:

> "Whether the rural milkmaid by her cow
> Sing in thy hearing, or thou liest now
> Alone in some deep dungeon's carless gloom."

In 1815 this was changed to :

> "Whether the all-cheering sun be free to shed
> His beams around thee, or thou rest thy head
> Pillowed in some dark dungeon's noisome den."

The ed. of 1820 reads :

> "Whether the whistling rustic tend his plough
> Within thy hearing, or thou liest now
> Buried in some deep dungeon's earless den."

The present text dates from 1827.

----

* For a much fuller account of Toussaint, see B. J. Lossing's article on " The Horrors of San Domingo," in *Harper's Magazine*, vol. xliii. p. 76 fol.

TOUSSAINT L'OUVERTURE.

WRITTEN IN LONDON, SEPTEMBER, 1802.

PUBLISHED in 1807. A prefatory note says :

" This was written immediately after my return from France to London, when I could not but be struck, as here described, with the vanity and parade of our own country, especially in great towns and cities, as contrasted with the quiet, and I may say the desolation, that the revolution had produced in France. This must be borne in mind, or else the reader may think that in this and the succeeding sonnets I have exaggerated the mischief engendered and fostered among us by undisturbed wealth. It would not be easy to conceive with what a depth of feeling I entered into the struggle carried on by the Spaniards for their deliverance from the usurped power of the French. Many times have I gone from Allan Bank in Grasmere vale, where we were then residing, to the top of the Raise-gap as it is called, so late as two o'clock in the morning, to meet the carrier bringing the newspaper from Keswick."

LONDON, 1802.

THIS sonnet, and the next two, were also written in September, 1802, and published in 1807.

8. *Manners.* "Courtesy springing from a chivalrous respect for our fellow-men " (T.).

14. *On herself.* Originally " on itself;" changed in 1820.

" IT IS NOT TO BE THOUGHT OF."

5, 6. *Roused though it be*, etc. The reading of 1807 (changed in 1827) was :

" Road by which all might come and go that would,
And bear out freights of worth to foreign lands."

" WHEN I HAVE BORNE IN MEMORY."

3. *Desert.* Apparently pronounced *desart*, as in sonnet *To B. R. Haydon*, 8. Cf. Shakespeare, *Sonnet* 49. 10 :

" Within the knowledge of mine own desert,
And this my hand against myself uprear,
To guard the lawful reason on thy part."

See also *Sonn.* 17. 2 and 72. 6.

6. *Now, when*, etc. Until 1845 the reading was " But when," etc.

TO THE DAISY.

THIS and the two following poems were written at Town-end, Grasmere, in 1802, and published in 1807.

The quotation from Wither (referring to his Muse) was prefixed in
1815. *Rustling*, in the 7th line (printed " rustelling " in some eds. of
Wordsworth), is a trisyllable. Cf. the lengthening of many similar words
in Shakespeare ; as *wrestler* in *As You Like It*, ii. 2. 13 : " The parts
and graces of this wrestler," etc.

7, 8. *And gladly*, etc. This is the original reading, restored in 1843
after having been changed in 1836 to

> " And Nature's love of thee partake,
>   Her much-loved Daisy ! "

9–12. *Thee Winter*, etc. The reading of 1807 was :

> " When soothed awhile by milder airs,
>   Thee Winter in his garland wears,
>   That thinly shades his few gray hairs ;
>   Spring cannot shun thee ; "

changed in 1827 to

> " When Winter decks his few gray hairs,
>   Thee in the scanty wreath he wears ;
>   Spring parts the clouds with softest airs,
>   That she may sun thee."

The text dates from 1836.

17. *A morrice train.* Like a company of the morrice-dancers associated with the old Mayday games of England. See Douce's *Illustrations of Shakespeare* or Scott's *Abbot*, chap. xiv., and the author's
note.

19–21. *Pleased at his greeting*, etc. The reading until 1836 was :

> " If welcome once. thou count'st it gain ;
>   Thou art not daunted,
>   Nor car'st if thou be set at naught."

25. *In their secret mews.* That is, in their hiding-places. The verb
mew originally meant to moult, or shed the feathers. Thence the noun,
applied to " the place, whether it be abroad or in the house, in which the
hawk is put during the time she casts, or doth change her feathers " (R.
Holmes's *Academy of Armory*). Cf. Spenser, *F. Q.* i. 5. 20 : " forth com-
ming from her darksome mew," etc. According to Pennant (*London*), the
royal stables in London were called *mews* from the original use of the
buildings for keeping the king's falcons.

37. *Should fare.* Cf. Milton, *P. L.* ii. 940 : " nigh founder'd on he
fares," etc.

47. *Chime.* A MS. note of the poet in the ed. of 1836 substitutes

" charm," but this does not appear in the more recent printed texts, with the exception of Knight's *Selections*.

57, 58. *Fresh-smitten by the morning ray*, etc.   The reading until 1836 was :

> " When, smitten by the morning ray,
> I see thee rise, alert and gay."

60–64. *With kindred gladness*, etc.   The original reading (changed in 1815) was :

> " With kindred motion.
> At dusk, I 've seldom marked thee press
> The ground, as if in thankfulness,
> Without some feeling, more or less,
> Of true devotion."

73–80. *Child of the year*, etc.   The reading of 1807 was :

> " Child of the year ! that round dost run
> Thy course, bold lover of the sun,
> And cheerful when the day 's begun
> As morning leveret,
> Thou long the poet's praise shalt gain;
> Thou wilt be more beloved by men
> In times to come ; thou not in vain
> Art Nature's favourite."

In 1815 lines 77–79 were made to read :

> " Thy long-lost praise thou shalt regain ;
> Dear shalt thou be to future men
> As in old time ;—thou not in vain," etc.

The text dates back to 1836.

Thy long-lost praise.   " See in Chaucer and the elder poets the honours formerly paid to this flower " (W.).   Note especially the prologue to *The Legende of Good Women*.

TO THE SAME FLOWER.

3. *Daisy, again I talk to thee.*   The reading of 1807 was "Sweet daisy, oft I talk to thee;" changed in 1843 to "Yet once again I talk to thee;" and in 1849 to the present text.

9, 10. *Oft on the dappled turf*, etc.   The reading of 1820, the original being :

> " Oft do I sit by thee at ease,
> And weave a web of similes."

41–46. *Bright flower*, etc.   In all the standard eds. the lines are pointed thus :

> " Bright *flower* ! for by that name at last,
> When all my reveries are past,
> I call thee, and to that cleave fast,
> Sweet silent creature !
> That breath'st with me in sun and air,
> Do thou, as thou art wont, repair," etc.

This cannot be right, but whether the division should be made at the end of the 3d line or of the 5th is not perfectly clear. The former seems preferable, and we point accordingly.

TO THE DAISY.

1-4. The reading of 2 in 1807 was "A pilgrim bold in Nature's care." The ed. of 1836 reads :

> "Confiding flower, by Nature's care
> Made bold,—who, lodging here or there,
> Art all the long year through the heir
> Of joy or sorrow."

The text is that of 1843.

6. *Some concord with humanity.* The original reading, changed in 1836 to "Communion with humanity," but restored in 1843.

8. *Thorough.* Used for *through*, to which it was anciently equivalent. Cf. Shakespeare, *M. N. D.* ii. 1. 3 : "Thorough bush, thorough briar," etc. See also *Yarrow Unvisited*, 38.

23. *Thy function apostolical.* "I have been censured for the last line but one—'thy function apostolical'—as being little less than profane. How could it be thought so? The word is adopted with reference to its derivation, implying something sent on a mission; and assuredly this little flower, especially when the subject of verse, may be regarded, in its humble degree, as administering both to moral and to spiritual purposes" (W.).

THE GREEN LINNET.

COMPOSED in 1803 " in the orchard, Town-end, Grasmere, where the bird was often seen as here described " (W.). It was first published in 1807.

1-8. *Beneath these fruit-tree boughs*, etc. The original reading was :

> "The May is come again;—how sweet
> To sit upon my orchard-seat !
> And birds and flowers once more to greet,
> My last year's friends together ;
> My thoughts they all by turns employ ;
> A whispering leaf is now my joy,
> And then a bird will be the toy
> That doth my fancy tether."

In 1815 "birds and flowers" was changed to "flowers and birds;" and in 1827 the present text was adopted.

20. *Sole.* Single. Cf. the law-term for an unmarried woman, *femme sole*.

25. *Amid yon tuft.* Knight, in his *Selections*, has "Upon yon tuft;" but he does not give that reading in his collation of the texts.

33–40. *My dazzled sight*, etc. The ed. of 1807 reads :

> " While thus before my eyes he gleams,
> A brother of the leaves he seems ;
> When in a moment forth he teems
>   His little song in gushes ;
> As if it pleased him to disdain
> And mock the form which he did feign,
> While he was dancing with the train
>   Of leaves among the bushes."

In 1820 line 38 was changed to its present form ; and in 1827 the stanza was made to read :

> " My sight he dazzles, half deceives,
> A bird so like the dancing leaves,"

with the remainder as in the text, which was finally settled in 1832.

K. remarks : " This, of all Wordsworth's poems, is the one most distinctively associated with the orchard at Town-end, Grasmere." Coleridge asks : " What can be more accurate, yet more lovely, than the two concluding stanzas ?"

TO A HIGHLAND GIRL.

WRITTEN in 1803, but not published until 1815. In his MS. notes the poet says : " This delightful creature and her demeanour are particularly described in my sister's Journal. The sort of prophecy with which the verses conclude has, through God's goodness, been realized ; and now, approaching the close of my 73d year, I have a most vivid remembrance of her and the beautiful objects with which she was surrounded."

5. *That household lawn.* The ed. of 1807 has " this," changed to *that* in 1836.

14. *When earthly cares are laid asleep.* After this line, the ed. of 1845 adds the couplet :

> " But, O fair creature ! in the light
> Of common day so heavenly bright,"

and changes the next line to " I bless thee, vision as thou art." The reading of this line in 1807 was " Yet dream and vision as thou art;" changed in 1836 as in the text.

18. *Thee neither know I*, etc. The reading until 1845 was " I neither know thee nor thy peers."

39. *Thy few words of English speech*, etc. Cf. Miss Wordsworth's *Journal :* " One of the girls was exceedingly beautiful ; and the figures of both of them, in gray plaids falling to their feet, their faces only being uncovered, excited our attention before we spoke to them ; but they answered us so sweetly that we were quite delighted, at the same time that they stared at us with an innocent look of wonder. I think I never heard the English language sound more sweetly than from the mouth of the elder of these girls, while she stood at the gate answering our inqui-

ries, her face flushed with the rain; her pronunciation was clear and distinct, without difficulty, yet slow, as if like a foreign speech."

44. *Beating up against the wind.* A nautical phrase for "making progress against the wind by alternate tacks in a zigzag line." The *New Eng. Dict.* gives no example of it used figuratively, as here. *Beat* is now more common among seamen than *beat up*.

47. *Happy pleasure.* No doubt the poet meant *happy* here to be taken in the sense of *fortunate*, like the Latin *felix*. Cf. the play upon the word in *Macbeth*, i. 3. 66: "Not so happy, yet much happier" (not so fortunate, but much more blessed).

54. *Have.* One of the English words that have no perfect rhyme, though the poets often use it in rhymes. Cf. Shakespeare, *Cymbeline*, iv. 2. 280:

> " Quiet consummation have,
> And renowned be thy grave ;"

and Milton, *Epitaph on Marchioness of Winchester*, 47 :

> " Gentle lady, may thy grave
> Peace and quiet ever have !"

In *Comus*, 238, it rhymes with *cave*, and in *Id.* 888 with *wave*.

Other imperfect or peculiar rhymes in the present volume are *calendar, year* (p. 43), *on, one* (49), *upon, one* (124), *no, do* (79), *nought, sought, remote* (92, 120), *creature, nature* (97, 127), *stature, nature* (144), *gushes, bushes* (99), *town, own* (103), *shadow, meadow* (104), *sullen, culling* (124), *forgetfulness, nakedness* (125), *weather, hither* (128), *meanderings, wanderings* (143), *gather, heather* (146) *sunshine, moonshine* (158). Note also the bad rhymes to *Yarrow* (*thorough, borough, sorrow*, etc.) in the *Yarrow* poems. Wordsworth, like Milton and many other poets, disregards the rule that words differing only by an initial *h* are not perfect rhymes. Thus, he has *arts, hearts* (70), *art, heart* (79, 91, 126, 147), *old, hold* (90, 113), *all, hall* (131), etc. See also on *When I have Borne in Memory*, 3.

72. *For I, methinks, till I grow old,* etc. Cf. Miss Wordsworth's *Journal :* "At this day the innocent merriment of the girls, with their kindness to us, and the beautiful face and figure of the elder, come to my mind whenever I think of the ferryhouse and waterfall of Loch Lomond, and I never think of the two girls but the whole image of that romantic spot is before me, a living image as it will be to my dying day."

THE SOLITARY REAPER.

WRITTEN in 1803, published in 1807.

5. *Alone she cuts and binds the grain,* etc. See p. 168 above.

10. *So sweetly to reposing bands.* The original reading, unfortunately changed in 1827 to " More welcome notes to weary bands."

13. *A voice so thrilling ne'er was heard.* The ed. of 1807 has " No

sweeter voice was ever heard;" and that of 1827 "Such thrilling voice was never heard." The text is that of 1836.

15. *The silence of the seas.* T. quotes *The Ancient Mariner:*

> " We were the first that ever burst
> Into that silent sea;"

and again :

> " And we did speak only to break
> The silence of the sea;"

16. *The farthest Hebrides.* Cf. *Lycidas*, 156: "beyond the stormy Hebrides."

29. *I listened till I had my fill.* The reading of 1807, which is clearly better than "I listened, motionless and still," to which it was changed in 1820.

30. *And when.* The ed. of 1807 had "And as," which was restored in 1836 after being changed to *And when* in 1827.

YARROW UNVISITED.

WRITTEN in 1803, published in 1807. The prefatory note says: "See the various poems the scene of which is laid upon the banks of the Yarrow; in particular the exquisite ballad of Hamilton, beginning :

> ' Busk ye, busk ye, my bonny, bonny bride,
> Busk ye, busk ye, my winsome marrow!' "

2. *The mazy Forth.* No note is needed on this and the other familiar Scotch rivers mentioned.

5. *Clovenford*, or *Clovenfords*, is on the Tweed, a few miles above Abbotsford. Dorothy Wordsworth says in her *Journal:* "At Clovenford, being so near to the Yarrow, we could not but think of the possibility of going thither, but came to the conclusion of reserving the pleasure for some future time, in consequence of which, after our return, William wrote the poem which I shall here transcribe."

6. *Marrow.* His sister. The word means "One of a pair, a mate, a companion, an equal, a sweetheart," etc. It appears in early English literature, but now survives only in the poetry and common speech of Scotland and the North of England.

8. *Braes.* Hillsides, sloping banks (Scotch).

9. *Let Yarrow folk*, etc. See p. 172 above. *Selkirk*, situated just below the confluence of the Yarrow and the Ettrick, is the market-town of the vicinity.

15. *Downward.* The eds. down to 1832 have "downwards."

17. *Galla Water.* The *Galla*, or *Gala*, is a branch of the Tweed, celebrated in an old ballad versified by Burns: " Braw, braw lads of Galla Water."

A *haugh* is low ground or meadows on the bank of a river. Cf. Burns, *Scotch Drink :* " Let husky wheat the haughs adorn."

19. *Dryborough.* Dryburgh, pronounced *Dryboro'*.

20. *Lintwhites.* Linnets. Cf. Tennyson, *Claribel :* " Her song the lintwhite swelleth."

21. *Tiviotdale.* More properly *Teviotdale*, the valley of the Teviot.

33. *Holms.* Meadows. Cf. *The Dowie Dens o' Yarrow :*

> " Down in a glen he spied nine armed men
> On the dowie holms o' Yarrow."

35. *Fair hangs the apple,* etc. The line is from Hamilton's ballad mentioned above. *Frae*=from; as in 9 above.

37. *Strath.* A broad river-valley. Cf. *Lady of the Lake*, iii. 87: " in lonely glen or strath."

38. *Thorough.* See on *To the Daisy*, 8 (p. 205 above).

43. *Saint Mary's Lake.* The source of the Yarrow. Scott refers to it in *Marmion*, introd. to canto ii. 147:

> " By lone Saint Mary's silent lake :
> Thou know'st it well,—nor fern nor sedge,
> Pollute the pure lake's crystal edge;
> Abrupt and sheer, the mountains sink
> At once upon the level brink,
> And just a trace of silver sand
> Marks where the water meets the land," etc.

In a note he says of the lake : " In the winter it is still frequented by flights of wild swans ; hence my friend Mr. Wordsworth's lines :

> 'The swans on sweet Saint Mary's Lake
> Float double, swan and shadow.' "

Wordsworth afterwards said to Aubrey De Vere : " Scott misquoted in one of his novels my lines on Yarrow. He makes me write :

> 'The swans on sweet Saint Mary's Lake
> Float double, swan and shadow;'

but I wrote ' The *swan* on *still* Saint Mary's Lake.' Never could I have written ' swans ' in the plural. The scene when I saw it, with its still and dim lake under the dusky hills, was one of utter loneliness;· there was *one* swan, and one only, stemming the water, and the pathetic loneliness of the region gave importance to the one companion of the swan—its own white image in the water. It was for that reason that I recorded the swan and the shadow. Had there been many swans and many shadows, they would have implied nothing as regards the character of the place, and I should have said nothing about them." He went on to comment on the fact that many who truly love Nature had yet no eye to discern her. " Indeed," he added, " I have hardly ever known any one but myself who had a true eye for Nature—one that thoroughly understood her meanings and her teachings."

But Scott, in his description of Saint Mary's Lake, dwells particularly on this very loneliness of the scene whereon Wordsworth lays such stress. The passage, partially quoted above, continues thus :

> " Far in the mirror, bright and blue,
> Each hill's huge outline you may view;

> Shaggy with heath, but lonely bare,
> Nor tree, nor bush, nor brake is there,
> Save where of land yon slender line
> Bears thwart the lake the scattered pine.
> Yet even this nakedness has power,
> And aids the feeling of the hour:
> Nor thicket, dell, nor copse you spy
> Where living thing concealed might lie;
> Nor point retiring hides a dell
> Where swain or woodman lone might dwell.
> There's nothing left to fancy's guess,
> You see that all is loneliness;
> And silence aids—though the steep hills
> Send to the lake a thousand rills;
> In summer time so soft they weep,
> The sound but lulls the ear asleep;
> Your horse's hoof-tread sounds too rude,
> So stilly is the solitude."

Surely we have here the "pathetic loneliness" of the "*still* Saint Mary's Lake." The *sweet* for *still* and the plural *swans* were merely a slip of memory, and the latter is explained by Scott's note, which shows that he was thinking of the "flights" of the birds in winter.

49–56. *Be Yarrow's stream*, etc. Shairp (*Aspects of Poetry*) comments on these lines thus: "And then the deep undertone of feeling which lay beneath all the lighter chaff and seeming disparagement breaks out in these two immortal stanzas" (as he prints the eight lines).

"After this ideal gleam," Shairp continues, "has for a moment broken over it, the light of common day again closes in, and the poem ends with the comforting thought that

> ' Should life be dull, and spirits low,
>   'T will soothe us in our sorrow
> That earth has something yet to show,
>   The bonnie holms of Yarrow.'

The whole poem, if it contains only two stanzas [49–56] pitched in Wordsworth's highest strain, is throughout in his most felicitous diction. The manner is that of the old ballad, with an infusion of modern reflection, which yet does not spoil its naturalness. The metre is that in which most of the old Yarrow ballads, from *The Dowie Dens* onward, are cast, with the second and the fourth lines in each stanza ending in double rhymes, to let the refrain fall full on the fine melodious name of Yarrow. It plays with the subject, rises and falls—now light-hearted, now serious, then back to homeliness, with a most graceful movement. It has in it something of that ethereality of thought and manner which belonged to Wordsworth's earlier lyrics—those composed during the last years of the preceding and the first few years of this century. This peculiar ethereality—which is a thing to feel rather than to describe—left him after about 1805, and though replaced in the best of his later poems by increased depth and mellowness of reflection, yet could no more be compensated than the fresh gleam of new-fledged leaves in spring can be made up for by their autumnal glory."

See also Mr. Hutton's criticism, p. 172 above.

"SHE WAS A PHANTOM OF DELIGHT."

WRITTEN at Town-end in 1804, and published in 1807. Wordsworth says that "the germ of the poem" was four lines (probably the
first four) "composed as a part of the verses on the Highland Girl."
He adds: "Though beginning in this way, it was written from my
heart, as is sufficiently obvious." As it stands, it is a tribute to his wife.

4. *To be a moment's ornament.* "To fill but one single moment with
beauty too bright and ethereal to last" (T.).

8. *From May-time,* etc. Changed in the ed. of 1836 (no other) to
" From May-time's brightest, liveliest dawn."

22. *The very pulse of the machine.* To our modern taste *machine*
does not seem a happy word, but, as K. remarks, it has become " more
limited and purely technical " since Wordsworth wrote. Cf. the eu-
phuistic use of the word in the one instance in which Shakespeare has
it—*Hamlet,* ii. 2. 124 : " while this machine is to him " (while this bod-
ily organism is his).

24. *Between life and death.* The first reading was " betwixt life and
death;" changed in 1832.

29. *And yet a spirit still,* etc. Cf. *The Prelude,* xiv. 268 :

> " She came, no more a phantom to adorn
> A moment, but an inmate of the heart,
> And yet a spirit, there for me enshrined
> To penetrate the lofty and the low."

30. *Of an angel light.* The original reading, changed in 1845 to " of
angelic light."

"I WANDERED LONELY AS A CLOUD."

WRITTEN at Town-end in 1804, and published in 1807. Wordsworth
says : " The daffodils grew and still grow on the margin of Ulleswater,
and probably may be seen to this day as beautiful in the month of March,
nodding their golden heads beside the dancing and foaming waves."

The following is from Miss Wordsworth's *Journal : " April* 15,
1802.—When we were in the woods below Gowbarrow Park we saw a
few daffodils close to the water-side. As we went along there were
more, and yet more; and, at last, under the boughs of the trees, we saw
there was a long belt of them along the shore. I never saw daffodils so
beautiful. They grew among the mossy stones about them; some rested their heads on the stones as on a pillow; the rest tossed, and reeled,
and danced, and seemed as if they verily danced with the wind, they
looked so gay and glancing." *Gowbarrow Park* is on the western shore
of Ulleswater.

See Mr. Hutton's comments on the poem, p. 170 above. Sara Coleridge exclaims : " How poetry multiplies bright images like a thousand-
fold kaleidoscope ! for how many ' inward eyes ' have those daffodils
danced and fluttered in the breeze, the waves dancing beside them !"

4. *Golden daffodils.* The ed. of 1807 has "dancing daffodils," and in the next line "Along the lake;" both changed in 1815.

6. *Fluttering and dancing in the breeze.* The ed. of 1807 has "Ten thousand dancing," etc.

7–12. *Continuous as the stars,* etc. This stanza was added in 1815.

15. *Could not but be gay.* The eds. down to 1836 have "be but."

16. *Jocund company.* The reading of 1815, the earlier being "laughing company."

21, 22. *They flash upon that inward eye,* etc. The poet tells us that these two lines were contributed by his wife.

THE AFFLICTION OF MARGARET.

WRITTEN at Town-end in 1804, published in 1807. The poet says: "This was taken from the case of a poor widow who lived in the town of Penrith. Her sorrow was well known to Mrs. Wordsworth, to my sister, and, I believe, to the whole town. She kept a shop, and when she saw a stranger passing by, she was in the habit of going out into the street to inquire of him after her son."

Coleridge refers to this poem as "that most affecting composition which no mother, and, if I may judge by my own experience, no parent can read without a tear."

10. *To have despaired, and have believed.* The original reading, for which the ed. of 1836 substitutes "To have despaired, have hoped, believed," with "been" for *be* in the next line.

24. *What power is in,* etc. The original reading (changed in 1832) was "What power hath even," etc.

50–56. *Perhaps some dungeon,* etc. Mr. Myers (p. 106), commenting upon Wordsworth's theory that "there neither is, nor can be, any essential difference between the language of prose and metrical composition," selects this stanza "from one of his simplest and most characteristic poems" to illustrate the inadequacy of the theory. He says:

"These lines, supposed to be uttered by 'a poor widow at Penrith,' afford a fair illustration of what Wordsworth calls 'the language really spoken by men,' with 'metre superadded.' 'What other distinction from prose,' he asks, 'would we have?' We may answer that we would have what he has actually given us, namely, an appropriate and attractive music, lying both in the rhythm and in the actual sound of the words used—a music whose complexity may be indicated here by drawing out some of its elements in detail, at the risk of appearing pedantic and technical. We observe, then (*a*), that the general movement of the lines is unusually slow. They contain a very large proportion of strong accents and long vowels, to suit the tone of deep and despairing sorrow. In six places only out of twenty-eight is the accent weak where it might be expected to be strong (in the second syllable, namely, of the iambic foot), and in each of these cases the omission of a possible accent throws greater weight on the next succeeding accent—on the accents, that is to say, contained in the words *inhuman, desert, lion, summoned, deep,* and *sleep.* (*b*) The first four lines contain subtle alliterations of the letters *d, h, m,* and *th.* In this connection it should be remembered that when consonants are thus repeated at the beginning of syllables, those syllables need not be at the beginning of words; and further, that repetitions scarcely more numerous than chance alone would have occasioned may be so placed by the poet as to produce a strongly-felt effect. If any one doubts the effectiveness of the unobvious alliterations here insisted on, let him read (1) 'jungle' for 'desert,' (2) 'maybe' for 'perhaps,' (3) 'tortured' for 'mangled,' (4) 'blown' for 'thrown,' and he will become sensible of the lack of the metrical support which the existing consonants give one another. The three last lines contain one or two similar alliterations on which I need not dwell. (*c*) The words *inheritest* and *summoned* are by no means such as 'a poor widow,' even at Penrith, would employ; they are used to intensify the imagined relation which connects the missing man with (1) the wild beasts who surround him, and (2) the invisible Power which leads; so that something mysterious and awful is added to his fate. (*d*) This impression is heightened by the use of the word *incommunicable* in an unusual sense, 'incapable of being communicated *with,*' instead of 'incapable of being communicated;' while (*e*) the expression 'to keep an incommunicable sleep' for 'to lie dead,' gives dignity to the occasion by carrying the mind back along a train of literary associations of which the well-known ἀτέρμονα νήγρετον ὕπνον of Moschus may be taken as the type.

"We must not, of course, suppose that Wordsworth consciously sought these alliterations, arranged these accents, resolved to introduce an unusual word in the last line, or hunted for a classical allusion. But what the poet's brain does not do consciously it does unconsciously; a selective action is going on in its recesses simultaneously with the overt train of thought, and on the degree of this unconscious suggestiveness the richness and melody of the poetry will depend.

"No rules can secure the attainment of these effects; and the very same artifices which are delightful when used by one man seem mechanical and offensive when used by another. Nor is it by any means always the case that the man who can most delicately appreciate the melody of the poetry of others will be able to produce similar melody himself. Nay, even if he can produce it one year, it by no means follows that he will be able to produce it the next. Of all qualifications for writing poetry this inventive music is the most arbitrarily distributed, and the most evanescent. But it is the more important to dwell on its necessity, inasmuch as both good and bad poets are tempted to ignore it. The good poet prefers to ascribe his success to higher qualities; to his imagination, elevation of thought, descriptive faculty. The bad poet can more easily urge that his thoughts are too advanced for mankind to appreciate than that his melody is too sweet for their ears to catch. And when the gift vanishes no poet is willing to confess that it is gone; so humiliating is it to lose power over mankind by the loss of something which seems quite independent of intellect or character. And yet so it is. For some twenty years at most (1798–1818) Wordsworth possessed this gift of melody. During those years he wrote works which profoundly influenced mankind. The gift then left him; he continued as wise and as earnest as ever, but his poems had no longer any potency, nor his existence much public importance." Cf. pp. 25 and 167–175 above.

60. *Between the living*, etc. The reading of 1807 (changed in 1832) was "Betwixt the living," etc. See on *She was a Phantom*, 24.

ODE TO DUTY.

WRITTEN in 1805, published in 1807. Wordsworth says of it: "This ode is on the model of Gray's *Ode to Adversity*, which is copied from Horace's *Ode to Fortune*. Many and many a time have I been twitted by my wife and sister for having forgotten this dedication of myself to the stern lawgiver. Transgressor indeed I have been, from hour to hour, from day to day: I would fain hope, however, not more flagrantly or in a worse way than most of my tuneful brethren. But these last words are in a wrong strain. We should be rigorous to ourselves and forbearing, if not indulgent, to others, and, if we make comparisons at all, it ought to be with those who have morally excelled us."

James Russell Lowell, in his address as president of the Wordsworth Society in 1884, refers to "the *Ode to Duty*, in which he speaks to us out of an ampler ether than in any other of his poems, and which may safely 'challenge insolent Greece and haughty Rome' for a comparison either in kind or degree."

The Dean of Salisbury, in a paper on "Wordsworth as an Ethical Teacher" (read before the Wordsworth Society in May, 1883), remarks: "The *Ode to Duty* all lovers of Wordsworth have, or ought to have, by heart. The poet evidently desires to bring into high relief the perfect play of a moral nature, wherein acts of virtue pass out of restraint into the glorious freedom and liberty which are proper to man."

5. *Thou who art victory and law*, etc. "Our sense of right gains the victory over imaginary terrors by making us feel that disobedience to the law of right within us should alone make us fear" (T.).

7. *From vain temptations*, etc. "Duty sets free from the influence of what only appears worth pursuing by rendering us morally incapable of acting otherwise than she bids; thus putting a stop to a moral struggle which mankind from their weakness find, even when successful, to be a 'weary strife'" (T.).

8. *And calm'st the weary strife*, etc. The ed. of 1807 reads: "From strife and from despair; a glorious ministry;" changed in 1815.

12. *The genial sense of youth.* The natural impulses of youthful innocence. See on *Tintern Abbey*, 113.

15, 16. *Long may the kindly impulse*, etc. The reading of 1827, which we prefer to the earlier or later forms. The ed. of 1807 has:

> " May joy be theirs while life shall last!
> And thou, if they should totter, teach them to stand fast!"

That of 1836 is :

> "Oh! if through confidence misplaced
> They fail, thy saving arms, dread Power! around them cast."

21, 22. *And they a blissful course*, etc.   The reading of 1807 (changed in 1827) was :

> "And blest are they who in the main
> This faith, even now, do entertain:
> Live in the spirit," etc.

This creed.   That is, this faith in joy and love to guide them.

24. *Yet seek thy firm support*, etc.   The reading of 1845.   The ed. of 1807 has, "Yet find that other strength, according to their need;" changed in 1836 to "Yet find they firm support, according to their need."

29-31. *And oft, when in my heart*, etc.   The reading of 1807 was :

> "Resolved that nothing e'er should press
> Upon my present happiness.
> I shoved unwelcome tasks away ;
> But thee I now would serve," etc.

That of 1815 was :

> "And oft when in my heart was heard
> Thy timely mandate, I deferred
> The task imposed from day to day;" etc.

The present reading was adopted in 1827.

36. *The quietness of thought.*   As "opposed to passion or feeling" (T.).

37. *Unchartered.*   Unrestricted; like national freedom unrestrained by a *charter*, or constitution.

40. *That ever is the same.*   Until 1827 the reading was "which ever is the same."

45-48. *Flowers laugh before thee*, etc.   The obedience of nature to physical law is beautifully compared to man's obedience to moral law. It is in keeping with Wordsworth's conception of nature as having "a true life of her own" and as being "the shape and image of right reason, reason in the highest sense, embodied and made visible in order, in stability, in conformity to eternal law" (Shairp).

53. *Lowly wise.*   Wise through humility.

TO A YOUNG LADY,

WHO HAD BEEN REPROACHED FOR TAKING LONG WALKS IN THE COUNTRY.

WRITTEN in 1805, and published in 1807.

5. *Thy own delightful days.*   The reading given by Matthew Arnold in his *Selections.*   The ed. of 1807 has "Thy slow delightful days," which was changed in 1836 to "Thy own heart-stirring days."

8, 9. *And treading among flowers of joy*, etc.   The reading of 1827, that of 1807 being

"As if thy heritage were joy,
And pleasure were thy trade."

16. *Serene and bright.* The ed. of 1807 had "alive and bright;" changed in 1815.

CHARACTER OF THE HAPPY WARRIOR.

WRITTEN in 1806, published in 1807. In the MS. notes on his poems, Wordsworth says: "The course of the great war with the French naturally fixed one's attention upon the military character, and, to the honour of our country, there were many illustrious instances of the qualities that constitute its highest excellence. Lord Nelson carried most of the virtues that the trials he was exposed to in his department of the service necessarily call forth and sustain, if they do not produce the contrary vices. But his public life was stained with one great crime, so that, though many passages of these lines were suggested by what was generally known as excellent in his conduct, I have not been able to connect his name with the poem as I could wish, or even to think of him with satisfaction in reference to the idea of what a warrior ought to be. For the sake of such of my friends as may happen to read this note I will add, that many elements of the character here pourtrayed were found in my brother John,* who perished by shipwreck as mentioned elsewhere. His messmates used to call him the Philosopher, from which it must be inferred that the qualities and dispositions I allude to had not escaped their notice. He often expressed his regret, after the war had continued some time, that he had not chosen the Naval, instead of the

---

* John was a few years younger than William, and captain of an East-Indiaman. In 1800 he had spent eight months with his brother at Grasmere. Myers (p. 69) says: "The two brothers had seen little of each other since childhood, and the poet had now the delight of discovering in the sailor a character congenial to his own, and an appreciation of poetry—and of the *Lyrical Ballads* especially—which was intense and delicate in an unusual degree. In both brothers, too, there was the same love of nature; and after John's departure, the poet pleased himself with imagining the visions of Grasmere which beguiled the watches of many a night at sea, or with tracing the pathway which the sailor's instinct had planned and trodden amid trees so thickly planted as to baffle a less practised skill. John Wordsworth, on the other hand, looked forward to Grasmere as the final goal of his wanderings, and intended to use his own savings to set the poet free from worldly cares.

"Two more voyages the sailor made with such hopes as these, and amid a frequent interchange of books and letters with his brother at home. Then, in February, 1805, he set sail from Portsmouth, in command of the 'Abergavenny' East-Indiaman, bound for India and China. Through the incompetence of the pilot who was taking her out of the Channel, the ship struck on the Shambles off the Bill of Portland, on February 5, 1805. 'She struck,' says Wordsworth, 'at 5 p.m. Guns were fired immediately, and were continued to be fired. She was gotten off the rock at half-past seven, but had taken in so much water, in spite of constant pumping, as to be water-logged. They had, however, hope that she might still be run upon Weymouth sands, and with this view continued pumping and bailing till eleven, when she went down. . . . A few minutes before the ship went down my brother was seen talking to the first mate with apparent cheerfulness; and he was standing on the hen coop, which is the point from which he could overlook the whole ship, the moment she went down—dying, as he had lived, in the very place and point where his duty stationed him.'"

East India Company's service, to which his family connection had led him. He greatly valued moral and religious instruction for youth, as tending to make good sailors. The best, he used to say, came from Scotland; the next to them, from the North of England, especially from Westmoreland and Cumberland, where, thanks to the piety and local attachments of our ancestors, endowed, or, as they are commonly called, free, schools abound."

Myers, commenting on this poem, asks (p. 79) : " Was there any man, by land or sea, who might serve as the poet's type of the ideal hero? To an Englishman, at least, this question carries its own reply. For by a singular destiny England, with a thousand years of noble history behind her, has chosen for her best-beloved, for her national hero, not an Arminius from the age of legend, not a Henri Quatre from the age of chivalry, but a man whom men still living have seen and known. For, indeed, England and all the world as to this man were of one accord; and when in victory, on his ship *Victory*, Nelson passed away, the thrill which shook mankind was of a nature such as perhaps was never felt at any other death—so unanimous was the feeling of friends and foes that earth had lost her crowning example of impassioned self-devotedness and of heroic honour.

"And yet it might have seemed that between Nelson's nature and Wordsworth's there was little in common. The obvious limitations of the great Admiral's culture and character were likely to be strongly felt by the philosophic poet. . . . Wordsworth was, in fact, hampered by some such feelings of disapproval. He even tells us, with that naïve affectionateness which often makes us smile, that he has had recourse to the character of his own brother John for the qualities in which the great Admiral appeared to him to have been deficient. But on these hesitations it would be unjust to dwell. I mention them only to bring out the fact that between these two men, so different in outward fates—between ' the adored, the incomparable Nelson ' and the homely poet, ' retired as noontide dew '—there was a moral likeness so profound that the ideal of the recluse was realized in the public life of the hero, and, on the other hand, the hero himself is only seen as completely heroic when his impetuous life stands out for us from the solemn background of the poet's calm. And surely these two natures taken together make the perfect Englishman. Nor is there any portrait fitter than that of *The Happy Warrior* to go forth to all lands as representing the English character at its height—a figure not ill-matching with ' Plutarch's men.'

" For indeed this short poem is in itself a manual of greatness; there is a Roman majesty in its simple and weighty speech. And what eulogy was ever nobler than that passage where, without definite allusion or quoted name, the poet depicts, as it were, the very summit of glory in the well-remembered aspect of the Admiral in his last and greatest hour ?

> Whose powers shed round him, in the common strife,
> Or mild concerns of ordinary life,
> A constant influence, a peculiar grace ;
> But who, if he be called upon to face

> Some awful moment to which Heaven has joined
> Great issues, good or bad for human kind,
> *Is happy as a lover, and attired*
> *With sudden brightness, like a man inspired.'*

Or again, where the hidden thought of Nelson's womanly tenderness, of his constant craving for the green earth and home affections in the midst of storm and war, melts the stern verses into a sudden change of tone :

> ' He who, though thus endued as with a sense
> And faculty for storm and turbulence,
> *Is yet a soul whose master-bias leans*
> *To homefelt pleasures and to gentle scenes;*
> Sweet images! which, wheresoe'er he be,
> Are at his heart, and such fidelity
> It is his darling passion to approve:
> More brave for this, that he hath much to love.'

Compare with this the end of the *Song at Brougham Castle*, where, at the words 'alas! the fervent harper did not know—' the strain changes from the very spirit of chivalry to the gentleness of nature's calm. Nothing can be more characteristic of Wordsworth than contrasts like this. They teach us to remember that his accustomed mildness is the fruit of no indolent or sentimental peace; and that, on the other hand, when his counsels are sternest, and 'his voice is still for war,' this is no voice of hardness or of vainglory, but the reluctant resolution of a heart which fain would yield itself to other energies, and have no message but of love.

   " There is one more point in which the character of Nelson has fallen in with one of the lessons which Wordsworth is never tired of enforcing, the lesson that virtue grows by the strenuousness of its exercise, that it gains strength as it wrestles with pain and difficulty, and converts the shocks of circumstance into an energy of its proper glow. The Happy Warrior is one,

> ' Who, doomed to go in company with Pain,
> And Fear, and Bloodshed, miserable train !
> Turns his necessity to glorious gain;
> In face of these doth exercise a power
> Which is our human nature's highest dower ;
> Controls them and subdues, transmutes, bereaves
> Of their bad influence, and their good receives ;
> By objects which might force the soul to abate
> Her feeling, rendered more compassionate ;'

and so further, in words which recall the womanly tenderness, the almost exaggerated feeling for others' pain, which showed itself memorably in face of the blazing 'Orient,' and in the harbour at Teneriffe, and in the cockpit at Trafalgar.

   " In such lessons as these—such lessons as *The Happy Warrior* or the Patriotic Sonnets teach—there is, of course, little that is absolutely novel. We were already aware that the ideal hero should be as gentle as he is brave, that he should act always from the highest motives, nor greatly care for any reward save the consciousness of having done his duty. We were aware that the true strength of a nation is moral, and not material; that dominion which rests on mere military force is destined quickly to decay; that the tyrant, however admired and prosperous, is in reality despicable, and miserable, and alone; that the true man should face death itself rather than parley with dishonour. These truths are *admitted* in all ages; yet it is scarcely stretching language to say that they are *known* to but few men. Or at least, though in a great nation there be many who will act on them instinctively, and approve them by a self-surrendering faith, there are few who can so put them forth in speech as to bring them home with a fresh conviction and an added glow; who can sum up, like Æschylus, the contrast between Hellenic freedom and barbarian despotism in 'one trump's peal that set all Greeks aflame;' can thrill, like Virgil, a world-wide empire with the recital of the august simplicities of early Rome.

"To those who would know these things with a vital knowledge—a conviction which would remain unshaken were the whole world in arms for wrong—it is before all things necessary to strengthen the inner monitions by the companionship of these noble souls. And if a poet, by strong concentration of thought, by striving in all things along the upward way, can leave us in a few pages, as it were, a summary of patriotism, a manual of national honour, he surely has his place among his country's benefactors not only by that kind of courtesy which the nation extends to men of letters of whom her masses take little heed, but with a title as assured as any warrior or statesman, and with no less direct a claim."

Mrs. Jameson, in her *Commonplace Book*, calls attention to the fact that if in this poem we make the experiment of "substituting the word *woman* for the word *warrior*, and changing the masculine for the feminine pronoun," we shall find that it "reads equally well." She prints lines 1–56 with these changes, and adds: "In all these fifty-six lines there is only one which cannot be feminized in its significance, . . . and which is totally at variance with our ideal of a Happy Woman. It is the line 'And in himself possess his own desire.' No woman could exist happily or virtuously in such complete independence of all external affections as these words express."

Miss Martineau, in her *Autobiography*, says: "Knowing that he had no objection to be talked to about his works, I told him I thought it might interest him to hear which of his poems was Dr. Channing's favourite. I told him I had not been a day in Dr. Channing's house when he brought me *The Happy Warrior*—a choice which I thought very characteristic also. 'Ay,' said Wordsworth, 'that was not on account of the *poetic conditions* being best fulfilled in that poem; but because it is' (solemnly) 'a chain of extremely *valooable* thoughts.—You see, it does not best fulfil the conditions of poetry; but it is' (solemnly) 'a chain of extremely valooable thoughts.'"

2. *That every man*, etc. The ed. of 1807 has, "Whom every man," etc. It was corrected in 1820, but in the last line of the poem not until 1845.

5. *Boyish thought.* The original reading (changed in 1845) was "childish thought."

7. *That makes.* Originally "That make;" corrected in 1827.

33. *He fixes good on good alone.* The reading of 1807, changed in 1836 to "He labours good on good to fix."

75, 76. *Persevering to the last,* etc. The ed. of 1807 has the following note on these lines :

> " ' For Knightes ever should be persevering.
> To seek honour without feintisse or slouth,
> Fro wele to better in all manner thing.'
>   CHAUCER—*The Floure and the Leaf.*"

79. *Or he must go to dust without his fame.* The reading of 1807, retained by Matthew Arnold. The ed. of 1836 reads : "Or he must fall, and sleep without his fame;" the *and* being made *to* in 1843.

THE POWER OF MUSIC.

WRITTEN in the spring of 1806, when Wordsworth spent two months in London, and published in 1807. "Taken from life," according to the author's MS. note.

3. *The stately Pantheon.* This building, successively a concert-hall, theatre, and bazar, still stands on Oxford Street, London (nearly opposite the Princess's Theatre), and is now (1889) a wine-warehouse. The popular accentuation of the name (*Panthéon,* as in the poem), though sustained by the dictionaries, is etymologically wrong.

15. *Dusky-browed,* Originally "dusky-faced;" changed in 1815.

37. *Mark that cripple.* The reading of 1827, that of 1807 being "There 's a cripple."

SONNETS.

"NUNS FRET NOT AT THEIR CONVENT'S NARROW ROOM."—Written in 1806, published in 1807 as a "Prefatory Sonnet" to the series of "Miscellaneous Sonnets."

3. *Their pensive citadels.* "That is, the world of thought, in which they shut themselves out from the world of action" (T.).

6. *Furness Fells.* Furness is a district in the northern part of Lancashire, adjoining Cumberland. The greater part of it is mountainous, the highest peaks being more than 2500 feet high. K. says : "In Wordsworth's time *Furness Fells* was a generic phrase for all the hills east of the Duddon, south of the Brathay, and west of Windermere." Furness Abbey, the ruins of which are the chief attraction of the extreme southern portion of the Furness district, was its centre in the olden time, when it had a much larger area.

8. *In truth the prison,* etc. T. quotes Lovelace, *To Althea from Prison :*

> "Stone walls do not a prison make,
> Nor iron bars a cage :
> Minds innocent and quiet take
> These for an hermitage "

9. *Hence for me.* It was "hence to me" until 1849.

13. *The weight of too much liberty.* Cf. *Ode to Duty*, 37 : " Me this unchartered freedom tires."

14. *Brief solace.* The reading of 1827, the earlier being "short solace."

" WINGS HAVE WE," ETC.—Written in 1806, printed in 1807.

9-12. *There find I personal themes*, etc. The reading of 1827. The ed. of 1807 has :

> " There do I find a never-failing store
> Of personal themes, and such as I love best ;
> Matter wherein right voluble I am.
> Two will I mention dearer than the rest."

13, 14. *The gentle lady.* The allusions to Shakespeare and Spenser need no explanation. Cf. the " Dedication " to *The White Doe of Rylstone :*

> " And, Mary, oft beside our blazing fire,
> When years of wedded life were as a day
> Whose current answers to the heart's desire,
> Did we together read in Spenser's lay
> How Una, sad of soul—in sad attire,
> The gentle Una, of celestial birth,
> To seek her knight went wandering o'er the earth ;"

and, in the next stanza, the reference to " The milk-white lamb which in a line she led."

In the preface to the ed. of 1815, Wordsworth says : " However imbued the surface might be with classical literature, he [Milton] was a Hebrew in soul ; and all things tended in him towards the sublime. Spenser, of a gentler nature, maintained his freedom by aid of his allegorical spirit, at one time inciting him to create persons out of abstractions ; and, at another, by a superior effort of genius, to give the universality and permanence of abstractions to his human beings, by means of attributes and emblems that belong to the highest moral truths and the purest sensations,—of which his character of Una is a glorious example."

" NOR CAN I NOT BELIEVE," ETC.—Written in 1806, published in 1807. It is a continuation of the preceding sonnet.

9-12. *Blessings be with them*, etc. These four lines are the inscription under Wordsworth's statue in Westminster Abbey. They were selected by Principal Shairp after Dean Stanley had said that he could not decide what quotation from the poet to use.

" THE WORLD IS TOO MUCH WITH US."—Written in 1806, published in 1807.

5. *The sea.* Misprinted " This sea " in Matthew Arnold's *Selections* (English ed.).

7. *Upgathered now like sleeping flowers.* The simile is thoroughly Wordsworthian.

11. *This pleasant lea.* The locality referred to is not known.

13. *Proteus rising from the sea.* The first reading (changed in 1827) was " Proteus coming from the sea." For the allusions to the changeable sea-god and *Triton,* cf. *Comus,* 871 :

> " By hoary Nereus' wrinkled look,
> And the Carpathian wizard's hook ;
> By scaly Triton's winding shell," etc.

Proteus is called *the Carpathian wizard* because of his prophetic power and his abode in the Carpathian sea; and a *hook,* or crook, is given him because he kept the herds of Neptune. He " represented the everlasting changes, united with ever-recurrent sameness, of the sea."

To SLEEP.—Written in 1806, published in 1807.

5. *Have all been thought,* etc. The ed. of 1807 has : " I 've thought of all by turns ; and still I lie;" that of 1836 : " I thought of all by turns, and yet I lie ;" and that of 1845 : " I have thought of all by turns, and yet do lie." We follow (as M. Arnold does) the text of 1827.

13. *Between day and day.* Until 1832 the reading was " betwixt day and day." See on *She was a Phantom,* 24, and *Affliction of Margaret,* 60. On the whole sonnet cf. Shakespeare, 2 *Henry IV.* iii. 1. 5 fol. :

> " O sleep, O gentle sleep,
> Nature's soft nurse, how have I frighted thee,
> That thou no more wilt weigh my eyelids down," etc.

ODE.

INTIMATIONS OF IMMORTALITY FROM RECOLLECTIONS OF EARLY CHILDHOOD.

WRITTEN in 1803–1806, published in 1807. The following is from the MS. notes of 1843 : " This was composed during my residence at Town-end, Grasmere. Two years at least passed between the writing of the four first stanzas and the remaining part. To the attentive and competent reader the whole sufficiently explains itself; but there may be no harm in adverting here to particular feelings or *experiences* of my own mind on which the structure of the poem partly rests. Nothing was more difficult for me in childhood than to admit the notion of death as a state applicable to my own being. I have said elsewhere—

> ' A simple child,
> That lightly draws its breath,
> And feels its life in every limb,
> What should it know of death?'

But it was not so much from feelings of animal vivacity that *my* difficulty came as from a sense of the indomitableness of the spirit within me. I used to brood over the stories of Enoch and Elijah, and almost to persuade myself that, whatever might become of others, I should be translated, in something of the same way, to heaven. With a feeling congenial to this, I was often unable to think of external things as having external existence, and I communed with all that I saw as something not apart from, but inherent in, my own immaterial nature. Many times while going to school have I grasped at a wall or tree to recall myself from this abyss of idealism to the reality. At that time I was afraid of such processes. In later periods of life I have deplored, as we have all reason to do, a subjugation of an opposite character, and have rejoiced over the remembrances, as is expressed in the lines—

> ' Obstinate questionings
> Of sense and outward things,
> Fallings from us, vanishings ;' etc.

To that dream-like vividness and splendour which invest objects of sight in childhood, every one, I believe, if he would look back, could bear testimony, and I need not dwell upon it here ; but having in the poem regarded it as presumptive evidence of a prior state of existence, I think it right to protest against a conclusion, which has given pain to some good and pious persons, that I meant to inculcate such a belief. It is far too shadowy a notion to be recommended to faith, as more than an element in our instincts of immortality. But let us bear in mind that, though the idea is not advanced in revelation, there is nothing there to contradict it, and the fall of man presents an analogy in its favour. Accordingly, a pre-existent state has entered into the popular creeds of many nations, and, among all persons acquainted with classic literature, is known as an ingredient in Platonic philosophy. Archimedes said that he could move the world if he had a point whereon to rest his machine. Who has not felt the same aspirations as regards the world of his own mind ? Having to wield some of its elements when I was impelled to write this poem on the ' Immortality of the Soul,' I took hold of the notion of pre-existence as having sufficient foundation in humanity for authorizing me to make for my purpose the best use of it I could as a poet."

Coleridge, in the *Biographia Literaria* (*Works*, Harper's ed. vol. iii. p. 489 fol.), remarks : "To the *Ode on the Intimations of Immortality* the poet might have prefixed the lines which Dante addresses to one of his own Canzoni—

> .   ' Canzone, i' credo, che saranno radi
> Color, che tua ragione intendan bene,
> Tanto lor sei faticoso ed alto.' *

> ' O lyric song, there will be few, think I,
>   Who may thy import understand aright,
> Thou art for *them* so arduous and so high!'

---

* *Canzoni Morali,* lib. iv. canz. i. *Tanto lor parli faticoso e forte* is the original third line. —S. C.

But the ode was intended for such readers only as had been accustomed to watch the flux and reflux of their inmost nature, to venture at times into the twilight realms of consciousness, and to feel a deep interest in modes of inmost being, to which they know that the attributes of time and space are inapplicable and alien, but which yet cannot be conveyed, save in symbols of time and space. For such readers the sense is sufficiently plain, and they will be as little disposed to charge Mr. Wordsworth with believing the Platonic pre-existence in the ordinary interpretation of the words, as I am to believe that Plato himself ever meant or taught it."

Emerson says of Wordsworth : "Alone in his time he treated the human mind well, and with an absolute trust. His adherence to his poetic creed rested on real inspirations. The *Ode on Immortality* is the high-water mark which the intellect has reached in this age." *

Lord Houghton (R. M. Milnes), in his address to the Wordsworth Society in 1885, remarks : "If I am asked . . . what is the greatest poem in the English language, I never for a moment hesitate to say, Wordsworth's *Ode on the Intimations of Immortality*. That poem is to me the greatest embodiment of philosophic poetry, which may decorate youth, and childhood itself, with the years of grave and philosophic manhood. It comprehends the life of man."

Lord Selborne, addressing the same society in 1886, and referring to this poem, says : "I have heard some very stanch upholders of orthodox dogmatic teaching find fault with it. All I can say is, I see nothing in it but this—though in some respects presented in a fanciful form —a recognition of the divine origin of the human soul. And if there is such a thing as a human soul, it has a divine origin, and whatever there be of true, beautiful, and divine comes from that origin, and from that alone. All that I seem to have learned from Wordsworth. I do not mention it controversially, but I mention it as part of the education of my mind by the reading of Wordsworth."

George William Curtis (*Harper's Magazine*, vol. xx. p. 127), commenting upon Wordsworth, says : "Lines of his are household words, like lines of Shakespeare; and it is Wordsworth who has written one of the great English poems—the *Ode upon Intimations of Immortality*. For sustained splendour of imagination, deep, solemn, and progressive thought, and exquisite variety of music, that poem is unsurpassed."

4. *Apparelled in celestial light.* Cf. *Westminster Bridge*, 4.

6. *As it hath been.* The ed. of 1807 has "as it has been;" changed in 1820.

25. *The cataracts blow their trumpets.* "A singularly bold metaphor, standing out in striking contrast to the studiously simple language of the second stanza" (T.).

26. *The season wrong.* As out of keeping with its joyousness.

28. *The fields of sleep.* "The regions of sleep, the early dawn."

* Cf. what Shairp says in the *Studies in Poetry* : "The *Ode on Immortality* marks the highest limit which the tide of poetic inspiration has reached in England within this century or indeed since the days of Milton."

As T. remarks, this interpretation is less prosaic than "the sleeping fields." K. paraphrases the passage thus: "The morning breeze blowing from the fields that were dark during the hours of sleep."

43. *When Earth herself.* Originally "While the Earth herself;" changed in 1827 to "While the Earth itself;" and in 1832 to "When the Earth herself." Finally, in 1836, *the* was dropped.

45. *Culling.* It was "pulling" until 1836. Neither word forms a perfect rhyme with *sullen.* Rhymes that suggest a vulgar pronunciation like *cullin'* are particularly objectionable. See on *Highland Girl,* 54.

51. *But there 's a tree,* etc. Cf. Browning, *May and Death:* "Only one little sight, one plant," etc.

58. *Our birth is but a sleep,* etc. "This ode, and especially this and the following stanza, are frequently called 'Platonic.' It must, however, be remembered that although Wordsworth coincides with Plato in assigning to mankind a life previous to their human one, he differs from him in making life 'a sleep and a forgetting,' while Plato makes life a tedious and imperfect process of ἀνάμνησις, or reminding. With Wordsworth the infant, with Plato the philosopher, approaches nearest to the previous more glorious state" (T.).

Cf. Tennyson, *Two Voices:*

> "As old mythologies relate,
> Some draught of Lethe might await
> The slipping through from state to state.
>
> . . . . . .
>
> And if I lapsed from nobler place,
> Some legend of a fallen race
> Alone might hint of my disgrace."

64. *Clouds of glory.* Like those "in thousand liveries dight" that accompany the Sun when he "begins his state" (*L'Allegro*).

66. *Heaven lies about us in our infancy!* This line has no rhyme; the only instance of the kind in the poem. In 185 there is apparently meant to be a "sectional" rhyme of *faith* and *death.*

72. *Priest.* The word, as T. notes, "includes the twofold notion of worshipper or ministrant and one who approaches nearest to the divinity."

88. *Fretted.* T. says that this "implies frequency, not vexation;" but is there not a suggestion of the latter? And is there not a touch of nature in this?

104. *Persons.* That is, *dramatis personæ.* The poet seems to have had in mind Shakespeare's "All the world's a stage," etc. (*As You Like It,* ii. 7. 139 fol.).

110. *Thou best philosopher,* etc. Coleridge criticises this passage severely in the *Biographia Literaria,* chap. xxii. Stopford Brooke, in his *Theology in the English Poets* (p. 273), says that it "is not Platonism, and indeed, as expressed, it runs close to nonsense. We can only catch the main idea among expressions of the child as the best philosopher. the eye among the blind, . . . the mighty prophet, the seer blest—expressions which taken separately have scarcely any recognizable meaning. By taking them all together, we feel rather than see that Words-

worth intended to say that the child, having lately come from a perfect existence, in which he saw truth directly, and was at home with God, retains, unknown to us, that vision—and, because he does, is the best philosopher, since he sees at once that which we through philosophy are endeavoring to reach; is the mighty prophet, because in his actions and speech he tells unconsciously the truths he sees, but the sight of which we have lost; is more closely haunted by God, more near to the immortal life, more purely and brightly free because he half shares in the pre-existent life and glory out of which he has come."

112. *That, deaf and silent,* etc.   Who, though deaf and dumb, dost understand the secrets of eternity.

114. *Prophet.*   "Rather in the biblical sense of 'teller forth' than that of 'fore-teller'" (T.).

117. *In darkness lost,* etc.   This line is not in the eds. of 1807 and 1815.

120. *Not to be put by.*   These lines follow in the eds. of 1807 and 1815:

> "To whom the grave
> Is but a lowly bed without the sense or sight
> Of day in the warm light,
> A place of thought where we in waiting lie."

122. *Of heaven-born freedom on thy being's height.*   "Childhood is, as it were, the mountain-top, the natural type of freedom and nearest heaven, from which men descend by easy steps into the vale of manhood" (T.).   The reading of 1807 (changed in 1815) was: "Of untamed pleasures, on thy being's height."

134. *Benediction.*   Until 1827 it was "benedictions."

137, 138. *Of childhood, whether busy,* etc.   The reading of 1815, the earlier being:

> "Of childhood, whether fluttering or at rest,
> With new-born hope forever in his breast."

143. *Fallings from us,* etc.   "The outward sensible universe, visible and tangible, seeming to fall away from us as unreal, to vanish in unsubstantiality" (K.).   Cf. Wordsworth's introductory note.

144. *Blank.*   "White, so undefined and unmeaning, like a colourless surface" (T.).   Cf. Tennyson, *Two Voices:*

> "Moreover, something is or seems,
> That touches me with mystic gleams,
> Like glimpses of forgotten dreams;
>
> Of something felt, like something here;
> Of something done, I know not where;
> Such as no language may declare."

153. *Uphold us,* etc.   The reading of 1807 (amplified in 1815) was: "Uphold us, cherish us, and make."

158. *Nor man nor boy.*   Neither manhood nor boyhood; the concrete for the abstract.

163. *That immortal sea.*   "As Wordsworth pictures the human soul drifting across the ocean of eternity to be tossed in its human birth upon

the shore of earth, so Longfellow, in his legend of *Hiawatha*, has pictured the soul drifting out again in death into the ocean sunset " (T.).

188. *Our loves.* The love which Nature seems to reciprocate. The reading is that of 1807, changed in 1836 to " Forebode not any severing," etc.

190. *One delight.* The *one* is antithetical to *habitual.*

196–199. *The clouds that gather,* etc. T. remarks: " This passage is rather obscure. The meaning seems to be—The falling sun, with his bright train of coloured clouds, yet brings the sobering thought of the race of men who, even in the poet's lifetime, had sunk to their setting, that their fellows might lord it in the zenith, crowned with victorious palm."

The same critic quotes the following Latin version of the last stanza :

" O nemora, O valles, O laeti gramine clivi,
Parcite discidium nostri praedicere amoris ;
Jam praesens imo agnosco sub pectore numen.
Quid si deposui puerilia gaudia mente,
Hoc magis aeterno vobis me foedere jungam :
Decurrentis aquae per adesas flumina ripas
Ipse pari passu quondam decurrere amabam,
Nunc quoque flumina amo : nascentis pura diei
Fax recreat ; quamquam O mihi moestior ire videtur
Sol quoties moriens caput inter nubila condit.
Haud aliter vidi mortalia saecla perire
Scilicet, et ruere hos, illos ut palma coronet.
Tangit enim pietas, tangunt mortalia pectus,
Spes agitat vitamque fovet : quo foedere florem
Contemplor quoties qui spirat humillimus, intus
Nescio quid lacrimis non enarrabile surgit."

Professor Henry Reed, in his edition of Wordsworth, cites, as parallel passages to this poem, the *Excursion*, ix.:

" Ah ! why in age
Do we revert so fondly to the walks
Of childhood—but that there the soul discerns
The dear memorial footsteps unimpaired
Of her own native vigour," etc.

and the *Prelude*, v.:

" Our childhood sits,
Our simple childhood, sits upon a throne
That hath more power," etc.

See also a fine passage in Ruskin's *Modern Painters*, vol. ii., beginning: " There was never yet the child of any promise," etc.

Knight quotes Henry Vaughan, *Silex Scintillans :*

" Happy those early days, when I
Shined in my angel infancy !
Before I understood this place
Appointed for my second race,
Or taught my soul to fancy aught
But a white, celestial thought :
When yet I had not walked above
A mile or two from my first Love,
And, looking back at that short space,
Could see a glimpse of His bright face ;
When on some gilded cloud or flower

My gazing soul would dwell an hour,
And in those weaker glories spy
Some shadows of eternity;
Before I taught my tongue to wound
My conscience with a sinful sound,
Or had the black art to dispense
A several sin to every sense,
But felt through all this fleshly dress
Bright shoots of everlastingness."

EAMONT BRIDGE.

SONG AT THE FEAST OF BROUGHAM CASTLE.

WRITTEN and published in 1807. The poet says: "This poem was composed at Coleorton while I was walking to and fro along the path that led from Sir George Beaumont's farm-house, where we resided, to the Hall which was building at that time."

The following explanatory note is appended to the poem in all the eds.:

"Henry Lord Clifford, etc., who is the subject of this poem, was the son of John Lord Clifford, who was slain at Towton Field, which John Lord Clifford, as is known to the reader of English History was the person who after the battle of Wakefield slew, in the pursuit, the young

Earl of Rutland, son of the Duke of York, who had fallen in the battle, 'in part of revenge' (say the authors of the *History of Cumberland and Westmoreland*), 'for the Earl's father had slain his.' A deed which worthily blemished the author (saith Speed); but who, as he adds, 'dare promise any thing temperate of himself in the heat of martial fury? chiefly, when it was resolved not to leave any branch of the York line standing; for so one maketh this Lord to speak.' This, no doubt, I would observe by the bye, was an action sufficiently in the vindictive spirit of the times, and yet not altogether so bad as represented; 'for the Earl was no child, as some writers would have him, but able to bear arms, being sixteen or seventeen years of age, as is evident from this,'— say the *Memoirs of the Countess of Pembroke*, who was laudably anxious to wipe away, as far as could be, this stigma from the illustrious name to which she was born,—' that he was the next child to King Edward the Fourth, which his mother had by Richard Duke of York, and that king was then eighteen years of age: and for the small distance betwixt her children, see Austin Vincent, in his *Book of Nobility*, p. 622, where he writes of them all.' It may further be observed, that Lord Clifford, who was then himself only twenty-five years of age, had been a leading man and commander two or three years together in the army of Lancaster before this time, and, therefore, would be less likely to think that the Earl of Rutland might be entitled to mercy from his youth. But, independent of this act, at best a cruel and savage one, the family of Clifford had done enough to draw upon them the vehement hatred of the House of York: so that after the Battle of Towton there was no hope for them but in flight and concealment. Henry, the subject of the poem, was deprived of his estate and honours during the space of twenty-four years; all which time he lived as a shepherd in Yorkshire, or in Cumberland, where the estate of his father-in-law (Sir Lancelot Threlkeld) lay. He was restored to his estate and honours in the first year of Henry the Seventh. It is recorded that, ' when called to Parliament, he behaved nobly and wisely; but otherwise came seldom to London or the Court; and rather delighted to live in the country, where he repaired several of his castles, which had gone to decay during the late troubles.' Thus far is chiefly collected from Nicholson and Burn; and I can add, from my own knowledge, that there is a tradition current in the village of Threlkeld and its neighbourhood, his principal retreat, that in the course of his shepherd-life he had acquired great astronomical knowledge. I cannot conclude this note without adding a word upon the subject of those numerous and noble feudal edifices spoken of in the poem, the ruins of some of which are at this day so great an ornament to that interesting country. The Cliffords had always been distinguished for an honourable pride in these castles, and we have seen that, after the wars of York and Lancaster, they were rebuilt; in the civil wars of Charles the First they were again laid waste, and again restored almost to their former magnificence by the celebrated Lady Anne Clifford, Countess of Pembroke, etc. Not more than twenty-five years after this was done, when the estates of Clifford had passed into the family of Tufton, three of these castles, namely, Brough, Brougham, and Pendragon, were demolished, and the timber and other materials sold by Thomas Earl of Thanet. We will hope that, when this order was issued, the earl had not consulted the text of Isaiah, 58th chap. 12th verse, to which the inscription placed over the gate of Pendragon Castle by the Countess of Pembroke (I believe his grandmother), at the time she repaired that structure, refers the reader:—'*And they that shall be of thee shall build the old waste places: thou shalt raise up the foundations of many generations ; and thou shalt be called, the repairer of the breach, the restorer of paths to dwell in.*' The Earl of Thanet, the present possessor of the estates, with a due respect for the memory of his ancestors, and a proper sense of the value and beauty of these remains of antiquity, has (I am told) given orders that they shall be preserved from all depredations."

1. *High in the breathless hall the minstrel sate.* Brougham Castle, now in ruins, is on the banks of the Eamont, about two miles from Penrith. The larger part of it was built by Roger Lord Clifford, son of Isabella de Veteripont. In 1412 it was attacked and laid waste by the Scots. In 1617 the Earl of Cumberland feasted James I. within its walls, on his return to Scotland. In 1651, having fallen into decay, it was restored, as stated above, by Lady Anne Clifford, Countess of Dorset, Pembroke, and Montgomery. After her time it was neglected and allowed to go to ruin.

7. *Her thirty years of winter past*, etc. The thirty years of the Wars of the Roses, 1455–1485.

11. *Both Roses flourish*, etc. Alluding to the union of the rival houses by the marriage of Henry VII. with Elizabeth of York.

27. *Earth helped him with the cry of blood.* "This line is from *The Battle of Bosworth Field*, by Sir John Beaumont (brother to the dramatist), whose poems are written with much spirit, elegance, and harmony, and have deservedly been reprinted lately in Chalmers's Collection of English Poets" (W.).

The allusion is to the death of Richard III. at Bosworth, the *cry of blood* doubtless referring to the murder of the young princes in the Tower.

35. *Their loyalty.* The reading of 1807, restored in 1820 after being altered to "their royalty" in 1815.

36. *Skipton.* The capital of the Craven district of Yorkshire. Its castle was the chief residence of the Cliffords. It was a *deserted tower* during the time that the "Shepherd Lord" was concealed in Cumberland. During the civil wars between Charles I. and the Parliament, it was held for the king, but was besieged and compelled to surrender in 1645. The following year it was ordered by the Parliament that the castle should be dismantled and henceforth be used only as a family residence. As such it still remains, being now, like Brougham Castle, in the possession of the Thanet family.

37. *Though she is but a lonely tower.* The ed. of 1807 adds:

> "Silent, deserted of her best,
> Without an inmate or a guest."

In 1820 these latter lines were made to read as in the text; but in 1845 they were omitted, and the preceding line changed to " Though lonely, a deserted tower." Line 41 suffers so much by the omission that one might almost fancy the couplet was accidentally dropped. The original reading of 41, by the way, was " Knight, squire, yeoman, page, or groom;" altered in 1836.

41. *Brougham.* The English pronunciation is *Broom.*

42. *How glad Pendragon,* etc. Pendragon Castle, near the source of the Eden, was another stronghold of the Cliffords. It was destroyed by the Scots in 1341, and remained in ruins for 140 years. To this the poet apparently refers in the next line. After being rebuilt it was again destroyed during the civil wars of the Stuarts, but was restored by Lady Anne Clifford in 1660. It was finally demolished in 1685.

46. *Rejoiced is Brough,* etc. The Castle of Brough-under-Stainmore (or Stanemore), on the banks of the Hillbeck, the *little humble stream,* also belonged to the Cliffords. It was destroyed by fire in 1519, and only in part restored by Lady Anne in 1660.

48. *And she that keepeth watch and ward,* etc. K. says this is "doubtless Appleby Castle," built before 1422. It was partially destroyed in 1648, and was afterwards repaired by Lady Anne. The *Eden* is the largest river in this part of England.

53. *One fair house.* Brougham Castle.

56. *Him and his lady-mother dear.* The " Shepherd Lord," and his mother, Lady Margaret, daughter and heiress of Lord Vesci, who married the Clifford of Shakespeare's *Henry VI.*

75. *On Carrock's side.* Carrock Fell (2174 feet) is opposite Bowscale Tarn, on the other side of the river Caldew.

91. *Mosedale's groves.* The valley referred to here is to the north of *Blencathara* or Saddleback (K.). This is a mountain, 2787 feet high, a few miles northeast of Keswick.

94. *Glenderamakin's lofty springs.* This river rises in the high ground north of Blencathara. It unites with St. John's Beck to form the Greta.

97. *Sir Lancelot Threlkeld.* See Wordsworth's note above.

118. *Simple glee.* Originally "solemn glee;" changed in 1845.

119. *Nor yet for higher sympathy.* The reading of 1845. That of 1807 was :

> " And a cheerful company,
> That learned of him submissive ways,
> And comforted his private days."

In 1836 the first line became " A spirit-soothing company."

124. *And both the undying fish,* etc. " It is imagined by the people of the country that there are two immortal fish, inhabitants of this tarn, which lies in the mountains not far from Threlkeld " (W.). *Bowscale Tarn* is to the north of Blencathara.

128, 129. *They moved about in open sight,* etc. The reading of 1807, changed in 1836 to :

> " And glancing, gleaming, dark or bright,
> Moved to and fro, for his delight."

131. *On the mountains.* Changed in 1836 to " Upon the mountains."

133. *And the caves.* Changed in 1836 to "And into caves."

137. *Face of thing.* The reading of 1807, that of 1836 being "The face of thing."

138, 139. *And if men*, etc. The reading of 1827, which differs from that of 1807 only in having *could* for "can." The ed. of 1836 has "And if that men;" and that of 1832 changes the next line to "His tongue could whisper words of might."

145. *On the blood of Clifford calls.* "The martial character of the Cliffords is well known; . . . and, besides several others who perished in the same manner, the four immediate progenitors of the person in whose hearing this is supposed to be spoken all died in the field" (W.).

159–160. *Alas! the fervent harper*, etc. This is the reading of 1807, changed in 1845 into:

> "Alas! the impassioned minstrel did not know
> How, by Heaven's grace, this Clifford's heart was framed;
> How he, long forced in humble walks to go," etc.

174. *The good lord Clifford.* After his restoration to his estates, he lived a comparatively quiet life. He was much at Bolton near by, where he studied astronomy and alchemy with the aid of the monks. In 1513, when nearly sixty years old, he was at Flodden, leading "the flower of Craven." He died in 1523, and was buried in the choir of Bolton Priory.

LAODAMIA.

WRITTEN at Rydal Mount in 1814, published in 1815. The MS. notes say: "The incident of the trees growing and withering put the subject into my thoughts, and I wrote with the hope of giving it a loftier tone than, so far as I know, has been given to it by any of the Ancients who have treated of it. It cost me more trouble than almost anything of equal length I have ever written."*

Myers (p. 113) remarks: "Under the powerful stimulus of the sixth *Æneid*—allusions to which pervade *Laodamia* † throughout—with unusual labour, and by a strenuous effort of the imagination, Wordsworth was enabled to depict his own love *in excelsis*, to imagine what aspect it might have worn, if it had been its destiny to deny itself at some heroic call, and to confront with nobleness an extreme emergency, and to be victor (as Plato has it) in an Olympian contest of the soul. For, indeed, the 'fervent, not ungovernable, love,' which is the ideal that Protesilaus is sent to teach, is on a great scale the same affection which we have

---

* And he appears to have had a proportionally high opinion of it. Mrs. Alaric Watts in her *Life of Watts*, says: "He asked me what I thought the finest elegiac composition in the language: and when I diffidently suggested *Lycidas*, he replied: 'You are not far wrong! It may, I think, be affirmed that Milton's *Lycidas* and my *Laodamia* are twin immortals.'"

† *Laodamia* should be read (as it is given in Mr. Matthew Arnold's admirable volume of selections) with the *earlier* conclusion; the *second* form is less satisfactory; and the *third*, with its sermonizing tone, "thus all in vain exhorted and reproved," is worst of all.

been considering in domesticity and peace : it is love considered not as a revolution but as a consummation; as a self - abandonment not to a laxer but to a sterner law; no longer as an invasive passion, but as the deliberate habit of the soul. It is that conception of love which springs into being in the last canto of Dante's *Purgatory*—which finds in English chivalry a noble voice—

> ' I could not love thee, dear, so much,
> Loved I not honour more.'

For, indeed (even as Plato says that Beauty is the splendour of Truth), so such a Love as this is the splendour of Virtue; it is the unexpected spark that flashes from self-forgetful soul to soul, it is man's standing evidence that he ' must lose himself to find himself,' and that only when the veil of his personality has lifted from around him can he recognize that he is already in heaven."

Mr. Aubrey de Vere, in his " Recollections of Wordsworth " (*Essays*, vol. ii. p. 289), says of his father, the late Sir Aubrey de Vere : " He had been one of Wordsworth's warmest admirers when their number was small, and in 1842 he dedicated a volume of poems to him. He taught me when a boy of eighteen years old to admire the great bard. I had been very enthusiastically praising Lord Byron's poetry. My father replied, ' Wordsworth is the great poet of modern times.' Much surprised, I asked, ' And what may his special merits be ?' The answer was, ' They are very various; as, for instance, depth, largeness, elevation, and, what is rare in modern poetry, an *entire* purity. In his noble *Laodamia* they are chiefly majesty and pathos.' A few weeks afterwards I chanced to take from the library shelves a volume of Wordsworth, and it opened on *Laodamia*. Some strong calm hand seemed to have been laid on my head, and bound me to the spot till I had come to the end. As I read, a new world, hitherto unimagined, opened itself out, stretching far away into serene infinitudes. The region was one to me unknown, but the harmony of the picture attested its reality. Above and around were indeed

> ' An ampler ether, a diviner air,
> And fields invested with purpureal gleams ;'

and when I reached the line, ' Calm pleasures there abide — majestic pains,' I felt that no tenants less stately were fit to walk in so lordly a precinct. I had been translated into another planet of song—one with larger movements and a longer year. A wider conception of poetry had become mine, and the Byronian enthusiasm fell from me like a bond broken by being outgrown. The incident illustrates poetry in one of its many characters—that of the ' Deliverer.' The ready sympathies and inexperienced imagination of youth make it surrender itself easily, despite its better aspirations, or in consequence of them, to a false greatness; and the true greatness, once revealed, sets it free. As early as 1824 Walter Savage Landor . . . had pronounced Wordsworth's *Laodamia* to be ' a composition such as Sophocles might have exulted to own, and a part of which might have been heard with shouts of rapture in the regions he describes '—the Elysian Fields."

Laodamia (or Laodameia, as some prefer to write it) was the daughter of Acastus, one of the Argonauts. She was the wife of Protesilaus, a Thessalian chief who devoted himself to the death predicted by the Delphic oracle for him who should first touch the Trojan shore. When the news of his fate reached Laodamia, she implored the gods that he might be allowed to return to the upper world. The prayer was granted, but only that he might remain three hours with her, and she died heartbroken when the brief reunion was over. It was said that the nymphs planted elms around the grave of Protesilaus which grew until they were high enough to command a view of Troy, when they withered away, springing up again from their roots only to wither again—"a constant interchange of growth and blight," as the poet relates.

1-4. *With sacrifice before the rising morn*, etc. The reading is that of 1815, retained by M. Arnold. In 1827 it was changed to

> " With sacrifice before the rising morn
>   Vows have I made by fruitless hope inspired ;
> And from the infernal gods, 'mid shades forlorn
>   Of night, my slaughtered lord have I required."

Sacrifices to the gods of the lower world were properly made before sunrise. Cf. Virgil, *Æneid*, vi. 242-258.

2. *Required.* In its etymological sense of "asked again." In Shakespeare the word often means to ask or beg; as in *Antony and Cleopatra*, iii. 12. 12 :

> " Lord of his fortunes, he salutes thee, and
> Requires to live in Egypt ; which not granted,
> He lessens his requests, and to thee sues
> To let him breathe between the heavens and earth,
> A private man in Athens."

11. *Her bosom heaves*, etc. Cf. *Æneid*, vi. 46 fol.

12. *And she expects the issue in repose.* After this stanza the MS. had these two stanzas, omitted in printing :

> " That rapture failing, the distracted queen
>   Knelt, and embraced the statue of the god:
> ' Mighty the boon I ask, but Earth has seen
>   Effects as awful from thy gracious nod.
> All-ruling Jove, unbind the mortal chain,
> Nor let the force of prayer be spent in vain !'
>
> Round the high-scaled temple a soft breeze
>   Along the column* sighed—all else was still—
> Mute, vacant as the face of summer seas,
>   No sign accorded of a favouring will.
> Dejected she withdraws—her palace-gate
> Enters—and, traversing a room of state,
>
> O terror ! what hath she perceived ?" etc.

19. *Mild Hermes spake.* The Greek god, with whom the Latin Mercury came to be identified. For his *wand*, see *Æneid*, iv. 242.

27. *But unsubstantial form*, etc. Cf. *Æneid*, ii. 794 or vi. 699.

45. *Could not withhold.* The reading of 1820, the earlier being "did not withhold."

---

* So Knight gives it, but we suspect a misprint for "columns."

46. *Generous.* Noble.

51. *Which then.* The ed. of 1815 had "That then;" changed in 1820.

58. *Thou shouldst elude.* The original reading, changed in 1845, was "That thou shouldst cheat."

65. *Parcæ.* The Fates.

66. *A Stygian hue.* A deathly pallor. See 93 below. *Stygian*= as of the lower world. Cf. the Latin *Stygius.*

68. *Know, virtue were not virtue,* etc. The reading of 1815, changed in 1836 to "Nor should the change be mourned, even if the joys," etc.

71. *Duly.* In due time, with the lapse of time. *Erebus*=the lower world; as often in Latin.

76. *A fervent, not ungovernable, love.* The reading of 1820, that of 1815 being "The fervor—not the impotence of love."

79. *Did not Hercules,* etc. The allusion is to the *Alcestis* of Euripides, where Hercules brings back the heroine from the lower world and restores her to her husband Admetus. Cf. Milton, *On his Deceased Wife :*

> "Methought I saw my late espoused saint
> Brought to me like Alcestis from the grave,
> Whom Jove's great son to her glad husband gave,
> Rescued from death by force though pale and faint."

82. *Vernal bloom.* The reading of 1815 (changed in 1827) was "beauty's bloom."

83. *Medea's spells,* etc. Æson, the father of Jason, was restored to youth by the magic of Medea. Cf. Shakespeare, *M. of V.* v. 1. 12 :

> "In such a night
> Medea gather'd the enchanted herbs
> That did renew old Æson."

90. *And though his favourite seat,* etc. An Alexandrine, like 157 below.

101, 102. *Spake of heroic arts,* etc. Cf. *Æneid,* vi. 653. The reading is that of 1827, that of 1815 being :

> "Spake, as a witness, of a second birth,
> For all that is most perfect upon earth."

Landor objected to the "second birth" on the ground that the expression had been "degraded by Conventiclers." Wordsworth defended it at the time, but evidently made up his mind afterwards that it suggested Christian rather than classical associations.

103. *Imaged.* The word, as T. remarks, "introduces the notion of the visionary, unsubstantial nature of the world of the dead."

105. *An ampler ether,* etc. Almost a translation of *Æneid,* vi. 640 :

> "Largior hic campos, aether et lumine vestit
> Purpureo, solemque suum, sua sidera norunt."

120. *What time the fleet at Aulis lay enchained. What time* (=at or during the time when) was a favourite idiom with the old poets, and was sometimes used in prose. Cf. *Ps.* lvi. 3, *Numb.* xxvi. 10, *Job,* vi. 17. The full phrase *at what time* occurs in *Dan.* iv. 5.

Aulis was a port at the mouth of the Euripus in Bœotia, where the

Greek fleet assembled before sailing for Troy, but was detained by a calm on account of the anger of Artemis, whom Agamemnon had offended. The goddess was at length appeased by the sacrifice of Iphigenia. Cf. Tennyson, *Dream of Fair Women*, etc.

122. *The oracle, upon the silent sea.* The reading of 1815 (changed in 1820) was: "Our future course, upon the silent sea."

131. *These fountains, flowers.* The *these* "brings back the attention to the presence of Protesilaus in his old home" (T.).

133. *Suspense.* Hesitation on our part.

137. *But lofty thought*, etc. My high resolve put into action set me free from this inward struggle.

139. *And thou, though strong in love, art all too weak.* Matthew Arnold, in his *Selections* (English ed.), puts a semicolon after *weak*, connecting *In reason* with what follows; but this is probably a misprint. All the standard eds. point as in the text.

143. *The invisible world*, etc. "Since the invisible world with thee hath sympathized so far as to permit my return, let thy fortitude draw this sympathy still closer by making thee more like the passionless happy beings of the other world" (T.).

146. *Towards a higher object.* The reading of 1815, changed in 1836 to "Seeking a higher object."

147. *That end.* Until 1827 it was "this end."

149. *Her bondage prove.* That the bonds of selfishness might prove the mere shadow of fetters when opposed to love. T. compares Tennyson, *Locksley Hall*:

> "Love took up the harp of life, and smote on all the chords with might—
>   Smote the chord of self that, trembling, passed in music out of sight."

We take it that *prove* is in the same construction as *be annulled;* but all the standard eds. and Arnold's *Selections* put a colon after *annulled*, apparently making *prove* imperative.

158–163. *Ah! judge her gently*, etc. The reading of 1815. See footnote on p. 232 above. Wordsworth made repeated efforts to improve the stanza, but only to its injury. The ed. of 1827 has:

> "By no weak pity might the gods be moved;
>   She who thus perished, not without the crime
> Of lovers that in reason's spite have loved,
>   Was doomed to wander in a grosser clime,
> Apart from happy ghosts that gather flowers
> Of blissful quiet 'mid unfading bowers."

In 1832 the 4th line of this was changed to "Was doomed to wear out her appointed time." In 1843 the first four lines took this form:

> "She—who, though warned, exhorted, and reproved,
>   Thus died, from passion desperate to a crime—
> By the just gods, whom no weak pity moved,
>   Was doomed to wear out her appointed time," etc.

In 1845, the first two lines were made:

> "Thus, all in vain exhorted and reproved,
>   She perished; and, as for a wilful crime," etc.

167. *Fondly.* Foolishly; the original meaning of the word, and the ordinary one in Shakespeare. Cf. *C. of E.* iv. 2. 57: "As if Time were in debt ! how fondly dost thou reason !"

173. *The trees' tall summits*, etc. Wordsworth adds this note : " For the account of these long-lived trees, see Pliny's *Natural History*, lib. xvi. cap. 44; and for the features in the character of Protesilaus see the *Iphigenia in Aulis* of Euripides. Virgil [*Æneid*, vi. 447] places the shade of Laodamia in a mournful region, among unhappy lovers,

'———His Laodamia,
It comes.' "

YARROW VISITED.

WRITTEN in September, 1814, and published in 1820. The poet says in the MS. notes of 1843 : "As mentioned in my verses on the death of the Ettrick Shepherd, my first visit to Yarrow was in his company.* We had lodged the night before at Traquhair, where Hogg had joined us and also Dr. Anderson, the editor of the British Poets, who was on a visit at the Manse. Dr. A. walked with us till we came in view of the Vale of Yarrow, and, being advanced in life, he then turned back. The old man was passionately fond of poetry, though with not much of a discriminating judgment, as the volumes he edited sufficiently show. But I was much pleased to meet with him, and to acknowledge my obligation to his collection, which had been my brother John's companion in more than one voyage to India, and which he gave me before his departure from Grasmere, never to return. Through these volumes I became first familiar with Chaucer, and so little money had I then to spare for books, that, in all probability, but for this same work, I should have known little of Drayton, Daniel, and other distinguished poets of the Elizabethan age, and their immediate successors, till a much later period of my life. I am glad to record this, not from any importance of its own, but as a tribute of gratitude to this simple-hearted old man, whom I never again had the pleasure of meeting. I seldom read or think of this poem without regretting that my dear sister was not of the party, as she would have had so much delight in recalling the time when, travelling together in Scotland, we declined going in search of this celebrated stream,† not altogether, I will frankly confess, for the reasons assigned in the poem on the occasion."

---

* In this *Extempore Effusion upon the Death of James Hogg*, written in November, 1835, the poet says :

" When first, descending from the moorlands,
    I saw the stream of Yarrow glide
  Along a bare and open valley,
    The Ettrick Shepherd was my guide."

† See the poem of *Yarrow Unvisited*, p. 103 above.

13. *Saint Mary's Lake.* See p. 209 above.

25. *Where was it that the famous Flower*, etc. Here, as Shairp notes in his *Aspects of Poetry*, "Wordsworth fell into an inaccuracy; for Mary Scott, the real 'Flower of Yarrow,' never did lie bleeding on Yarrow, but became the wife of Wat of Harden and the mother of a wide-branching race. Yet Wordsworth speaks of *his* bed, evidently confounding the lady 'Flower of Yarrow' with that 'slaughtered youth' for whom so many ballads had sung lament. This slight divergence from fact, however, no way mars the truth of feeling, which makes the poet long to pierce into the dumb past, and know something of the pathetic histories that have immortalized these braes." Cf. Scott's note on *Saint Mary's Lake*, partly quoted on p. 209 above : " Near the lower extremity of the lake are the ruins of Dryhope Tower, the birthplace of Mary Scott, daughter of Philip Scott of Dryhope, and famous by the traditional name of the Flower of Yarrow."

31. *The water-wraith ascended thrice.* Cf. Logan, *The Braes of Yarrow :*
> " Scarce was he gone, I saw his ghost :
> It vanished with a shriek of sorrow ;
> Thrice did the water-wraith ascend
> And gave a doleful groan through Yarrow."

38. *Sorrow.* For the rhyme, see on *Highland Girl*, 54 ; also for *stature, nature* (50, 52) and *gather, heather* (66, 68) below.

45-48. *Meek loveliness*, etc. " No words in the language penetrate more truly and deeply into the very heart of nature. It was one of Wordsworth's great gifts to be able to concentrate the whole feeling of a wide scene into a few words, simple, strong, penetrating to the very core. Many a time, and for many a varied scene, he has done this, but perhaps he has never put forth this power more happily than in the four lines in which he has summed up for all time the true quality of Yarrow. You look on Yarrow, you repeat these four lines over to yourself, and you feel that the finer, more subtle essence of nature has never been more perfectly uttered in human words. There it stands complete. No poet coming after Wordsworth need try to do it again, for it has been done once, perfectly and forever" (Shairp).

55. *Newark's towers.* The scene of Scott's *Lay of the Last Minstrel.* The castle was built by James II. of Scotland. A massive square tower, now unroofed and ruinous, surrounded by an outward wall, is all that remains of it. It is on the banks of the Yarrow, about three miles from Selkirk.

62-64. *A covert for protection*, etc. The reading of 1827, that of 1820 being :
> " It promises protection
> To all the nestling brood of thoughts
> Sustained by chaste affection."

66. *Wild wood.* The original reading (changed in 1827) was "wild wood's."

87. *Will dwell with me*, etc. " Having traversed the stream from St. Mary's Loch to Newark and Bowhill, he leaves it with the impression that sight has not destroyed imagination—the actual not effaced the ideal." Cf. the closing stanzas of *Yarrow Unvisited.*

TO B. R. HAYDON.

WRITTEN in 1815; published in the *Examiner*, March 31, 1816, and afterwards in the ed. of 1820. No alterations have been made in the text.

Sending this sonnet to Haydon, December 21, 1815, Wordsworth said that it " was occasioned, I might say inspired, by your last letter." This was probably Haydon's letter of November 27, in which he says : " I have benefited and have been supported in the troubles of life by your poetry. I will bear want, pain, misery, and blindness; but I will never yield one step I have gained on the road I am determined to travel over."

8. *Desert.* For the rhyme, see p. 202 above.

NOVEMBER 1.

WRITTEN in 1815 ; published in the *Examiner*, Jan. 28, 1816, and later in the ed. of 1820.

3. *Smooth as the sky can shed.* The reading of 1837. As first printed it was " as smooth as Heaven can shed;" changed in 1832 to " smooth as the heaven can shed."

14. *Has filled.* The reading of 1845, that of 1816 being " I have filled."

INSIDE OF KING'S COLLEGE CHAPEL, CAMBRIDGE.

WRITTEN in 1821, published in 1822.

1. *The royal saint.* Henry VI., who founded the college in 1440, and himself laid the first stone of the chapel, which is the most famous and the most beautiful of all the buildings of the University. The great effect of the interior is due to its height (78 feet), to the beauty and splendour of the stained glass, and to the magnificent fan-tracery of the roof.

TO A SKYLARK.

WRITTEN at Rydal Mount in 1825, published in 1827.

In the eds. from 1827 to 1843 the following was printed as a second stanza :

> " To the last point of vision, and beyond,
> Mount, daring warbler! that love-prompted strain
> ('Twixt thee and thine a never-failing bond)
> Thrills not the less the bosom of the plain:
> Yet might'st thou seem, proud privilege ! to sing
> All independent of the leafy spring."

It now appears as the eighth stanza of a poem entitled *A Morning Exercise*, and dated 1828 by Knight.   In a note to that piece Wordsworth says: "I could wish the last five stanzas of this to be read with the poem addressed to the skylark."   They are as follows (with the next preceding stanza, without which the *kinds* in the first line that follows might be supposed a misprint for *birds*):

> The daisy sleeps upon the dewy lawn,
>   Not lifting yet the head that evening bowed;
> But *he* is risen, a later star of dawn,
>   Glittering and twinkling near yon rosy cloud;
> Bright gem instinct with music, vocal spark;
> The happiest bird that sprang out of the Ark!
>
> Hail, blest above all kinds!—Supremely skilled
>   Restless with fixed to balance, high with low.
> Thou leav'st the halcyon free her hopes to build
>   On such forbearance as the deep may show;
> Perpetual flight, unchecked by earthly ties,
> Leav'st to the wandering bird of paradise.
>
> Faithful, though swift as lightning, the meek dove;
>   Yet more hath Nature reconciled in thee;
> So constant with thy downward eye of love,
>   Yet, in aërial singleness, so free;
> So humble, yet so ready to rejoice
> In power of wing and never-wearied voice.
>
> To the last point of vision, and beyond, etc. (as above).
>
> How would it please old Ocean to partake,
>   With sailors longing for a breeze in vain,
> The harmony thy notes most gladly make
>   Where earth resembles most his own domain!
> Urania's self might welcome with pleased ear
> These matins mounting towards her native sphere.
>
> Chanter by heaven attracted, whom no bars
>   To daylight known deter from that pursuit,
> 'T is well that some sage instinct, when the stars
>   Come forth at evening, keeps thee still and mute;
> For not an eyelid could to sleep incline
> Wert thou among them, singing as they shine!

10. *With instinct.*   Until 1832 the reading was "with rapture."

12. *True to the kindred points of heaven and home.*   Stopford Brooke remarks: "It is one of Wordsworth's poetic customs to see things in the ideal and the real, and to make each make the other poetical.   He places the lark in a 'privacy of glorious light,' but he brings him home at last to his 'nest upon the dewy ground.'   It is the very thing that he always does for man."   Cf. Hogg, *The Lark:* "Thy lay is in heaven—thy love is on earth."

ACCORDING to the author, "composed almost extempore [in 1827] in a short walk on the western side of Rydal Lake;" and published the same year. Cf. the sonnet, "Nuns fret not," etc., p. 119 above.

3. *Shakespeare unlocked his heart.* Cf. Browning, *House :*

> " ' Hoity-toity ! A street to explore,
> Your house the exception ! *"With this same key*
> *Shakespeare unlocked his heart"* once more !'
> Did Shakespeare ? If so, the less Shakespeare he !"

Mr. Swinburne replies : "No whit the less like Shakespeare, but undoubtedly the less like Browning." Coleridge, Sir Henry Taylor, Rossetti, and Victor Hugo agree with Wordsworth and Swinburne in regarding Shakespeare's *Sonnets* as autobiographical. The only *poet* besides Browning on the other side, so far as we are aware, is R. H. Stoddard.

4. *Petrarch's wound.* His unrequited love for Laura.

5. *Tasso.* His works include two volumes of sonnets, published in 1581 and 1592.

6. *Camoens.* Luis de Camoens, the epic poet of Portugal, who was banished to Macao in 1556 (on account of his satire, *Disparates na India*), and while in exile wrote the *Lusiad*, and also many sonnets, lyrics, etc. His name is usually accented on the first syllable in English, but Wordsworth follows the Portuguese pronunciation.

8. *Dante.* See his *Vita Nuova.*

10. *It cheered mild Spenser*, etc. Spenser wrote 92 sonnets; and in the 80th he says :

> " After so long a race as I have run
> Through Faery land, which those six books compile,
> Give leave to rest me being halfe fordonne,
> And gather to myselfe new breath awhile."

14. *Too few.* Milton wrote only 23 sonnets, including those in Italian.

THE WISHING-GATE.

WRITTEN at Rydal Mount in 1828; published in the *Keepsake*, 1829, and in the ed. of 1832.

" In the vale of Grasmere, by the side of the old highway leading to Ambleside, is a gate, which, time out of mind, has been called the Wishing-gate, from a belief that wishes formed or indulged there have a favourable issue " (W.). See cut on p. 151.

31. *Yea ! even.* The reading of 1829 (changed in 1832) was " Yes ! even."

40. *The local genius.* The *Genius loci.*

16

64. *And yearn.* In 1836 this was made "And thirst."
67. *The church-clock's knell.* The bell of Grasmere church.

THE PRIMROSE OF THE ROCK.

WRITTEN at Rydal Mount in 1831, published in 1835. Wordsworth says: "The rock stands on the right hand a little way leading up the middle road from Rydal to Grasmere. We have been in the habit of calling it the Glowworm Rock from the number of glowworms we have often seen hanging on it as described. The tuft of primrose has, I fear, been washed away by the heavy rains." The *rock* is easily recognized now, though the primrose is gone.

See Mr. Hutton's comments on the poem, p. 171 above.

21. *To her sphere.* That is, to her orbit. As *sphere* is used by Shakespeare, Milton, and other of our old writers, it means the crystalline sphere, in which, according to the Ptolemaic astronomy, the heavenly body was fixed and by whose motion it was carried round. Cf. Milton, *Hymn on Nativity*, 125: "Ring out, ye crystal spheres," etc.

YARROW REVISITED.

WRITTEN in 1831, published in 1835. In the preface to the volume (*Yarrow Revisited, and Other Poems*), Wordsworth says:

"In the autumn of 1831, my daughter and I set off from Rydal to visit Sir Walter Scott before his departure for Italy. This journey had been delayed by an inflammation in my eyes till we found that the time appointed for his leaving home would be too near for him to receive us without considerable inconvenience. Nevertheless we proceeded and reached Abbotsford on Monday. I was then scarcely able to lift up my eyes to the light. How sadly changed did I find him from the man I had seen so healthy, gay, and hopeful, a few years before, when he said at the inn at Patterdale, in my presence, his daughter Anne also being there, with Mr. Lockhart, my own wife and daughter, and Mr. Quillinan,—'I mean to live till I am *eighty*, and shall write as long as I live.' But to return to Abbotsford, the inmates and guests we found there were Sir Walter, Major Scott, Anne Scott, and Mr. and Mrs. Lockhart, Mr. Liddell, his lady and brother, and Mr. Allan the painter, and Mr. Laidlow, a very old friend of Sir Walter's. One of Burns's sons, an officer in the Indian service, had left the house a day or two before, and had kindly expressed his regret that he could not await my arrival, a regret that I may truly say was mutual. In the evening, Mr. and Mrs. Liddell sang, and Mrs. Lockhart chanted old ballads to her harp; and Mr. Allan, hanging over the back of a chair, told and acted odd stories in a humorous way. With this exhibition and his daughter's singing, Sir Walter was much amused, as indeed were we all as far as circumstances would allow. But what is most worthy of mention is the admirable demeanour of Major Scott during the following evening, when the Liddells were gone and only ourselves and Mr. Allan were present. He had much to suffer from the sight of his father's infirmities and from the great change that was about to take place at the residence he had built, and where he had long lived in so much prosperity and happiness. But what struck me most was the patient kindness with which he supported himself under the many fretful expressions that his sister Anne addressed to him or uttered in his hearing. She, poor thing, as mistress of that house, had been subject, after her mother's death, to a heavier load of care and responsibility and greater sacrifices of time than one of such a constitution of body and mind was able to bear. Of this Dora and I were made so sensible that, as soon as we had crossed the Tweed on our departure, we gave vent at the same moment to our apprehensions that her brain would fail and she would go out of her mind, or that she would sink under the trials she had passed and those which awaited her. On Tuesday morning Sir Walter Scott accompanied us and most of the party to Newark Castle on the Yarrow. When we alighted from the carriages he walked pretty stoutly, and had great pleasure in revisiting those his favourite haunts. Of that excursion the verses *Yarrow Revisited* are a memorial. Notwithstanding the romance that pervades Sir Walter's works and attaches to many of his habits, there is too much pressure of fact for these verses to harmonize as much as I could wish with other poems. On our return in the afternoon we had to cross the Tweed directly opposite Abbotsford. The wheels of our carriage grated upon the pebbles in the bed of the stream, that there flows somewhat rapidly; a rich but sad light of rather a purple than a golden hue was spread over the Eildon hills at that moment; and, thinking it probable that it might be the last time Sir Walter would cross the stream, I was not a little moved, and expressed some of my feelings in the sonnet beginning—'A trouble, not of clouds, or weeping rain.' At noon on Thursday we left Abbotsford, and in the morning of that day Sir Walter and I had a serious conversation *tête-à-tête*, when he spoke with gratitude of the happy life which upon the whole he had led. He had written in my daughter's album, before he came into the breakfast-room that morning, a few stanzas addressed to her, and, while putting the book into her hand, in his own study, standing by his desk, he said to her in my presence—'I should not have done anything of this kind but for your father's sake : they are probably the last verses I shall ever write.' They show how much his mind was impaired, not by the strain of thought, but by the execution, some of the lines being imperfect, and one stanza wanting corresponding rhymes : one letter, the initial S, had been omitted in the spelling of his own name. In this interview also it was that, upon my expressing a hope of his health being benefited by the climate of the country to which he was going, and by the interest he would take in the classic remembrances of Italy, he made use of the quotation from *Yarrow Unvisited* as recorded by me in the *Musings at Aquapendente* six years afterwards. Mr. Lockhart has mentioned in his Life of him what I heard from several quarters while abroad, both at Rome and elsewhere, that little seemed to interest him but what he could collect or heard of the fugitive Stuarts and their adherents who had followed them into exile. Both the *Yarrow Revisited* and the sonnet were sent him before his departure from England. Some further particulars of the conversations which occurred during this visit I should have set down had they not been already accurately recorded by Mr. Lockhart. I first became acquainted with this great and amiable man —Sir Walter Scott—in the year 1803, when my sister and I, making a tour in Scotland, were hospitably received by him in Lasswade upon the banks of the Esk, where he was then living. We saw a good deal of him in the course of the following week : the particulars are given in my sister's Journal of that tour."

The following is the passage in the *Musings at Aquapendente* to which Wordsworth refers above :

> " One there surely was.
> ' The Wizard of the North,' with anxious hope
> Brought to this genial climate, when disease
> Preyed upon body and mind—yet not the less
> Had his sunk eye kindled at those dear words
> That spake of bards and minstrels ; and his spirit
> Had flown with mine to old Helvellyn's brow,
> Where once together, in his day of strength,
> We stood rejoicing, as if earth were free
> From sorrow, like the sky above our heads.
>   Years followed years, and when, upon the eve
> Of his last going from Tweed-side, thought turned,
> Or by another's sympathy was led,
> To this bright land, Hope was for him no friend,
> Knowledge no help ; Imagination shaped
> No promise. Still, in more than ear-deep seats,
> Survives for me, and cannot but survive,
> The tone of voice which wedded borrowed words
> To sadness not their own, when, with faint smile
> Forced by intent to take from speech its edge,
> He said, ' When I am there, although 't is fair,
> 'T will be another Yarrow.' Prophecy
> More than fulfilled, as gay Campania's shores
> Soon witnessed, and the City of Seven Hills.
> Her sparkling fountains and her mouldering tombs ;
> And more than all, that eminence which showed
> Her splendours, seen, not felt, the while he stood
> A few short steps—painful they were—apart
> From Tasso's convent-haven and retired grave.'

In a note on the passage,

> " yet not the less
> Had his sunk eye kindled," etc.

the poet says : " His, Sir Walter Scott's eye, *did* in fact kindle at them, for the lines ' Places forsaken now,' and the two that follow* were

---

* " Places forsaken now, though living still
The muses, as they loved them in the days
Of the old minstrels and the Border bards."

These lines occur in a reference to the scenery of Cumberland and the Border which precedes the passage in the *Musings* quoted above.

adopted from a poem of mine which nearly forty years ago was in part read to him, and he never forgot them."

Again, on the reference to "old Helvellyn's brow," Wordsworth says : "Sir Humphry Davy was with us at the time. We had ascended from Patterdale, and I could not but admire the vigour with which Scott scrambled along that horn of the mountain called 'Striding Edge.' Our progress was necessarily slow, and was beguiled by Scott's telling many stories and amusing anecdotes, as was his custom. Sir H. Davy would have probably been better pleased if other topics had occasionally been interspersed, and some discussion entered upon : at all events he did not remain with us long at the top of the mountain, but left us to find our way down its steep side together into the vale of Grasmere, where, at my cottage, Mrs. Scott was to meet us at dinner."

There is also the following note on the line, "A few short steps—painful they were—apart :" "This, though introduced here, I did not know till it was told me at Rome by Miss Mackenzie of Seaforth. . . . She accompanied Sir Walter to the Janicular Mount, and, after showing him the grave of Tasso in the church upon the top, and a mural monument there erected to his memory, they left the church and stood together on the brow of the hill overlooking the city of Rome : his daughter Anne was with them, and she, naturally desirous, for the sake of Miss Mackenzie especially, to have some expression of pleasure from her father, half reproached him for showing nothing of that kind either by his looks or voice : 'How can I,' replied he, 'having only one leg to stand upon, and that in extreme pain !' so that the prophecy was more than fulfilled."

Shairp, in his *Aspects of Poetry*, remarks : "The poem is a memorial of the very last visit Scott ever paid, not to Yarrow only, but to any scene in that land which he had so loved and glorified. A memorial of that day, struck off on the spot, even by an inferior hand, would have been precious. But when no less a poet than Wordsworth was there to commemorate this, Scott's last day by his native streams, and when into that record he poured so much of the mellow music of his autumnal genius, the whole poem reaches to a quite tragic pathos. As you croon over its solemn cadences, and think of the circumstances out of which it arose and the sequel that was so soon to follow, you seem to overhear in every line 'the still sad music of humanity.'"

2. *Winsome Marrow.* See on *Yarrow Unvisited*, 6 above.

5. *Newark's castle-gate.* See on *Yarrow Visited*, 55 above.

47. *And Care waylays.* The ed. of 1835 has "waylay;" changed in 1837.

50. *Eildon-hill.* The *Trementium* of the Romans (cf. "Eildon's triple height" in the next poem), to the south of Melrose. The highest summit is 1385 feet above the level of the sea. According to the old legend, the hill was originally a uniform cone, but a demon, at the direction of Michael Scott, divided it into three peaks. Cf. the *Lay of the Last Minstrel*, ii. 144 :

> "And, warrior, I could say to thee
> The words that cleft Eildon Hills in three."

53. *Sorrento's breezy waves.*   On the southern shore of the Bay of Naples.

70. *Wherever they.*   The reading of 1835 (changed in 1837) was " Where'er thy path."

81. *And what, for this frail world*, etc.   " After the expression of the hope of what Italy may do to restore Scott, Wordsworth passes on to reflect on the power of ' localized Romance ' to elevate and beautify existence, . . . and then the poem closes with a farewell benediction to the stream whose immemorial charm his own three poems have so greatly enhanced " (Shairp).

93. *Ah, no !*   Knight, in his *Selections*, has " Oh, no !" for which his collation of the texts gives no authority.

102. *Too timidly.*   Cf. *Lay of Last Minstrel*, introd. 27 :

> " He passed where Newark's stately tower
> Looks out from Yarrow's birchen bower;
> The Minstrel gazed with wishful eye—
> No humbler resting-place was nigh.
> With hesitating step at last
> The embattled portal arch he passed," etc.

103. *Not the last !*   Cf. line 8 above.

ON THE DEPARTURE OF SIR WALTER SCOTT FROM ABBOTSFORD FOR NAPLES.

WRITTEN in 1831, published in 1835.

3. *Eildon's triple height.*   See on *Yarrow Revisited*, 50.

13. *The midland sea.*   The Mediterranean.

14. *Parthenope.*   Naples, which was built on the site of an ancient place called *Parthenope* after the Siren of that name.   Wordsworth follows Virgil and Ovid in referring to Naples as *Parthenope*.   Cf. Milton, *Comus*, 879 : " By dead Parthenope's dear tomb."

DEVOTIONAL INCITEMENTS.

WRITTEN at Rydal Mount in 1832, published in 1835.   See Mr. Hutton's comments on the style, p. 169 above.

50-53. *The priests*, etc.   The reading of 1835 (changed in 1836) was :

> " The solemn rites, the awful forms,
> Founder amid fanatic storms;
> The priests are from their altars thrust,
> The temples levelled with the dust."

69. *The Eternal Will.*   The reading until 1836 was " the Almighty Will."

71. *Divine monition Nature yields.* The ed. of 1835 has " Her admonitions Nature yields ;" and that of 1836 " Divine admonishment she yields." The text dates from 1845.

MOSSGIEL FARM.

WRITTEN in 1833, published in 1835. The poet says : " Mossgiel was thus pointed out to me by a young man on the top of the coach on my way from Glasgow to Kilmarnock. It is remarkable that, though Burns lived some time here, and during much the most productive period of his poetical life, he nowhere adverts to the splendid prospects stretching towards the sea and bounded by the peaks of Arran on one part, which in clear weather he must have had daily before his eyes. In one of his poetical effusions he speaks of describing ' fair Nature's face ' as a privilege on which he sets a high value; nevertheless, natural appearances rarely take a lead in his poetry. It is as a human being, eminently sensitive and intelligent, and not as a poet, clad in his priestly robes and carrying the ensigns of sacerdotal office, that he interests and affects us. Whenever he speaks of rivers, hills, and woods, it is not so much on account of the properties with which they are absolutely endowed, as relatively to local patriotic remembrances and associations, or as they ministered to personal feelings, especially those of love, whether happy or otherwise;—yet it is not always so. Soon after we had passed Mossgiel Farm we crossed the Ayr, murmuring and winding through a narrow woody hollow. His line—' Auld hermit Ayr strays through his woods '—came at once to my mind with Irwin, Lugar, Ayr, and Doon,—Ayrshire streams over which he breathes a sigh as being unnamed in song; and surely his own attempts to make them known were as successful as his heart could desire."

4. *The daisy.* Cf. Burns's *To a Mountain Daisy*, written " on turning one down with the plough, in April, 1786."

6. *The peaks of Arran.* Arran is a mountainous island off the coast of Ayrshire, at the mouth of the Firth of Clyde.

9. *Bield.* Shelter (Scottish). The quotation is from the poem mentioned above.

"MOST SWEET IT IS WITH UNUPLIFTED EYES."

WRITTEN in 1833, published in 1835.

5-8. *Pleased rather*, etc. The MS. reading was :

> " Pleased rather with that soothing after-time
> Whose seat is in the mind. occasion's queen !
> Else nature's noblest objects were, I ween,
> A yoke endured, a penance undergone."

10. *Commerce.* Communion, intercourse. Cf. *Hamlet*, iii 1. 110: " Could beauty have better commerce than with honesty ?" Milton uses the verb in a similar way; as in *Il Penseroso*, 39: "And looks commercing with the skies."

"A POET!—HE HATH PUT HIS HEART TO SCHOOL."

WRITTEN and published in 1842. Wordsworth says: "I was impelled to write this sonnet by the disgusting frequency with which the word *artistical*, imported with other impertinences from the Germans, is employed by writers of the present day: for *artistical* let them substitute *artificial*, and the poetry written on this system, both at home and abroad, will be for the most part much better characterized."

Cf. Wordsworth's picture of the true poet in *A Poet's Epitaph :*

> "But who is he, with modest looks
>   And clad in homely russet brown?
> He murmurs near the running brooks
>   A music sweeter than their own.
>
> He is retired as noontide dew,
>   Or fountain in a noonday grove;
> And you must love him ere to you
>   He will seem worthy of your love.
>
> The outward shows of sky and earth,
>   Of hill and valley he has viewed;
> And impulses of deeper birth
>   Have come to him in solitude.
>
> In common things that round us lie
>   Some random themes he can impart,—
> The harvest of a quiet eye
>   That broods and sleeps on his own heart."

5. *Thy art be nature.* Cf. the *Winter's Tale*, iv. 4. 89:

> "Yet nature is made better by no mean
> But nature makes that mean; so, over that art
> Which you say adds to nature, is an art
> That nature makes. . . .
>   This is an art
> Which does mend nature—change it rather; but
> The art itself is nature."

"GLAD SIGHT WHEREVER NEW WITH OLD."

WRITTEN and published in 1845.

7, 8. *Unless, while with admiring eye*, etc. "It is benignly ordained that green fields, clear blue skies, running streams of pure water, rich groves and woods, orchards, and all the ordinary varieties of rural nature should find an easy way to the affections of all men. But a taste beyond this, however desirable it may be that every one should possess it, is not to be implanted at once; it must be gradually developed both in nations and individuals. Rocks and mountains, torrents and wide-spread waters, and all those features of nature which go to the composition of such scenes as this part of England is, distinguished for, cannot, in their finer relations to the human mind, be comprehended, or even very imperfectly conceived, without processes of culture or opportunity of observation in some degree habitual" (W.).

ADDENDA.

"WORDSWORTHSHIRE."—The English Lake District, or "Wordsworthshire," as James Russell Lowell has aptly called it, occupies a portion of the three counties of Cumberland, Westmoreland, and Lancashire, which is about forty-five miles in extreme length and breadth. It is a charming region, but how much has the poet added to its attractions! Even its market value has been immensely enhanced by the process. Some one has said that the mere mention of a locality by Scott has increased its value more than the highest farming could do; and the same is true of this district and Wordsworth. It would have been a resort for tourists if he had not lived and sung there, but by no means to the extent that it now is; and some portions of it would be quite unknown and unvisited were it not that Wordsworth found them out in his lonely "tramps" among the hills, and made them famous by his verse.

Windermere, or more properly *Winandermere*, is perhaps the most noted of the lakes, and is the one which the tourist, coming from the south by rail, usually visits first. It is about eleven miles long, and averages about a mile in breadth. In some places it is 240 feet deep. Bowness, situated near the middle of the lake, on its eastern shore, is a favourite point of view and centre of excursions. At the Ferry (see cut on p. 159), about three quarters of a mile south of Bowness, the banks approach each other so that the passage across is not more than a quarter of a mile. A short distance above Bowness there is a fine view of the lake (see cut on p. 37) from a hill on the road to Ambleside. A mile and a quarter beyond this pleasant little town, and rather more than two miles from the upper end of Windermere, we reach *Rydal*, a village near the lower end of *Rydal Water* (p. 46),a lakelet scarcely half a mile in length, and a quarter of a mile in breadth. Nab Scar (1300 feet high) rises from its northern bank, and a little way up its side is *Rydal Mount**(p. 8), the poet's residence for thirty-seven years. "It seems

---

* Myers, in his interesting chapter on "The English Lakes" (p. 49), says: "Rydal Mount has probably been oftener described than any other English poet's home since Shakespeare; and few homes, certainly, have been moulded into such close accordance with their inmates' nature. The house, which has been altered since Wordsworth's day, stands, looking southward, on the rocky side of Nab Scar, above Rydal Lake. The garden was described by Bishop Wordsworth immediately after his uncle's death, while every terrace-walk and flowering alley spoke of the poet's loving care. He tells of the 'tall ash-tree, in which a thrush has sung, for hours together, during many years;' of the 'laburnum in which the osier cage of the doves was hung;' of the stone steps ' in the interstices of which grow the yellow flowering poppy, and the wild geranium or

to have been ingeniously set aside out of the common road, though not completely isolated. It is a kind of bird's-nest upon the rugged bosom of the mountain. Interlaced around it with care are all species of thickly growing shrubs and vines. Its front windows have a splendid prospect over the deeply scooped vale of Rydal Water and Grasmere, and the mountains beyond. It is a very plain and almost rough dwelling externally, though with a peerless site." Higher up the hill is *Rydal Hall*, the seat of the *De Flemings*, in the midst of a fine park with many grand old trees. The celebrated *Rydal Falls* are at the back of the hall. There are two falls, nearly half a mile apart, the lower one (p. 36) being the more beautiful. Seen through a window of the old summer-house hard by, it appears like a picture set in a frame.

"A short way on from Rydal Mere, and strung to it by a silver streamlet, is the heart of all the lakes, *Grasmere*, which is somewhat larger than its sister mere. As the road creeping around under Nab Scar passes the middle part of the lake, it runs near the *Wishing-gate* (p. 151) sung by Wordsworth in those tripping verses with such solemn ending. Here one looks down upon one of the most lovely and softly peaceful scenes on earth, and yet with a certain sober grandeur about it quite impossible to describe."

A little further on we come to *Town-end*, a small group of houses, among which is the cottage that was the first home of Wordsworth in the district (p. 15) and to which he brought his young bride in 1802. We soon reach the village of Grasmere, which is at the head of the lake, four miles from Ambleside. The parish church of St. Oswald (p. 176) is a quaint little edifice, and adjoining it is the burying-ground with the modest tombstones of the poet, his sister, his wife and her sister (p. 16), his only daughter Dora, and her husband Edward Quillinan (p. 167). Wordsworth's is of black slate, and is the middle one in the group (p. 167). The marble tablet, shown on p. 34, is within the church, over the pew which he frequently occupied.

Allan Bank (p. 16) is on higher ground behind the village. After Wordsworth removed to the rectory (p. 16), it was for some time occupied by De Quincey.

Following the common track of tourists who have but a few days for the Lakes, we should keep on by the same road over the pass of *Dunmail Raise* (p. 135), the summit of which is 783 feet above the sea. A heap of stones at this point is said to mark the scene of a battle between Dunmail, King of Cumberland, and the Saxon Edmund, in 945. The former was defeated and slain, the eyes of his two sons were put out by

---

Poor Robin '—
                                  ' gay
        With his red stalks upon a sunny day.'

And then of the terraces—one levelled for Miss Fenwick's use, and welcome to himself in aged years; and one [p. 9] ascending, and leading to the 'far terrace' on the mountain's side, where the poet was wont to murmur his verses as they came. Within the house were disposed his simple treasures: the ancestral almery [p. 10], on which the names of unknown Wordsworths may be deciphered still; Sir George Beaumont's pictures, . . . and the cuckoo clock which brought vernal thoughts to cheer the sleepless bed of age, and which sounded its noonday summons when his spirit fled.".

order of Edmund, and the territory was given to Malcolm, King of Scotland. The ascent of this pass was a favourite walk of Wordsworth's.* The summit is two miles and a half from Grasmere, and *Helvellyn* (3118 feet) then comes in sight on the other side, with the lake of *Thirlmere* (p. 115) at its base. Presently we reach the small inn and church of *Wythburn* (p. 129)—

> " a humble house of prayer,
> Where Silence dwells, a maid immaculate.
> Save when the Sabbath and the priest are there,
> And some few hungry souls for manna wait."

The eastern shore of Thirlmere† is now skirted for nearly two miles. The lake itself is a mile longer, but only a quarter of a mile wide. At one point it is so narrow that a picturesque foot-bridge has been thrown across it.

The stream issuing from Thirlmere flows through the *Vale of St. John* (p. 123), the entrance to which soon appears on the right of the road, with Blencathara (see p. 231) at the farther end. As we go on we get a good view of the famous *Castle Rock*, the scene of Scott's *Bridal of Triermain*. As the poem tells us,

> " With toil his way the king pursued
> By lonely Threlkeld's waste and wood,
> Till on his course obliquely shone
> The narrow Valley of Saint John
> Down sloping to the western sky,
> Where lingering sunbeams love to lie.
>   *   *   *   *   *
> But midmost of the vale a mound
> Arose, with airy turrets crowned,
> Buttress and rampire's circling bound,
>   And mighty keep and tower ;
> Seemed some primeval giant's hand
> The castle's massive walls had planned,
> A ponderous bulwark to withstand
>   Ambitious Nimrod's power."

From some points of view the resemblance to a castle is very striking.

---

* Cf. p. 202 above, where he tells of climbing it at two o'clock in the morning to get the latest news from France.

† Myers (p. 51) remarks : " It is chiefly round two lines of road leading from Grasmere that Wordsworth's associations cluster—the route over Dunmail Raise, which led him to Keswick, to Coleridge and Southey at Greta Hall, and to other friends in that neighbourhood ; and the route over Kirkstone, which led him to Ulleswater, and the friendly houses of Patterdale, Hallsteads, and Lowther Castle. The first of these two routes .   . skirts the lovely shore of Thirlmere—a lonely sheet of water, of exquisite irregularity of outline, and fringed with delicate verdure, which the Corporation of Manchester has lately bought to embank it into a reservoir. *Dedecorum pretiosus emptor !* This lake was a favourite haunt of Wordsworth's ; and upon a rock on its margin, where he and Coleridge, coming from Keswick and Grasmere, would often meet, the two poets, with the other members of Wordsworth's loving household group, inscribed the initial letters of their names. To the 'monumental power' of this Rock of Names Wordsworth appeals, in lines written when the happy company who engraved them had already been severed by distance and death :

> ' O thought of pain,
> That would impair it or profane !
> And fail not Thou, loved Rock, to keep
> Thy charge when we are laid asleep,'

The rock may still be seen, but is to be submerged in the new reservoir."

There is nothing more of special interest on the road to Keswick until we reach a height called *Castle Rigg*, a mile from the town. Here we get a beautiful view of Derwentwater and Bassenthwaite lakes, with the valley of the Derwent between them, the two peaks of Skiddaw, and the Newland Mountains. Southey and Coleridge thought this the finest part of the Lake Region; and the poet Gray declared that, on leaving Keswick, when he turned round at this place to take a parting look at the landscape, he was so charmed that he " had almost a mind to go back again."

Derwentwater (p. 57) is half a mile from Keswick. It is about three miles long, and a mile and a half wide, "expanding within an amphitheatre of mountains, rocky but not vast, broken into many fantastic shapes, peaked, splintered, impending, sometimes pyramidal, opening by narrow valleys to the view of rocks that rise immediately beyond, and are again overlooked by others."

Greta Hall, long the residence of Southey, is near Keswick, and he lies buried in the Crosthwaite churchyard, about three quarters of a mile distant.

A favourite excursion from Keswick is by the east side of Derwentwater to *Borrowdale*, the valley through which the Derwent flows into the lake. The *Lodore* empties at nearly the same point, and a little way up the stream is the fall that Southey has immortalized ; but only after heavy rains is it at all true to his description.

Eagle Crag (p. 93) is seen towering on the left as we go up the Borrowdale valley. Farther on the steep ascent of Borrowdale Hause begins. The pass is 1190 feet high, and commands admirable views of the valley we have left. On the other side *Honister Crag* (p. iv.), the grandest in the district, lifts an almost perpendicular wall of rock to the height of 1500 feet. The road descends rapidly into the *Buttermere* valley to the lake (p. 75) from which it derives its name. This is but a little more than a mile in length and half a mile in breadth, and hemmed in by some of the highest and steepest of the Cumbrian mountains. A small brook connects it with the larger lake of Crummock. The return to Keswick is usually made by a more direct but less beautiful road through the Newlands Valley.

Ulleswater (p. 145) is generally visited either from Ambleside or Keswick. The lake, which has been compared to the Swiss Lucerne, is nine miles long, with an extreme breadth of three quarters of a mile. It is zigzag in shape, forming three "reaches" of unequal length, closed in by mountains. It disputes the palm with Derwentwater for varied wildness and beauty. The *Eamont* (p. 228) is the outlet of Ulleswater.

The *Langdale Pikes* (p. 87) are a pair of mountains known respectively as Harrison Stickle (2401 feet) and Pike o' Stickle (2323 feet). Though neither so lofty nor so massive as many heights in the district, they are conspicuous from so many points that none are more familiar to the tourist. They are a little north of west from Ambleside, at a distance of about seven miles, and are oftenest visited from that town. *Stickle Tarn* (p. 256) lies at the base of Harrison Stickle.

" WORDSWORTHSHIRE."

TO THE CUCKOO.

O BLITHE new-comer! I have heard,
    I hear thee and rejoice.
O cuckoo! shall I call thee bird,
    Or but a wandering voice?

While I am lying on the grass
    Thy twofold shout I hear;
From hill to hill it seems to pass,
    At once far off and near,

Though babbling only to the vale
    Of sunshine and of flowers,   10
Thou bringest unto me a tale
    Of visionary hours.

Thrice welcome, darling of the Spring!
    Even yet thou art to me
No bird, but an invisible thing,
    A voice, a mystery;

The same whom in my schoolboy days
    I listened to—that cry
Which made me look a thousand ways
    In bush and tree and sky,   20

To seek thee did I often rove
    Through woods and on the green;
And thou wert still a hope, a love,
    Still longed for, never seen.

And I can listen to thee yet,
    Can lie upon the plain
And listen, till I do beget
    That golden time again.

O blessed bird! the earth we pace
    Again appears to be   30
An unsubstantial, faery place,
    That is fit home for thee!

The above poem (see preface) should have followed *Yarrow Unvisited*, p. 106. It was composed in 1804 in the orchard at Town-end, and published in 1807. Of all his poems this was Wordsworth's special favourite; but the critics of the time regarded it as ridiculous and affected. Palgrave says of it : " This poem has an exaltation and a glory, joined with an exquisiteness of expression, which place it in the highest rank amongst the many masterpieces of its illustrious author."

3, 4. *Shall I call thee bird*, etc. In the preface to the ed. of 1815, Wordsworth cites these lines as an example of imagination : " This concise interrogation characterizes the seeming ubiquity of the voice of the cuckoo, and dispossesses the creature almost of a corporeal existence ; the imagination being tempted to this exertion of her power by a consciousness in the memory that the cuckoo is almost perpetually heard throughout the season of spring, but seldom becomes an object of sight."

6-8. *Thy twofold shout*, etc. The reading of 1807 was :

> " I hear thy restless shout:
> From hill to hill it seems to pass
> About, and all about !"

That of 1815 was :

> " Thy loud note smites my ear !—
> From hill to hill it seems to pass,
> At once far off and near !"

In 1820 it was changed to the present text, which was restored in 1845 after having been changed in 1832 to

> " Thy twofold shout I hear,
> That seems to fill the whole air's space,
> As loud far off as near."

9-11. *Though babbling only*, etc. The ed. of 1807 reads :

> " To me, no babbler with a tale
> Of sunshine and of flowers,
> Thou tellest, cuckoo ! in the vale," etc.

That of 1815 has :

> " I hear thee babbling to the vale
> Of sunshine and of flowers,
> And unto me thou bring'st a tale," etc.

That of 1820 reads the same except that *And* in the last line is changed to *But*. In 1827 the text was finally settled as it now stands.

17. *The same whom*. " The same that " would be better, aside from the use of *whom* for a bird, which may be justified by the personification, as in *Brougham Castle*, 16.

HART-LEAP WELL (p. 191).—The locality is close to a wayside inn called the *Halfpenny House*, which is on the direct road from Leyburn to Richmond. All the stones have now disappeared, and only one of the trees overhanging the well was left a few years ago. Very likely this last relic of Sir Walter's pleasure-house may now be gone.

STICKLE TARN.

INDEX OF WORDS AND PHRASES EXPLAINED.

17

THIRLMERE.

AFTERNOONS WITH THE POETS.

AFTERNOONS WITH THE POETS. By C. D. DESHLER.
Post 8vo, Cloth, $1 75.

This pleasing work is made up of citations from the poets, accompanied with easy and familiar discussions of their merits and peculiarities. Seven afternoons are thus agreeably occupied, and take the shape of as many interesting chapters. The participants are the " Professor " and his pupil, who are represented as on terms of the utmost intimacy, and express their sentiments to each other with perfect freedom. * * * Mr. Deshler has happily selected the sonnet, and confined his view of the poets to their productions in this single species of verse. * * * The author's extensive research has been accompanied by minute scrutiny, faithful comparison, and judicious discrimination. His critical observations are frank, honest, good-natured, yet just, discreet, comprehensive, and full of instruction. It would be difficult to find a volume that in so small a compass offers equal aid for the cultivation of literary taste, and for reaching an easy acquaintance with all the great poets of the English tongue. The style is pure and transparent, and though colloquial in form, it is exceedingly correct and elegant, embodying every chaste adornment of which language is capable.—*Boston Transcript.*

A very unconventional and pleasant book.—*N. Y. Herald.*

The substance of the book is decidedly meritorious, far better than most of the criticism published in these days. It shows careful study, extensive reading, a nice taste and discrimination, and also a genuine appreciation and insight which are rare.—*N. Y. Evening Express.*

A volume of much literary interest, and is very pleasantly written.* * * Mr. Deshler's discussions of literature are extremely interesting. * * * It will be a source of enjoyment to all who have a taste for poetry, and can appreciate the highest triumphs of poetic art as displayed in the sonnet. —*Hartford Post.*

We have to thank Mr. Deshler for a collection of some of the most exquisite sonnets in the English language, with an animated, appreciative, and suggestive comment which shows a fine poetical taste and is an interesting and instructive guide in a charming field.—*N. Y. Mail.*

PUBLISHED BY HARPER & BROTHERS, NEW YORK.

☞ HARPER & BROTHERS *will send the above work by mail, postage prepaid, to any part of the United States or Canada, on receipt of the price.*

ENGLISH MEN OF LETTERS.

EDITED BY JOHN MORLEY.

The following volumes are now ready:

SAMUEL JOHNSON....................By Leslie Stephen.
EDWARD GIBBON....................By J. C. Morison.
SIR WALTER SCOTT ....By R. H. Hutton.
PERCY BYSSHE SHELLEY...........By J. A. Symonds.
DAVID HUME........................By T. H. Huxley.
OLIVER GOLDSMITH.................By William Black.
DANIEL DEFOE......................By William Minto.
ROBERT BURNS.....................By Principal Shairp.
EDMUND SPENSER..................By R. W. Church.
WILLIAM M. THACKERAY.........By Anthony Trollope.
EDMUND BURKE....................By John Morley.
JOHN MILTON........................By Mark Pattison.
NATHANIEL HAWTHORNE..........By Henry James, Jr.
ROBERT SOUTHEY..................By Edward Dowden.
GEOFFREY CHAUCER...............By A. W. Ward.
JOHN BUNYAN ....By J. A. Froude.
WILLIAM COWPER..................By Goldwin Smith.
ALEXANDER POPE.................By Leslie Stephen.
LORD BYRON ....By John Nichol.
JOHN LOCKE........................By Thomas Fowler.
WILLIAM WORDSWORTH...........By F. W. H. Myers.
JOHN DRYDEN......................By G. Saintsbury.
WALTER SAVAGE LANDOR..... ....By Sidney Colvin.
THOMAS DE QUINCEY ....By David Masson.
CHARLES LAMB.....................By Alfred Ainger.
RICHARD BENTLEY ....By R. C. Jebb.
CHARLES DICKENS.................By A. W. Ward.
THOMAS GRAY.......................By E. W. Gosse.
JONATHAN SWIFT...................By Leslie Stephen.
LAURENCE STERNE.................By H. D. Traill.
THOMAS B. MACAULAY............By J. C. Morison.
HENRY FIELDING...................By Austin Dobson.
RICHARD BRINSLEY SHERIDAN.......By Mrs. Oliphant.
JOSEPH ADDISON..................By W. J. Courthope.
LORD BACON......................By R. W. Church.
SAMUEL TAYLOR COLERIDGE..........By H. D. Traill.
SIR PHILIP SIDNEY................By J. A. Symonds.
JOHN KEATS ....By Sidney Colvin.

12mo, Cloth, 75 cents per volume.

Published by HARPER & BROTHERS, New York.

THOMAS GRAY.

SELECT POEMS OF THOMAS GRAY. Edited, with Notes, by WILLIAM J. ROLFE, A.M., formerly Head Master of the High School, Cambridge, Mass. Illustrated. Square 16mo, Paper, 40 cents; Cloth, 56 cents. (*Uniform with Rolfe's Shakespeare.*)

Mr. Rolfe has done his work in a manner that comes as near to perfection as man can approach. He knows his subject so well that he is competent to instruct all in it; and readers will find an immense amount of knowledge in his elegant volume, all set forth in the most admirable order, and breathing the most liberal and enlightened spirit, he being a warm appreciator of the divinity of genius.—*Boston Traveller.*

The great merit of these books lies in their carefully edited text, and in the fulness of their explanatory notes. Mr. Rolfe is not satisfied with simply expounding, but he explores the entire field of English literature, and therefrom gathers a multitude of illustrations that are interesting in themselves and valuable as a commentary on the text. He not only instructs, but stimulates his readers to fresh exertion; and it is this stimulation that makes his labor so productive in the school-room.—*Saturday Evening Gazette*, Boston.

Mr. William J. Rolfe, to whom English literature is largely indebted for annotated and richly illustrated editions of several of Shakespeare's Plays, has treated the "Select Poems of Thomas Gray" in the same way —just as he had previously dealt with the best of Goldsmith's poems.— *Philadelphia Press.*

Mr. Rolfe's edition of Thomas Gray's select poems is marked by the same discriminating taste as his other classics.—*Springfield Republican.*

Mr. Rolfe's rare abilities as a teacher and his fine scholarly tastes enable him to prepare a classic like this in the best manner for school use. There could be no better exercise for the advanced classes in our schools than the critical study of our best authors, and the volumes that Mr. Rolfe has prepared will hasten the time when the study of mere form will give place to the study of the spirit of our literature.—*Louisville Courier-Journal.*

An elegant and scholarly little volume.—*Christian Intelligencer*, N. Y.

PUBLISHED BY HARPER & BROTHERS, NEW YORK.

☞ *Sent by mail, postage prepaid, to any part of the United States or Canada, on receipt of the price.*

ROBERT BROWNING.

SELECT POEMS OF ROBERT BROWNING. Edited, with Notes, by WILLIAM J. ROLFE, A.M., formerly Head Master of the High School, Cambridge, Mass., and HELOISE E. HERSEY. Illustrated. 16mo, Paper, 40 cents ; Cloth, 56 cents. (*Uniform with Rolfe's Shakespeare.*)

Probably no critic yet has gone to the heart of Browning's true significance as does Miss Hersey. There is something in the fineness of her insight and her subtle, spiritual sympathy that truly interprets him, while others write in a more or less scholarly manner about him. Miss Hersey's work indicates the blending of two exceptional qualities—the poetic sympathy and the critical judgments. She feels intuitively all the poet's subtle meanings ; she is responsible to them by virtue of temperament ; yet added to this is the critical faculty, keen, logical, and constructive.—*Boston Traveller.*

To say that the selections have been made by Mr. Rolfe is to say that they have not only been made by a careful and accurate scholar, but by a man of pure and beautiful taste. . . . The Notes, which fill some thirty pages, are admirable in their scope and brevity.—*N. Y. Mail and Express.*

We can conscientiously say that both the arrangement of the selections and the fulness, as well as the illuminating character, of the annotations are all that the most exacting taste could require ; and the whole work is well fitted to charm the poet's established admirers, and to awaken in others who have not been among these a new sense of Browning's strength and beauty as a writer.—*Hartford Times.*

The "Select Poems of Robert Browning" is a marvel of industrious editing, wise, choice, and excellent judgment in comment. . . . An introduction, a brief account of Browning's life and works, a chronological table of his works, and a series of extracted critical comments on the poet, precede the series of selections. Besides these there are at the end of the book very extensive, valuable, and minutely illustrative notes, together with addenda supplied by Browning himself on points which the editors were unable fully to clear up.—*N. Y. Star.*

PUBLISHED BY HARPER & BROTHERS, NEW YORK.

☞ HARPER & BROTHERS *will send the above work by mail, postage prepaid, to any part of the United States or Canada, on receipt of the price.*

ROBERT BROWNING.

A BLOT IN THE 'SCUTCHEON AND OTHER DRA-
MAS. By ROBERT BROWNING. Edited, with notes, by
WILLIAM J. ROLFE, A.M., and HELOISE E. HERSEY.
With Portrait. 16mo, Paper. 40 cents ; Cloth, 56 cents.
(*Uniform with Rolfe's Shakespeare.*)

Prepared in the same thorough manner as the previous volume upon
the Select Poems of the same author and the numerous manuals of Mr.
Rolfe. No poet needs, for the average reader, such an interpretation
as is here given more than Browning. Read carefully, with reference to
the notes of the editors, the richness of the great poet's thoughts and
fancies will be the better apprehended. —*Zion's Herald,* Boston.

Out of the eight dramas which the poet wrote between 1837 and 1845
the three most characteristic ones have been selected, and a full idea of
his dramatic power may be gained from them. A synopsis of critical
opinions of Mr. Browning's works is included in the volume. The same
careful scholarship that marked Professor Rolfe's editions of Shakespeare
is shown in this edition of Browning. The lovers of the poet will be
pleased to have old favorites in this attractive form, while many new
readers will be attracted to the author by it. Robert Browning will fill
a larger space in the world's eye in the future than he has done already.
—*Brooklyn Union.*

The introduction and notes are all that could be desired.—*N. Y. Sun.*

The book itself is not only a compact compilation of the three plays,
but it is valuable for the commentatory notes. The editing work has
been done in an able manner by Professor Rolfe and Miss Hersey, who
has gained a high place among the modern Browning students.—*Philadelphia Bulletin.*

This dainty volume, with flexible covers and red edges, contains not
merely Browning's dramas, with the author's latest emendations and cor-
rections, but notes and estimates, critical and explanatory, in such volume, and from sources so exalted, that we have not the temerity to add
one jot or tittle to the aggregate.—*N. Y. Commercial Advertiser.*

PUBLISHED BY HARPER & BROTHERS, NEW YORK.

☞ HARPER & BROTHERS *will send the above work by mail, postage prepaid, to any
part of the United States or Canada, on receipt of the price.*

OLIVER GOLDSMITH.

SELECT POEMS OF OLIVER GOLDSMITH. Edited, with Notes, by WILLIAM J. ROLFE, A.M., formerly Head Master of the High School, Cambridge, Mass. Illustrated. 16mo, Paper, 40 cents ; Cloth, 56 cents. (*Uniform with Rolfe's Shakespeare.*)

The carefully arranged editions of " The Merchant of Venice " and other of Shakespeare's plays prepared by Mr. William J. Rolfe for the use of students will be remembered with pleasure by many readers, and they will welcome another volume of a similar character from the same source, in the form of the " Select Poems of Oliver Goldsmith," edited with notes fuller than those of any other known edition, many of them original with the editor.—*Boston Transcript.*

Mr. Rolfe is doing very useful work in the preparation of compact hand-books for study in English literature. His own personal culture and his long experience as a teacher give him good knowledge of what is wanted in this way.—*The Congregationalist,* Boston.

Mr. Rolfe has prefixed to the Poems selections illustrative of Goldsmith's character as a man, and grade as a poet, from sketches by Macaulay, Thackeray, George Colman, Thomas Campbell, John Forster, and Washington Irving. He has also appended at the end of the volume a body of scholarly notes explaining and illustrating the poems, and dealing with the times in which they were written, as well as the incidents and circumstances attending their composition. — *Christian Intelligencer,* N. Y.

The notes are just and discriminating in tone, and supply all that is necessary either for understanding the thought of the several poems, or for a critical study of the language. The use of such books in the schoolroom cannot but contribute largely towards putting the study of English literature upon a sound basis ; and many an adult reader would find in the present volume an excellent opportunity for becoming critically acquainted with one of the greatest of last century's poets.—*Appleton's Journal,* N. Y.

PUBLISHED BY HARPER & BROTHERS, NEW YORK.

☞ *Sent by mail, postage prepaid, to any part of the United States or Canada, on receipt of the price.*

SHAKESPEARE.

WITH NOTES BY WM. J. ROLFE, A.M.

The Merchant of Venice.
The Tempest.
Julius Cæsar.
Hamlet.
As You Like it.
Henry the Fifth.
Macbeth.
Henry the Eighth.
A Midsummer-Night's Dream.
Richard the Second.
Richard the Third.
Much Ado About Nothing.
Antony and Cleopatra.
Romeo and Juliet.
Othello.
Twelfth Night.
The Winter's Tale.
King John.
Henry IV. Part I.
Henry IV. Part II.

King Lear.
The Taming of the Shrew.
All 's Well That Ends Well.
Coriolanus.
Comedy of Errors.
Cymbeline.
Merry Wives of Windsor.
Measure for Measure.
Two Gentlemen of Verona.
Love's Labour 's Lost.
Timon of Athens.
Henry VI. Part I.
Henry VI. Part II.
Henry VI. Part III.
Troilus and Cressida.
Pericles, Prince of Tyre.
The Two Noble Kinsmen.
Poems.
Sonnets.
Titus Andronicus.

Illustrated. 16mo, Cloth, 56 cents per vol. ; Paper, 40 cents per vol.

FRIENDLY EDITION, complete in 20 vols., 16mo, Cloth, $30 00 ; Half Calf, $60 00. (*Sold only in Sets.*)

In the preparation of this edition of the English Classics it has been the aim to adapt them for school and home reading, in essentially the same way as Greek and Latin Classics are edited for educational purposes. The chief requisites are a pure text (expurgated, if necessary), and the notes needed for its thorough explanation and illustration.

Each of Shakespeare's plays is complete in one volume, and is preceded by an Introduction containing the "History of the Play," the "Sources of the Plot," and "Critical Comments on the Play."

From HORACE HOWARD FURNESS, Ph.D., LL.D., *Editor of the "New Variorum Shakespeare."*

No one can examine these volumes and fail to be impressed with the conscientious accuracy and scholarly completeness with which they are edited. The educational purposes for which the notes are written Mr. Rolfe never loses sight of, but like "a well-experienced archer hits the mark his eye doth level at."

From F. J. FURNIVALL, *Director of the New Shakspere Society, London.*

The merit I see in Mr. Rolfe's school editions of Shakspere's Plays over those most widely used in England is that Mr. Rolfe edits the plays as works of a poet, and not only as productions in Tudor English. Some editors think that all they have to do with a play is to state its source and explain its hard words and allusions ; they treat it as they would a charter or a catalogue of household furniture, and then rest satisfied. But Mr. Rolfe, while clearing up all verbal difficulties as carefully as any Dryasdust, always adds the choicest extracts he can find, on the spirit and special "note" of each play, and on the leading characteristics of its chief personages. He does *not* leave the student without help in getting at Shakspere's chief attributes, his characterization and poetic power. And every practical teacher knows that while every boy can look out hard words in a lexicon for himself, not one in a score can, unhelped, catch points of and realize character, and feel and express the distinctive individuality of each play as a poetic creation.

From Prof. EDWARD DOWDEN, LL.D., *of the University of Dublin, Author of "Shakspere: His Mind and Art."*

I incline to think that no edition is likely to be so useful for school and home reading as yours. Your notes contain so much accúrate instruction, with so little that is superfluous ; you do not neglect the æsthetic study of the play ; and in externals, paper, type, binding, etc., you make a book "pleasant to the eye" (as well as "to be desired to make one wise")—no small matter, I think, with young readers and with old.

From EDWIN A. ABBOTT, M.A., *Author of "Shakespearian Grammar."*

I have not seen any edition that compresses so much necessary information into so small a space, nor any that so completely avoids the common faults of commentaries on Shakespeare—needless repetition, superfluous explanation, and unscholar-like ignoring of difficulties.

From HIRAM CORSON, M.A., *Professor of Anglo-Saxon and English Literature, Cornell University, Ithaca, N.Y.*

In the way of annotated editions of separate plays of Shakespeare, for educational purposes, I know of none quite up to Rolfe's.

From Prof. F. J. CHILD, *of Harvard University.*

I read your " Merchant of Venice " with my class, and found it in every respect an excellent edition. I do not agree with my friend White in the opinion that Shakespeare requires but few notes—that is, if he is to be thoroughly understood. Doubtless he may be enjoyed, and many a hard place slid over. Your notes give all the help a young student requires, and yet the reader for pleasure will easily get at just what he wants. You have indeed been conscientiously concise.

Under date of July 25, 1879, Prof. CHILD *adds:* Mr. Rolfe's editions of plays of Shakespeare are very valuable and convenient books, whether for a college class or for private study. I have used them with my students, and I welcome every addition that is made to the series. They show care, research, and good judgment, and are fully up to the time in scholarship. I fully agree with the opinion that experienced teachers have expressed of the excellence of these books.

From Rev. A. P. PEABODY, D.D., *Professor in Harvard University.*

I regard your own work as of the highest merit, while you have turned the labors of others to the best possible account. I want to have the higher classes of our schools introduced to Shakespeare chief of all, and then to other standard English authors ; but this cannot be done to advantage unless under a teacher of equally rare gifts and abundant leisure, or through editions specially prepared for such use. I trust that you will have the requisite encouragement to proceed with a work so happily begun.

From the Examiner and Chronicle, N. Y.

We repeat what we have often said, that there is no edition of Shakespeare which seems to us preferable to Mr. Rolfe's. As mere specimens of the printer's and binder's art they are unexcelled, and their other merits are equally high. Mr. Rolfe, having learned by the practical experience of the class-room what aid the average student really needs in order to read Shakespeare intelligently, has put just that amount of aid into his notes, and no more. Having said what needs to be said, he stops there. It is a rare virtue in the editor of a classic, and we are proportionately grateful for it.

From the N. Y. Times.

This work has been done so well that it could hardly have been done better. It shows throughout knowledge, taste, discriminating judgment, and, what is rarer and of yet higher value, a sympathetic appreciation of the poet's moods and purposes.

From the Pacific School Journal, San Francisco.

This edition of Shakespeare's plays bids fair to be the most valuable aid to the study of English literature yet published. For educational purposes it is beyond praise. Each of the plays is printed in large clear type and on excellent paper. Every difficulty of the text is clearly explained by copious notes. It is remarkable how many new beauties one may discern in Shakespeare with the aid of the glossaries attached to these books. . . . Teachers can do no higher, better work than to inculcate a love for the best literature, and such books as these will best aid them in cultivating a pure and refined taste.

From the Christian Union, N. Y.

Mr. W. J. Rolfe's capital edition of Shakespeare . . . by far the best edition for school and parlor use. We speak after some practical use of it in a village Shakespeare Club. The notes are brief but useful ; and the necessary expurgations are managed with discriminating skill.

From the Academy, London.

Mr. Rolfe's excellent series of school editions of the Plays of Shakespeare . . . they differ from some of the English ones in looking on the plays as something more than word-puzzles. They give the student helps and hints on the characters and meanings of the plays, while the word-notes are also full and posted up to the latest date. . . . Mr. Rolfe also adds to each of his books a most useful "Index of Words and Phrases Explained."

PUBLISHED BY HARPER & BROTHERS, NEW YORK.

☞ *Any of the above works will be sent by mail, postage prepaid, to any part of the United States or Canada, on receipt of the price.*